I0822867

HOUSE HAMILTON

House Hamilton

10 RULES TO SURVIVE MONSTER HUNTING

Jeanette Stevenson

To my three most dedicated readers. My husband, who encouraged me to get it written so that he didn't have to listen to me ramble anymore. My father, who knew I could before I did. My brother and my toughest critic who never settled for less than my best.

Also, to the Mysterious Galaxy Writing Group for butchering every substandard sentence and being Mia's greatest advocate when I lost her voice.

Contents

Rule # 1: When in doubt, myth it out.

1.1: A slight change of plans.

This was not how I imagined starting this guide to hunting monsters. I figured I would be sitting in my study wearing a robe worthy of the late, Mr. Heffner and smoking a bubble pipe. Why bubbles? Because nicotine is gross, that's why. Anyhow, nothing like hands on learning. When Mrs. Chambers showed up for school looking like she'd spent the weekend purging every ounce of her humanity in a vomit fest, I figured better now than never.

***

My classmates and I herded into the sophomore calculus lesson with the single-minded mentality of pack animals. The squeaking sneakers and body odor made up the average Monday experience. Not to mention the combined halitosis of 24 teenagers returning to class after lunch. If you send your kid, spouse or even self to work or school with leftover fish you are exactly what is wrong with humanity, just FYI.

Demi, my best friend, took her seat two rows away from me. Brushing a lock of her dark hair back, the green tipped ends were barely contained behind her ear. She shot me an ironic smile and placed her palms together looking toward the ceiling. I could practically hear the choir of angels singing. Mrs. Chambers stood up and

I waited for the usual 'proclamation of serenity', not to be confused with a prayer. I did a double take, though, as I glanced up from my backpack.

On the previous Friday, Harmony Chambers had been an average sized, middle-aged woman with an unfortunate obsession with long, flowery muumuu-like dresses. The woman struggling to lift the ten-pound brick, also known as our textbook, had skin that hung loosely on her spindly arms. Sunken eyes stared out at us, overly bright and unblinking. Her mouth hung in a loose gape as if she were asleep standing up.

After picking my own jaw up off the ground, I tilted my head from side to side cracking the vertebrae in my neck. This lesson just got interesting.

I pulled out a leather notebook. Gold embroidered letters stamped across the front read: 'House Hamilton.' Flipping through the pages, I settled on a section titled 'Doppelganger.' I retrieved a plain legal pad from my bag and prepared to diagnose the exact variety of monster Mrs. Chambers had become.

Facts: a devout Christian, *bless her heart,* Chambers never took a single sip of the devil's nectar in her life. She, also, wasn't the type to turn up suddenly pregnant or develop a dangerous eating disorder. You might be saying it's a long leap to assume my teacher had become some kind of supernatural beast. Perhaps she's on a rapid weight loss diet or got really aggressive liposuction. That's not how my life works. Stick around, you'll see.

Just for a sanity check, I looked over at Demi. She pointed to Chambers then curled her three middle fingers toward her palm leaving the thumb and pinky sticking out. She tapped this on her chin. American Sign Language for, "Somethings wrong with her." I nodded and signed back, "I got this."

Looking around the room, I discovered that the rest of my classmates didn't seem to find anything strange about the droning lecture. At least two of them were asleep. Popular girl, Kiera Weinhard had a look of abject disgust on her face. I thought that had less to do with the string of drool hanging from the corner of Chamber's lip than the pattern of her dress. I tended to agree, the flora was indeed distractingly heinous.

As Chambers fumbled through her lesson it seemed like her words hissed out of her mouth faster than the puppeteer could work the jawbone. Honestly, that's not to say she was the world's greatest orator before. For my part, I was taking copious notes. Albeit not about the mathematical properties of integration. I'll be real with you; I don't see much point in studying calculus as it applies to the real world. I know at least enough to detect a fellow amateur at work.

I found it cute that Chambers thought we wouldn't notice her over large snack hidden under her desk. A relic of the 1960's, the desk had about an inch of exposure between the floor and its solid metal plated front. The unmistakable crease of a plumber's crack could be easily, and I must say rather distractingly, seen from my unfortunate vantage point. I figured, by process of elimination, that the top of those dimpled butt cheeks belonged to William Forester our only 'absent' classmate.

I scratched off Draugr from my list. They didn't eat live meat. Plus, Harmony Chambers wasn't greedy, just judgy. Will's bottom appeared pink and healthy throughout the lesson. Putting my pen down I looked pointedly at the ceiling. This monster was starting to annoy me.

Firstly, they chose to pick my fifth period instructor. That meant I had a large peanut butter sandwich only just beginning to digest in my stomach. That was going to make me sluggish. Secondly, I was most definitely going to be late to my next class because I now had to save Forester's sorry pimple-ridden behind. Then get rid of the evidence in the allotted ten minutes between class times. Lastly, I was kind of insulted. This was Salem High in Salem Massachusetts. Hamilton territory. The greatest, longest lasting family of Smyths that ever lived, and I am Amelia Ann Hamilton.

1.2: Why calculus is pointless.

Okay, so I might have gotten ahead of myself there for a minute in my indignation. Let me back up. The Smyths are a league of people who hunt down all the things that go bump in the night. My family was one of the oldest members. When I say, the poorly fitted beast now releasing our class at the bell should have known not to come here, it was not a boast. The pure stupidity of coming to this city and pretending to be my teacher boggled my mind. I've been killing monsters long before my necessity for the, ever handy, sports bra.

As the lesson concluded I marveled at the fact that almost none of my classmates spotted our teacher's possible descent into anorexia. Demi looked at me quizzically as the class packed up. I tapped my thumb against my chest while the rest of my fingers remained straight. ASL for, "Fine."

Demi was deaf but that made her even better at recognizing the unusual. If I had to guess, reading Mrs. Chambers' lips while her mouth moved in bizarre ways must have been base level impossible. I signed to Demi telling her to leave and I would take care of the thing masquerading as our teacher.

Instead of being the last one of my fellow students out of the door I turned the aptly named dead bolt toward the locked position. I pulled my stretchy jeans a little higher up my hips. With a waistline just a little wider than Marilyn Monroe, my curves tended to wiggle my jeans down past the fashionably appropriate rise. I rescued a hair tie from my pocket and secured my mahogany curls back away from my face.

Chambers' head was buried under the desk, probably getting a good whiff of her snack. I sat back down at my station and purposefully screeched the legs against the tile. The monster froze. Slowly she lifted her head up. I saw her dislocated jaw snap back from its hyperextended position. I wasn't scared, just a touch disgusted. I redoubled my composure.

Half of Chambers face drooped expressionless, as if she'd suddenly developed Bell's Palsy. "What can I do for you my dear?"

What was this, though? Little red riding hood. *And what excellent swallowing ability you have Mrs. Chambers.* "I suppose I have a question," I began as I clinically poised my pen over my notes. "How long ago did you hatch?"

Her loose jaw fell open in a look of surprise, but I was pretty sure that was unintentional. I got the suspicion she was more confused than surprised.

"I'm not sure what you mean?" she replied.

'Hatch' was a trigger word for her. I crossed off Kitsune from my list. They didn't come from pods. Not to mention that as far as I could see there was no characteristic fox shaped shadow. She didn't appear to have recently become a red head either.

Mrs. Chambers shuffled. Her hungry eyes kept wandering down toward the prize beneath her desk. "Did you need help with your notes?" Her tone made it clear that she hoped I didn't.

"You know I think I might, thanks." I was enjoying the way my presence made her squirm. "I have studied hard today. I noticed quite a few things that lead me to believe I've got the right answer now. I can only assume that you must have just hatched because whoever sired you really didn't set you up for success here."

Chambers began to splutter incoherent things that sounded like denial. I reached down and pulled my garrote from my bag. I smiled at the look of pure snarling hatred that she gave the object now glittering on my desk. "Pretty, isn't it? The silver here was blessed by monks at Meteora over one hundred years ago." I ran my finger along its razor thin edge. Chambers' body remained tense, so I continued.

"I've spent this lesson puzzling this out. It wasn't difficult to nail down your species. Let's get real, only a few creatures go around thinking they can wear a human meat suit and not bother to tailor it to size." Chambers looked down at her loosely hanging skin. I couldn't help it; the smirk just took over my lips. This thing was completely clueless. "So, after careful observation the only conclusion I can come up with is that *you,* my dear, are a ghoul."

I had already gripped the oak handles of the garrote, my fingers hugging the grooves of its runes when Chambers moved. She let out a pitiful…oh no I mean *truly horrifying* roar. I kicked my desk toward it and the creature stumbled. I can't truthfully say if the desk was the cause of it tripping. The thing was having difficulty navigating the long flowy dress and heels. I kinda, just a little, felt bad for it.

Before I could make it around the desk, Chambers sprang up. The benefit of a newly hatched ghoul was that it was depressingly naive. On the downside they were incredibly strong. Now that I let slip that I knew what it was, the ghoul moved in its more natural way.

Chambers scuttled on the floor on all fours. Claws tore through the skin of her fingertips letting out an ooze of congealed blood. The ghoul jumped at me, sinking its nasty talons into the arm of my favorite leather jacket. The thick fabric saved me from needing a tetanus shot but ripped mercilessly in long strips. That made my blood boil. Leather sucks to repair. I kicked Chambers in the gut and the beast fell. It was shockingly easy to wrap the garrote around its neck once it was on the ground. I put my knee against its spine and held it there for a moment.

Not even out of breath I paused, blowing a lock of hair out of my eyes. "Can I ask you something?" If I was going to be late for my next class, the thing could have at least given me a workout.

"Did you raise your hand?" wheezed the creature formerly known as Mrs. Chambers.

"Funny," I really did laugh. I do love a little low brow humor from time to time. "What possessed you to come to Salem? Didn't your sire warn you?"

"Mother said don't go east. Is this east?" The ghoul's voice was childlike.

"Well, that depends on where you started out. Considering you're about to lose your head I suspect you went east."

The last thing that escaped the ghoul was a whispered curse. The sound hissed out of its severed vocal cords as its head parted company from its neck.

1.3: Cleaning Sucks.

Forget every convenient monster movie and TV show you've ever seen. Baddies don't go poof and disappear when you've killed them. Nope, usually they make a terrible mess that's most often bloody or stinky. In Chambers' case it was both.

My teacher must not have been dead very long, considering the freshness of the blood and bile flowing from her neck. She was probably killed recently most likely by the ghoul itself.

As the dead ghoul oozed, I went around her desk and kneeled to get a look at Will. He was in good shape, no bite marks. I removed the gag and cut his hands free from the shoestrings binding his wrists. He scrambled out from under the desk mercifully pulling up his sagging pants. We both looked down at the decapitated form of our calculus teacher.

Will shook violently and wiped tears from his face. "What *was* that thing?"

I nudged the corpse with the toe of my boot. "Ghoul. A baby, I think."

Will made a face halfway between shock and disapproval. "You killed a baby?"

I looked over at him incredulously, "I don't think there have been any studies regarding ghoul maturity, but yeah. It couldn't have hatched any more than five days ago."

"It was so strong though." Will backed away from the corpse. "I mean, I just wanted to get some advice on this week's homework then it got me." He gestured with one hand while miming, pretending to snatch something from the air.

I clapped the kid on the shoulder companionably. "Brown nosing can kill William. Remember that."

"Shut up Mia." He sounded embarrassed. Couldn't blame him. "Thanks though."

"No worries," I shrugged my shoulders. "Shall we get started?"

The nice thing about saving someone's life, especially a person who knows all about the supernatural, was that you got help lifting the body. Will Forester's mother was a witch so the whole dead teacher thing didn't rattle him as much as the average mortal. I counted myself lucky that Salem was Wicca heavy. It made for less awkward interactions when saving lives.

Now for the dirty work. From my bag I retrieved the essentials that no girl should ever go without: black trash bags and duct tape. Will and I wrapped and taped up the remnants of the ghoul placing the head in its hands for safe keeping. We wheeled the package out on top of a trolly typically used for the class's projector. Then we dumped it in the trunk of my car, a 1966 Volvo Amazon. Owing to her age, my ride had a huge trunk for a sedan. Because I'm no novice, the interior was coated in an easy to clean polyvinyl chloride.

Marveling at my pristinely kept classic car Will said, "I thought your birthday wasn't till October. Don't you need to be 16 to drive?"

"I'm surprised you could even ask that question. You're finally getting some use out of that half-witch blood of yours." I reached in and I held up an ornate bag I kept hooked on the rearview mirror. It had small turquoise beads stitched into the leather. "A little magic goes a long way. This little baby deflects all awkward questions. Except from you, I guess. Anyway, thanks for helping me drag her out. I already sent a text to Edgar about the mess he says he'll take care of it. Your mom owes him some of her white chocolate macadamia cookies, though."

Will laughed, his voice still a little hoarse and rattled. "I can make that happen." Looking suddenly worried again Will continued, "Wont Edgar be pissed?"

"Janitors are always pissed off. Smyth janitors in charge of wayward teens, more than most." I sat down behind the wheel and turned the key eliciting a hefty growl from the engine. "Why don't you put in an order for those cookies for me too while you're at it."

"You got it Mia. Thanks again." Will waved as I put the car in gear.

I selected a playlist that began with Metallica's 'For whom the bell tolls.' As I drove off, I blasted the music. A few modern comforts could be added to my classic Amazon princess, but air conditioning wasn't one of them. I cranked the windows down and banged my hands on the steering wheel in rhythm with the song's drumbeat.

On the drive to the funeral home the open windows kept most of the toxic decaying smell from overwhelming me. I did have a few moments where I wanted to stop and beat the ever-loving crap out of the bag's contents. I blame Will Smith and the movie *Independence Day* for the impulse. I suspected dead aliens smelled just about as rancid as dead ghouls.

You might be asking yourself why on earth was I taking a decapitated schoolteacher to a funeral home? The simple answer: in this town, and let's face it in most, the mortuary was run by Smyths.

One of the perks of having a beast of a car like my Amazon was that people knew when you were coming. My baby had a healthy purr. The engine sounded like a small plane landing. So, I wasn't surprised when Alan Pollocks met me at the double doors of the Valley Mortuary and Crematorium. A thin man, balding with severe age lines, from scowling no doubt, Pollocks looked at me warily. Clearly, I'm not his favorite customer.

I put my head out of the window so he could see me better. "Hey Mr. Pollocks. Got a ripe one for you." I gave him my most charming smile.

"Amelia, you know better. Go to the back door. I'm not unloading through the front," Alan growled. He was so agitated that his suit wrinkled.

Pollocks was right. I did know better but it made me smile to see the panic in his eyes. I pulled around to the back door and waited while he wove his way through the inner workings of his business. Alan pushed the door open and a new man I didn't know wheeled out a sleek metal table.

"Got yourself an intern, huh?" I nodded to the new guy.

Pollocks, busy examining the trash bag encased body nodded and gestured vaguely toward his companion. "This is Nguyen."

Nguyen reached out and offered me his hand. I shook it, noting his warm brown eyes and thin but lightly muscled frame. "I'm Mia, nice to meet you."

"You can call me Ben, and the pleasure is all mine." Ben let go of my hand and smiled.

Pollocks snapped on some gloves excessively loud, "Flirt later. I want this done quickly."

I rolled my eyes and waited while the two men loaded up the body and wheeled it inside. Before Alan shut the door, he looked down the empty driveway.

"Relax, Mr. Pollocks. You know me, I'm always careful," I winked at Ben. "No one followed me. No one is headed this way. Plus, as a bonus I kept the ghoul in one piece. Or two but still pretty solid."

"You people know I hate this." A Smyth by virtue of his occupation, Alan was one of the rare few that hadn't grown up in the trade. He accepted his role reluctantly.

Ben came around the table and handed Pollocks a pair of scissors. "Did you say ghoul?"

I paused looking from one man to the other. Surely the intern knew about the supernatural, right? Pollocks glanced up noting the awkward silence. "It's his first creature but he's already gotten the 'speech.'" I sighed, relieved that I didn't need to burst that bubble. We should have made pamphlets. Something easy to hand over and tell people that we'd be back *after* their head exploded.

Ben peered into the neck cavity of the decapitated woman, "Where is the monster?"

"It's just as dead as Miss Harmony Chambers here." I picked up a long metal tube I think was used for embalming and held it in my hands like a teacher at a lectern. "Ghouls have physical forms but they're kind of like tape worms. They climb in and puppet the host sort of like the person is possessed."

Ben examined the flesh on Chambers face and furrowed his eyebrows. "This body has been dead for days, but she's been walking around? These ligature marks are fresh though. Did someone decapitate her today?"

Alan huffed in exasperation and handed me a tub of Vick's Vapor rub. I put a healthy portion under my nose. "Guilty."

Ben's flirtatious attention turned wary. "Oh, I see. Wont someone notice she's missing?"

"Yes and no," I conceded. "See, situations like this are where the Smyth infrastructure comes in." Ben still looked confused. "It will go something like this: busybody Karen, who, by the way, notices everything except that her neighbor was body snatched, will call in the missing person's report. This report is sent to detectives, aka Smyths. For a few weeks the news will be all over this case: an innocent, widowed, spinster schoolteacher doesn't just up and disappear. News outlets will report any tantalizing 'facts' they can dig up about

Mrs. Chambers. That one time she went to a midnight showing of *Rocky Horror Picture Show* dressed as Magenta will cast her character in a salacious light. Even though the photo is nearly twenty years old." Mr. Pollocks cut through the bag, and Ben helped him remove the jewelry from the body's fingers and ears while listening closely to my tale.

"You don't suppose she has a belly button ring or anything?" Pollocks addressed me. He had settled into the routine detached objectivity that was necessary for his job. I shook my head not liking the image, but he cut open her dress anyway to be sure.

As Pollocks looked over Mrs. Chambers' body clinically, he waved away Ben's hands. The younger man took off his gloves then scrubbed himself clean over at the sink. With out looking at me Ben asked, "Then what?"

"Well, maddeningly as it might be to hear, her past will be rung out on a court of public opinion. The conclusion will be that her 'experimental youth' and 'lonely, widowed status' left her vulnerable to potential unwanted solicitous attention. In short, it was her fault she went and got herself disappeared."

"That's cold," Ben surmised.

"It's a cold, cruel world Mr. Nyugen." Ben shook his head looking over Chambers body with sympathy. Determined I finished the story, "After a while only cold case detectives (also Smyths) will care about the file collecting dust and only enough to deflect others from opening inquiries about it. In conclusion, as my English teacher likes to see me write, Harmony Chambers' ashes will have no further attention than the exclamations of how beautiful this year's geraniums have bloomed."

1.4: If the founding fathers could see us now.

After my visit with the funeral home director and his cute assistant, I made my way downtown to my dad's bar. My dad could have joined the police, a profession that attracts a lot of Smyth members, but the Hamilton's have run this town since damn near day one. Our business had been established in 1785 by a great, great, who knows, relation. It's a go-to location for other Smyths; a safe place to talk openly about their recent hunting expeditions.

The exterior was just the same as many of the buildings in downtown Salem. Apparently, architects back in the day were very fond of the story of the *Three Little Pigs*. At least the third one and his house of brick. Russet tones of red filled the streets, plastered on building facades, mailboxes, retaining walls, you name it. The awnings tented over the wide glass windows were black and the sign beside the door read, Hamilton's Bar.

My status as a minor wasn't questioned by the bouncer. A burly man named Rudy waved me inside. His name was short for Rudolph, but I suggest you use it only if you want to have your head caved in. I pushed the heavy oak doors open. I knew from the moment I stepped inside that I was in trouble. None of the usual daytime patrons would look me in the eye. All their voices muted into murmured conversation as I slid behind the bar and ran my fingers on the polished granite surface of the counter. The bartender, Wendy, a pretty, older woman with the face and strong muscled physique of a biker tossed me a clean rag.

"I take it he's not here yet." I took the rag and started drying off dishes.

"Nope. He ran out of here a good hour ago." Wendy's voice sounded like she'd gargled shards of glass every morning. "I guess someone didn't show for her afternoon classes. Again."

I sucked in a breath through my teeth, "Yeah, um, anyway..."

Wendy laughed like a chainsaw revving up. "Better work on them excuses. He ain't gonna be happy after talkin' to that stick-up-the-ass that you call a principle." She snapped her own towel at me whipping it against my hip. A ding from the kitchen announced that one of our patron's orders was up. "Hold down the fort for me?" I nodded and set to cleaning the counters.

The door of the bar creaked open, and a boy came in. He strode over and sat down on a stool facing me. I called him a boy for lack of a better word. He had the swagger of a man but also a patch of unshaven stubble at the left side of his Adam's apple and the pock-like markings of recent acne on his jaw line. He was handsome despite his outward signs of youth. Confidence twinkled in his hazel eyes. He 'tried' to order a whiskey on the rocks.

I couldn't help it and smiled. "That's funny kiddo. How about you try one of these." I handed him a shot of holy water. We keep it on tap. Always bless your pipes. Good for demon repelling and avoiding plumbing disasters. Even though we ran a bar specifically for Smyths we got many a bold hell spawn willing to risk being surrounded to take out an influential member of the organization like my father.

"You sure I'm ready for that?" He was cocky in an attractive sort of way. I tried hard not to blush.

"I don't know, my friend. Afraid of a little water?" I pushed the glass toward him, innocently. I was so ready for another fight. The decapitation of the ghoul was like a sampler platter of adrenalin; I wanted more.

He lifted the shot glass to his lips and knocked the whole thing down his throat. I watched his face closely but there was no reaction. Not a demon. The window of potential threats narrowed exponentially. This boy was human. Human but clearly stupid.

"I need to see Mitch," the boy stated. The room, which was already mostly quiet, went dead silent. I could tell that the boy noticed but he didn't take his eyes off me. His shoulders tensed; he looked ready for a fight. I could respect that.

"Mitch isn't here yet." I stood up straighter. "He's not fond of strangers either."

"He and I go way back." The slight curve of his smile brought up a long-forgotten memory. I had met him before, but I couldn't exactly pinpoint from when.

Wendy came out from the kitchen with a large tray balancing a good six dishes of food. She shot me a curious glance, but I scrunched my nose and shook my head, no need for her to worry.

"Alright then," I addressed the boy. "Come on back but it's going to be water or soda for you. I don't care what lies your fake ID has to offer." He smirked and followed me as I led him to the back meeting rooms.

Before he entered the furthest room down the hallway, he ran his fingers on the door frame along the runes imbedded there. Sitting down comfortably he threw his arms over the top of the rounded couch cushions taking up as much space as his man-spreading body could manage. He cleared his throat and said, "Mitch, sweety, I need to speak with Mitch."

I swallowed the bile rising in my throat and grabbed the nearest chair. I spun it around so that the rear of the chair faced him and straddled the thing. Hooking my arms over the back rest I leaned my chin against my interlocked fingers.

"That's not how this works, my friend," my tone was growing impatient.

Completely unabashed, he didn't so much as change his posture. I found that both infuriating and cute at the same time. We stared each other down for a few moments before he realized that he was the one making inquiries and I had no obligation to answer them. Pulling his arms away from the top of the cushions he rested them on his knees. He sighed, clearly a touch frustrated that I wasn't relenting. "I'm Harrison Monroe. My brother was John Monroe. He's... he's gone." The hitch in Harrison's throat broke down my steely demeanor. "I need Mitch's help. John always said that if anything ever happened, I should find Mitch. Is he here?"

Monroe. I knew about the Monroe's. They were a family as old as mine, dating back to the foundation of our country. My father spoke very fondly about John. If John was dead that wasn't good news for the Smyths. John was an incredible hunter: savvy, street smart, and fierce.

I pulled my cell phone out and sent a quick text to my dad. "Need you in conference room 4. Safe. Sorry." As the phone buzzed in my hand, I already knew what it would say. "He's coming. I'm Mia by the way."

"Amelia Hamilton. I know. I remember." There was no trace of cockiness in his expression, just appraisal and curiosity. "You've grown up a lot."

I really did blush this time but turned my face away hoping he couldn't see. He ran his fingers through his chestnut brown hair that curled up a good inch off the top of his head. As the light caught the sparse blonde strands mixed in, I began to remember. We had met just once before. The circumstances of that day had become muddled in the dramatics that occurred shortly after. I remembered

Harrison Monroe. I remembered the reason he wasn't permitted anywhere near Salem, Massachusetts.

1.5: Training interruptus.

The nice thing about this memory is that it gives us another chance to discuss an interesting monster. I was twelve at the time and only about a few months into the required Smyth training hours. Our previous excursion had proven to be nothing more than investigating a witch. Turned out she was not, in fact, poisoning her patrons. Witch was just really, really bad at potion making.

On the day that I met Harrison my father had promised a juicy hunt. We headed to Asheville, North Carolina and Mount Mitchell, the highest peak in the Appalachian Mountains. I think the prideful part of my dad enjoyed seeing his name on all the road signs.

On the drive, dad quizzed me on the case. “Ok, Mia, what do the reports say?”

I opened the binder I prepared for the investigation. I liked to keep things orderly, so each section was neatly labeled with color coded tabs. I flipped to the place where the police reports were. “Looks like at least six attacks by a ‘giant mountain lion’ and two missing campers.”

My sister, Molly, scoffed from the front passenger seat. “Sounds like the perfect place for a family camping trip.” To her credit we did drag her along with us. Fun family time was hard to schedule in the life of a Smyth. Sometimes you had to double up.

"You should appreciate a chance to connect with nature," dad said. "Doesn't your coven have an earth magic portion to their initiation standards? You have less than a year to prepare then you'll be 18 and ready to do the ceremony." Molly didn't respond. I could practically feel her eyes rolling even in the back seat.

The clearing of our campsite was an established spot. The pad designed for pitching our abode away from home was framed in two-by-fours and packed in fine gravel. It also included a quality picnic bench equipped with warped-wood, splinter seating and rusted metal legs.

Whereas I was less than impressed, Molly looked downright traumatized. She'd pulled out her phone and went live on some social-media platform. She found the right spot to let her shoulder length dark brown hair flow interestingly in the wind. "Omg guys can you believe this. I'm out here with bugs and filthy blankets..."

"And really cute boys," a voice interrupted. A teenage boy came out of the bushes with a wide grin. The gaunt look of a post growth spurt hung around his limbs, but his voice was steady and deep. He only had eyes for my sister whose crop top accented her flat stomach and perfectly developed chest. Ending her video, Molly looked at him like he was a roach. I enjoyed that more than I'd like to admit.

From around our truck a man walked amiably with my dad. Their boisterous voices carried over to us in a crescendo, "I heard you took out that pack of Bakru." My dad clapped the other man on the shoulder. "Nice one. I thought every magician knew better than to summon those little devils."

"I think it's the Pinocchio aspect of it. Little wooden children made specially to do your bidding. These conjurers need a taste of real parenthood. If they had any clue, they'd know that kids are no good at following orders, right Harris?"

The boy beside us tried and failed to look abashed. "I got here in the end, didn't I?"

"Dang, that's Harrison? Time flies, huh?" My dad dusted his Indiana Jones styled Panama hat by banging it against his leg.

The older man stepped back and put his hand over his heart. "Your one to talk. That can't be little Molly. Last time I saw her she was just about to start kindergarten."

A shadow of something passed over my dad's face as if the memory of that last time sparked something odd. He was quick to disguise it. "Girls, this is John Monroe, his brother Harrison, and his son Lincoln."

Molly let out a little laugh. "Brother?"

John raised an eyebrow at Molly. My sister blushed and cast her eyes down. John had the ashy brown kind of hair that made you think it had been blonde when he was young. Pale, a little stocky and on the shorter side he had the commanding swagger of a man not afraid of being in the spotlight. Harris was taller with mocha colored skin and more importantly was at least half John's age.

Harris laughed at the tension building. "It's okay, old man. I wouldn't believe it either." Harris nudged John in the ribs eliciting a smile. Side by side you could see the resemblance in how one corner of their lips lifted a little higher than the other and the deep dimples in their cheeks. "You see Molly, our dad had a pretty lengthy active period." Harris explained.

"Ew." I whispered under my breath.

Lincoln chuckled and caught my eye. He looked about my age. Owing to our preteen status I was much taller than him. My training bra and poorly shaven legs were not nearly as embarrassing as his voice squeaking from low to high as he tried to say "hello."

John smiled at the boy and rubbed the top of his blonde head. It looked mortifying, a gesture ill befitting his hopes of appearing mature. "I'd bet you guys aren't just out here for a family camping trip. I got wind of the 'mountain lion' reports as well. Guess I should have called the hotline to make sure someone else hadn't marked it down for investigation. We just decided to head this way two days ago. Harris got rid of a poltergeist in Knoxville in record time."

"That's alright, we can always use extra hands." If I was nearby, I would have stamped on my father's foot. Being too far away I merely glared. I needed this kill.

John and his boys set up camp beside us. As the day wore on, I grew tired of the great tales of Harris' success. His monster count was annoyingly large. In true adolescent dramatics, I huffily went into our tent, zipped it up as aggressively as one can with a zipper. Then I slammed a few books around for good measure.

By the time dusk rolled around I stopped turning the pages of one of my monster textbooks ferociously. It was hunting time and I was determined to get there first. Of course, we all left as one pack. Everyone but Molly, who stayed back to film a few videos of herself complaining how lame camping was.

Decked out in a utility-belt and the kind of vest fisherman wear, my dad had his shotgun held at the ready. I suspected his vest was not full of hooks and lures. More likely the pockets contained potions and charms. Camp was already far enough behind us that we could no longer see the smoke from the fire.

Dad pulled out a flashlight and cast its beam through the trees. "Hunting near nightfall is helpful for two reasons. Name them."

I jumped in quickly so that no one else could answer first. "Most monsters are nocturnal. 'Things that go bump in the night' is not just a euphemism. Also, most corporeal monsters have that tapetum lucidum." I looked back to see that Harris and Link were both very confused. "It's a reflective structure in the eyes that creates the appearance that they glow at night. Kinda like cats do."

John cleared his throat and nudged Harris; it was his turn to show off. "I'm pretty sure we are looking for a Wendigo." John gave him a 'go on' gesture. "Their diets are mostly human, and they live in the mountains. Normally people describe them as having horns like a dear or the face of a wolf."

My dad and I came to the same conclusion. Though the mountain lion description was a bit of a stretch, all the other factors led to Wendigo. We were all confident in our assessment until we found the tracks. The creature we were looking for either had a two-legged friend with similar feet or the thing had six legs. The prints in the mud were enormous, about the size of a dinner plate. They led to a den dug into the root of a tall pine. I was pretty sure you could park a minivan inside.

Bending down to examine the tracks my dad picked up a piece of dirt and crumbled it. "I say we set up a watch. This creature is clearly not what we thought it was. The tracks here look like they head in. I don't see any going out. Any arguments?" No one disagreed so we settled near the entrance convinced that the creature was inside.

1.6: Memory Lane's resident alley cat.

We were wrong. I had fallen asleep propped upright sitting back-to-back with my dad. The night was silent but for the wind and the hooting of owls. I opened my eyes briefly and caught the glint of a reflective yellow iris three inches from my face. I closed my eyes sleepily for just another second before I snapped awake and jerked enough to dislodge my father from his position on the ground. This was lucky since the creature leapt at us and missed.

We scrambled to our feet and got the first good look at the monster in our midst. It was enormous, roughly the exact height and width of a dumpster. With the head of a cougar the rest of its body was also distinctly feline. Its tail and legs were where things got weird. The tail was long and tapered like a cat but at the end of it there was a ball with spike-like quills. It did indeed have six legs though it appeared the front two were mostly for maiming its victims. They were curved, bent inward almost like human arms. The clawed paws had razor sharp talons. Its powerful back legs were heavily muscled and looked as if the creature could spring itself forward with deadly accuracy.

The beast swung its tail at John, who ducked, and the spikes got lodged in a nearby tree. John told Link to run but the kid was sitting terrified huddled under a blanket. Thankfully, the monster was well distracted. Harris pulled a semi-automatic handgun from the holster at his side and opened fire aiming directly at the beast's chest. This seemed to annoy it more than cause any significant damage. My father tried to slash its legs with his hunting knife, but the creature's skin seemed almost impenetrable. The blade only left the tiniest of paper cuts.

I backed away, making space, trying to assess. I wracked my brain struggling to remember what my textbook had said about this beast. "It's a Wampus cat."

Reloading his gun Harris muttered, "Great, now we know what it's called. How do we kill it?"

Wringing my hands, I examined the creature's skin for vulnerability. The Wampus let out a blood curdling scream and dove at my dad who quickly dashed behind a tree avoiding the strike. "My book said that it mostly went after livestock and wild animals. I didn't even think about it for this case."

Fashioning a torch out of a big stick and a piece of torn cloth, John kept one eye on Link's crouched form. The youngest Monroe was still frozen in place.

Harris cocked his gun and aimed for the beast's maw. "Not helpful seeing as this one has gotten a taste for man flesh."

Okay Mia, think. Smyths in the past mostly scared them off because killing one was really freaking difficult. Great, another super helpful fact. The answer was somewhere in my memory of the text. My father called out, "Rule number one: When in doubt, myth it out."

Right. Whenever something didn't quite make sense, it was sometimes necessary to go back to the origin of the myth. The three men narrowly avoided the vicious swipes and advances of the creature. "Okay, the Wampus is a Cherokee legend," I called. "It came from a 'fruit of the tree of knowledge' sort of story. Those always paint women who want to learn as evil, and sin ridden. Rude."

Harris' gun skittered into the woods as the beast's tail dislodged from the tree and jabbed its spikes into his palm. "Get to the point!"

"The woman from the myth had hidden under a blanket to listen in on an, all male, elder's council. She had been cursed into becoming this creature. Wait. Blanket!"

"Is she serious? Are we going to cuddle the thing to death?" Harris complained behind a tree digging quills out of his hand.

I rushed over to where Link hid and snatched the blanket, he cowered under, away from him. It happened from the tiniest grazing of his fingers and mine. Suddenly, I felt like my skin glued to his. As I tried to look into his eyes a vision passed between us. Or at least it looked like he saw what I did.

The experience was strange, like watching an apparition in front of you while being able to see reality beyond it. All at once I could see Link's shocked face, his eyes rolled up into his head and only the whites showing. I could also see if I focused, a square box like a television playing out the scene in front of the creature's den. The vision sped up in time, past what was happening around us. The image showed John shoving Harris aside as the claw of the Wampus came down. It scraped against John's back. My dad leapt at the creature and tried to sink his knife in its eye. He managed it but moments later its jaws clamped down on his neck and shoulder. His flesh was ripped away in an instant and he fell to the ground twitching and inches from death.

I don't remember pushing Link away from me. At least not with my hands. I turned around and saw just as I had before, John shoving Harris aside and receiving long gashes down his back from the beast's claws. As my father approached, I screamed, "Daddy no!" I pushed my hands out toward him out of instinct and an invisible force threw him back.

I sprang toward the Wampus, the blanket around my shoulder, and climbed up its rear legs. Then I wrapped the covering around its head, smothering it. It immediately began to wheeze. For good measure I drove my own hunting knife into its eye socket and the thing went down like a ton of bricks.

Of course, a lot of weird stuff just happened there. I know, I'll get to that but first a happy dance for my first kill. I not only knew what it was, but I also kicked its ass. Who says you can't be a nerd and a bad bitch at the same time?

Back to our story. So, John got badly messed up and Harris' hand needed attention. We went to camp so that Molly could throw some stitches in and apply a healing poultice to each injury. My dad and John decided to bury the Wampus remains at first light. Given that sunrise was only a few hours away we lit a campfire and sat staring at each other for a long, awkward, while.

I cleared my throat before speaking, "So, do your eyes often glow in the dark, Link?

The boy's eyebrows knit together, "My eyes were glowing?"

I nodded. "Bright blue, like little flashlights."

John stiffened, "No, that was a first for us." He turned to my dad. "The telekinesis?"

"Brand new." Dad didn't meet anyone's glance. I couldn't help but think moving things with my mind was kinda awesome, but my dad had a somberness to his expression that suggested otherwise.

John sighed. With his fist clenched he massaged his temple with his knuckles. "What happened with you two?"

I looked over at Link. His hunched shoulders and darting glances made me wonder what the vision was like for him. Taking pity on the boy, I took a crack at answering. "It was like some kind of vision. It was like watching TV, but I could still see everything else around me. I saw what was about to happen and I decided to stop it."

"And what was going to happen?" Dad had his elbows on his knees and his hands clasped in front of his face as if in prayer.

"That monster was going to rip you in half." Link was dead pale and his voice, though squeaky, was solid and sure. My dad looked over to me and I nodded confirming my vision was the same.

Dad sat up straighter and dusted some of the dirt off his cargo pants. "I think you kids best head off to sleep. You can get a few hours before we need to pack up. John and I will bury the cat." He seemed calm, so I started to protest. "Damn it, Mia! Just do what you're told for once."

I shut up immediately. I could feel the light prick of tears in the corners of my eyes. I had seen a vision of my favorite person in the whole world die right in front of me. Then I had to save his life with powers that I didn't understand nor trust. Now he was yelling at me? Molly got up and took me by the arm leading me back to our tent.

Safely inside, I flopped down on my bed roll and turned to the tent wall so that Molly wouldn't see me cry. She sat down next to me and stroked my hair. "He's scared." I huffed. Her fingers through my hair were calming me despite my agitation. "The witch stuff is always a sore spot for him."

"I don't want to be a witch!" I tried for indignant, but the quaver in my voice made it come out more petulant.

"Smyths don't move things with their mind, Mi." Molly stopped stroking my hair and ran her nails down the center of my spine in a light scratch that a masseuse might envy.

"It was one time. It's not fair. I didn't mean to do it." I yawned and rolled over.

Molly brushed my hair off my face. "I know, kid. Try to sleep."

I did.

When I woke up, I was uncomfortably warm. Before I could make an unholy amount of noise trying to extricate myself from the sleeping bag, I heard my sister and my dad talking outside the tent. I stiffened, listening hard.

"John's gonna keep them all on the opposite side of the country. It won't be an issue." Dad sounded agitated like he'd been answering many similar questions.

"Magic doesn't work that way and you know it." Molly was being way more assertive than I was used to.

"It's going to work this time. I'm going to make sure of it," Dad snapped.

"If they are part of a prophetic pairing there's nothing you can do."

"Stop it, Molly," Dad hissed. "There is no prophecy. No runes, no tarot reading. It's a fluke and they just need to keep away from each other."

Molly let out a disbelieving 'pfft' sound. "Is this because of Momma Sara?" I started holding my breath not wanting to miss a single word. Sara was my mother's name.

"Don't call her that." I could almost hear my dad's words struggling past what I assumed were gritted teeth.

"She's the only mother I remember," Molly said, defensively.

"Well, there is a good chance she killed your actual mother, Molly. Not to mention what she did to Mia so forgive me for not remembering her fondly."

"Sara's witch-blood is in Mia. One day Mi is going to have to embrace that."

My dad's voice dropped to a low baritone, "Not today and never around Lincoln Monroe." Molly made to protest farther but my dad cut her off. "This subject is closed. Consider it buried."

And that was that. If Mitchel Hamilton buried something it stayed dead. I never took a crack at asking about it. Maybe part of me didn't want to know. Now that the Monroe's were back in town, I might have to change that assertion.

Rule # 2: Do your research.

2.1: No cat calls in the lunch line.

I didn't get to hear my father talk to Harrison Monroe, but I also didn't get in trouble for taking care of ghoulie Mrs. Chambers. I put that down as a win.

Let me be real. I did, for a little minute there, think that I was going to get away with not talking to you about my telekinetic powers. Seeing Harris again made me realize that's not going to work. I don't have a solid explanation for why this strange but highly useful gift got tossed my way. Nor do I fully understand what Link had to do with it.

It happened, and my dad didn't offer any helpful hints. I know that he doesn't like it when I use it and doesn't want me to go anywhere near Lincoln Monroe. This was why I found it strange that my father agreed to let them stay in Salem. I didn't get to ask him if I was supposed to avoid the boy or not. I wasn't about to engage him in more conversation that could lead to punishment.

Harris and Link were on campus signing up for classes the next morning. I wasn't the first to notice the pair. Demi spotted them when they arrived. I tapped her on the shoulder as I approached. With my hands splayed facing me, I lightly flicked my bent middle fingers touching my chest and moving up. ASL for, "What's up."

She pointed out the Monroe boys with a quizzical look on her face. I confirmed that those were the ones I was texting her about last night. She signed, “Kinda cute, don’t you think?” She eyed me knowingly as I appraised Harris marching into the building. Cocky, kind of aloof and knee deep in the Smyth culture, just my type. I gave her a half smile of acknowledgement.

This was the first time I got a good look at Link since we were both kids. Tall and only slightly gangly, he walked with a hunch shouldered gate that suggested an ill-established confidence level. “Good genes in that family,” I signed to Demi with a little nudge to her shoulder as her eyes stared at Link’s blonde curls and sky-blue eyes. My friend wiggled her eyebrows in a mock seductive kind of way. She liked to date the melanin impaired. Something about the contrast against her own bronzed skin appealed to her.

As if by some internal radar, Link looked back toward me. When his eyes locked on mine, I felt an unexpected wave of vertigo. He moved almost unintentionally toward me before Harris turned him away and steered him into the school. Demi had to tap me hard on the shoulder before I turned around. I was a few feet toward the school from where I started. She pointed to me and signed the letters O and K.

“Yeah,” I signed back. “I’m okay.”

Link wasn’t assigned to any of my classes before lunch. The mysterious magnetic need to get closer to him didn’t strike until after I had filled up my tray from the lunch line. Being ahead of him, I stood chatting animatedly with our lunch ladies. I really hated how high school shows and movies always depicted these women. The images of them as large spinsters with warts and hairnets dishing piles of slop on flimsy plastic trays were deeply unappealing.

The supervisor in the kitchen handed me my Tuesday usual, Chef salad. She looked extra radiant this afternoon decked in a brand new, royal blue hoody. "Look at you Ms. Diana," I began. "Did Bobby get into Salem State by any chance?"

With a wink she gave me an extra dinner roll. She turned around briefly so that I could see the Viking mascot with his classic horned helmet and shield held up. "Early admission," she confirmed. "The little smarty pants will start classes in the spring."

"Congrats!" I took a bite of my extra roll. If you want to get in good with your local adults, ask about their kids. In leu of kids, try fur-babies. If they don't have either, run!

I got this tingle on the back of my neck and when I turned around Link was three kids behind me staring. "Looks like you have a not-so-secret admirer," Diana commented.

I raised my eyebrows at him intending an obvious dismissal, but he didn't look away. I could feel my feet longing to move closer to him, but I was back in command. "Secret death wish, more like," I murmured.

Turning to serve the next kid, Diana laughed. "Give the boy a break Amelia. What else is he to do standing in the presence of such a beautiful girl?"

Admonishing her, I shook my half-eaten roll in her direction. "We are far too woke a generation to keep indulging that nonsense. Boys can control their eyeballs. I do it all the time. It's not hard."

Diana held her hands up in surrender smiling kindly at me. I returned the expression and took my tray over to sit beside Demi. As I plopped down next to her, I noticed her writing on a sheet of paper before sliding it back to another girl. Most of the other students at our school held conversations with Demi this way. As the only one willing to learn ASL to speak with her I didn't need to carry an extra notebook. Backpacks can be extremely heavy.

Demi narrowed her eyes at the paper while the other girl wrote. Digging into my salad I tried to remember the other girl's name. She was a year ahead of us, so I didn't have much cause to interact with her. Since she belonged to one of our Wiccan families, she probably knew I was a Smyth. Our groups worked mostly in tandem with each other since peace treaties were established in the late 1600's. Basically a 'we won't hunt you if you don't curse us' kind of thing.

Even upside-down Demi could tell what the girl was writing. She turned to me and relayed the information in sign. "This is Kate, she lives two houses down from me."

"Hey," I took the paper Demi handed me. According to the note, Kate's aunt had been acting strangely since she got word that her son, a Marine, had been killed overseas. The aunt would no longer allow her niece to come visit. She had secluded herself in her home and shut down her candle shop in town. "Sorry to hear about your cousin."

"Thanks," there was a catch in Kate's voice, but she didn't cry. "It's been hard for the whole family, but my poor aunt is devastated. I just don't want something bad to happen to her too."

I gripped her hand briefly to reassure her. "I'll look into it, try not to worry."

This sort of thing happens all the time. When you are notorious, in certain circles, for your famous family of monster killers, tips and requests come with the territory. It's an exhilarating job and someone has to do it, might as well be me.

2.2: What a Wiccan game to play.

After school I headed downtown. Brooks Candle Shop was dark, the closed sign turned toward the street. A thick layer of autumn leaves accumulated around the airgap of the front door. The tinted and stylistically swirled glass of the shop windows made the interior look like a mess of vague shapes. Making my way to the alley behind the building I tried the back door, but it was locked.

Before committing a crime such as breaking and entering, I usually liked to check in with my dad. Pulling out my phone I pressed ICE on my contacts list, in case of emergency. A girl should always be prepared. It rang twice before my dad answered. "What's wrong?"

I rolled my eyes, "Nothing."

He made a sound of disbelief, "Isn't calling someone on the phone considered passee these days? Wouldn't you rather send me an incomprehensible slew of emoji hieroglyphs?"

"Ha, ha. I'm over at Willow Brooks' shop, her niece is worried about her. Since that thing happened to her son, she closed the doors and won't talk to the rest of the family."

"It's a damn shame about Matthew. He was a good kid."

I didn't know him so I couldn't answer that. "Permission to take a look around?"

"Don't you have homework?"

"Not much, plus this shouldn't take too long." There was a long silence at the other end of the call. "Come on, it's just the shop I won't go to Willow's house till after school tomorrow, deal?"

"Alright but I better see at least a B on that English paper."

"Please, it's going to be an A, easy." Considering that I had not written a word of the five-page essay, I figured it was going to be a long night. If I could start the evening with a little mystery, that might just carry me over all the hours that I would be glued to my laptop later.

"Fine, permission granted. Be home before dinner." Another warning but this time with less ferocity. I agreed and he hung up.

From my backpack I pulled out a tension wrench, pick and rake. Not the long-handled gardening tool but a small bulb-hilted piece of thin metal about the length of a butter knife. The end was skinny and ridged, ideal for scraping against lock mechanisms to release them. Applying pressure lightly to the keyhole with the wrench I then pushed each pin inside the lock up with the pick. A satisfying click let me know that I succeeded.

The back of the shop was crowded with boxes and smelled like a bath bomb exploded in the tiny storage space. I pinched my nose shut. There was such a thing as too much perfume. I cast the beam of my flashlight around the room and found the door that led into the shop. The main shop floor had mostly the same floral aroma except that there was the distinct tinny smell of iron. Somewhere, beyond all the scented candles and incense, a pool of blood leaked pungently into the air.

I shined my light around and spotted a pair of feet poking out from behind the register. Scanning the room once more I determined we were alone. As I knelt beside the girl, I saw a perfect, circle-shaped hole in her chest. Her heart had been removed. By the precision of the hole, I assumed that the damage was done by magic. She must have been in her early twenties. Probably an attendant of Ms. Brooks. Her face was peaceful in death. With a napkin I pulled from my pocket I brushed a stray lock of auburn hair from her cheek.

I've seen a lot of death. It's practically my occupation to kill things. It's different, though, to come across a dead human. Monsters make their choices, mostly its nature. Killing them doesn't feel as much like a triumph. It's more like a preventative measure for the next poor soul that could run afoul of them. This girl and the others that I've seen lose their lives did so for gain, not by animal instinct. Her heart taken for use in a spell. Her life ended to bring another one back. Willow Brooks was trying to raise her son from the dead.

2.3: I work alone.

Part of me wanted to stalk over and pound on Willow's door demanding to know why she had done it. You want your kid back sure but why murder that poor girl? Convenience was why. But I promised my dad I'd come straight home.

I found him in the office painstakingly typing with his typical hunt and peck method. His broad shoulders stretched the fabric of his favorite flannel shirt. Despite our encouragement, he never accepted that Molly and I had his best interest at heart when we advised him that the lumberjack look would never come back in style.

When I tossed my backpack down, he looked up at me over the rim of his reading glasses. "Who died?" It was a serious question.

"Pauline Norman. According to her driver's license she was 23, wore corrective lenses and was an organ doner." I suspected she hadn't intended that last fact to be taken as an invitation for murder.

Returning to his work he pushed his glasses higher on the bridge of his nose. "You call Uncle Wes?" I nodded. Wesley Field wasn't my dad's brother, but as a permanent fixture in my life he got his uncle title.

"And he's going to handle it."

Though not exactly a question I felt compelled to answer. "He's taking care of the girl, but Willow is still mine."

Pausing in his search for the correct letter on his keyboard he locked eyes with me. I set my jaw in a hard line trying not to betray an ounce of trepidation. "You know what you're up against?" Strictly speaking, no, but I wasn't about to admit it. My dad rubbed his fingers into his eyes tiredly. I was exasperating him, I could tell. "Tell me what you know?"

The Mia in my mind did a little happy dance. Asking me questions was his admission of acquiescence. "The heart had been removed by a spell. So, it can't be a monster. Willow isn't powerful enough to pull this off with her own magic. She's got to be working with a demon."

Dad resumed his 'typing'. "You could have made that connection when you were in the second grade. You need to be more specific."

I sat back and thought about it. Over the span of human history, the fear of the unknown has manifested in malevolent spirits in many different cultures. To say that the only real demons were those that serve the Christian devil was wildly limiting. Although Christians have drummed up a lot of those little buggers.

"It's got to be Faust." Seeing dad's displeased expression I amended, "Mephisto. You knew what I meant."

As always, my father came prepared. He tossed me a copy of 'The Tragical History of Doctor Faustus' by Christopher Marlowe. As I'd read it twice already, I decided it would do nicely to double as the subject of my essay. "Thanks dad."

I left him to the dullness of his inventory spreadsheets for the bar and made my way to my room. I wanted nothing more than to dive head-first into my four-poster bed, but my laptop's blank screen beckoned me. I spun in my computer chair letting the light blue walls blur. Then I kicked against the floor shooting myself forward toward the desk. Like most things in our home, it was solid wood and really old. It took me three hours to finish the paper owing to all the tedious MLA formatting for siting my sources.

Frustrated, I tried to imagine the next day. I'd be sitting behind a small wooden desk with dried gum on its underbelly and a wobbly leg. Tomorrow, I had to listen to some classmate as they gave their report. Droning on about how incredibly rebellious Holden Caulfield was in 'Catcher in the Rye.' I could be out saving a life instead of hearing the glorification of some angsty teen. And yes, I am aware that made me a hypocrite. Attendance was non-negotiable with my dad.

Using my telekinesis, I imagined the toggle of the light switch between my fingers and pressed down. The light went out immediately. I perked up staring at the wall and imagined the switch in the up position. Before I could finish the image in my mind the light came on again. I swung my legs off the side of the bed, sitting up. Never, not once in the three years since Mount Mitchell had my ability come that naturally. It usually took a great deal of mental coaxing unless I was feeling strong emotions. You should see how quick a spider can fly through a room when it surprises me.

The combination of mental strain and the fear of becoming a lab rat kept me from using the power much at all. My heart hammered in my chest. My phone, resting on the cordless charging port began to play my Jimi Hendrix playlist. My go-to guy for calming my ass down. I wondered if the song was my doing or some new invention of the internet algorithm reading my thoughts again. Those app tycoons had a magic of their own I swear. As "All Along the Watchtower" played my heart rate slowed.

Typically, I am good with weird, but the day had been jammed packed with it. Link and his strange magnetism, a stollen heart and now this. I'd thought back on that night in the woods many times. The implications of a single touch awakening something dormant in me. I knew then that telekinesis wasn't something I acquired on that mountain. It had always been there. What I didn't understand was why it came out then and why it got stronger now? The ties to

Lincoln Monroe were too hard to ignore but I'd never experienced magic like this. Honestly, it scared me. Getting up I flipped the switch off with my real deal fingers and went to bed.

2.4: If you've got it, forge it.

The next morning, I drove up to school prepared to suffer through the day. I spotted Demi in her usual spot sitting on a rock overlooking the main entrance. Up close I could see dark circles under her eyes. I waved, then signed, "Rough night?"

Holding her index finger in the air she made soft circular motions with her palm facing her chest. "Always."

"Dreams again?" I sympathized.

Demi nodded with a far way look in her eyes. As with most people who find the loss of one of their senses, she gained prowess in others. Not to mention she was the daughter of a witch and a Lakota medicine man. Demi's premonitions unfortunately came in the form of dreams. She liked to come to school early and be in the peace of the morning calm.

"Did you see them?" I didn't need to specify; my best friend knew the Monroe boys were on the top of my spy list.

She brought her index and middle fingers down to rest on the underside of her thumb, "No."

Strange. I was practically late as evidenced by the ringing of the bell moments later. If Demi didn't see them, they weren't here at all.

Why show up on a Tuesday and then dip out the next morning? Why bother to register for school if you didn't plan to attend?

In my mind's eye I saw the paper that Willow's niece, Kate, had crumpled up and threw in the trash. I could imagine that idiot boy Harris dig it out and discover what I was looking into. Damnit. I bet they went straight to her house and barged in without a care to what awaited them. Of course, no one had confronted Willow yet since I made Uncle Wes promise that I could have her.

About to say a quick goodbye, Demi clutched my arm. Her eyes were glazed over as if remembering something. She fingerspelled F U R Y; a clue from her dream. Great. Not only did those stupid boys run into a hunt without an ounce of preparation but they dove headfirst into a nest of Furies. I told Demi to make an excuse for me in the office and I bolted to my car.

Pressing the button to open the glove box I shuffled through the registration and insurance. I moved aside a large camera and found the charm I was looking for. Believe it or not the medallion had the symbol of a speaker and the sound waves coming out of it. It was the same one that you see at the bottom of your computer screen or alongside your phone's volume control. With a circle of silver around the symbol and a slash through it the message was clear enough. 'No noise.' Sometimes even modern ideas can have magical effects. Most of the ancient signs started out as mere carvings after all.

With the noise dampening charm resting around my rearview mirror, I made my way back home. I needed supplies but if my father was there, I would be in serious trouble. I figured if I cruised by and saw his car I could head to the bar, where we kept a lot of the same equipment. If I drove up the road with my engine at full volume, there would be no mistake that it was me. No one else in the neighborhood had a classic car like mine.

Thankfully, my dad wasn't home. I only had time for a smash and grab. Sprinting through the house past the kitchen I flew down the steps to the basement. Bumping my hip painfully into the wrought iron anvil, I skidded to a stop. The zipper of my backpack stuck momentarily as I hastily flayed it open. I had already packed some essentials for a demon extrication, but I wasn't prepared for the Furies. Passing over the raw materials that were used for weapon making in the propane forge I opened the drawers of a tall red tool-cabinet.

Demi gave me invaluable information when she told me about the Furies. Though Greek and Roman mythology paint the Furies as goddesses they were more accurately monsters. Sometimes a god inspires the myth and other times a creature is retrofitted into a god. I opened the drawers that housed our bronze weapons. If you have a Greek problem, bronze was the only solution.

Despite its seemingly normal exterior the red tool-cabinet was not the dumping ground for rusting sockets and long forgotten screw drivers. Each drawer was labeled, and the contents were snugly laid out in shadow foam marking their designated place. Selecting a dagger, I tossed it into the bag. I grabbed five rounds of bronze tipped shotgun shells then turned to the standing safe beside the toolbox. Spinning the dial my fingers naturally stopped at the right numbers to unlock it. I grabbed a short-barreled Remington from its depths and loaded it.

On another shelf inside the safe I scanned the labeled boxes till I found the one I needed. The overhead tube lighting caught in the sparkling metal of the medallion. A spray of aquamarine crystals along the bottom represented the ocean. The burst of vertical fanned tangerine quartz signified the sunrise. The stones worked harmoniously to reduce stress and increase childlike wonder. Both of which the Furies found repulsive. Most importantly, the medallion eliminated the sound of a Fury's cry. The horrifying noise can incapacitate anyone who hears it. Which, I would have told the two geniuses trapped in Ms. Brooks' house if they had bothered to ask.

With my loot obtained I crashed through the door at the top of the basement stairs. Startled, Molly jolted her full mug of coffee sending the scorching brown contents all over her shirt. Sitting on a barstool at the counter she cursed heavily as her skin reddened in angry splotches.

Seething, she said, "Oh girl, you are in so much trouble."

"I don't have time for this. The morons Monroe are about to get themselves killed." I hitched my bag up on my shoulder and started to walk out.

"You know, Mi, there are these people, I think they are called 'adults,' who can do these kinds of things too." Molly snapped, cleaning the coffee off her ruined shirt.

"Cut the sarcasm, Moll, you don't wear it as good as I do."

As I ran off, she shouted, "Go to school!"

"Nobody likes a snitch!" I yelled back.

I didn't really expect her not to tell. Daddy's perfect little angel would never let an injustice like mine go unnoticed. Plus, the school office probably already informed him that I was missing, again. This was my hunt. I'd done the research as per the family rule book. The Monroe boys were already trying and failing to step on my toes. Explaining what went wrong would only waste time. These justifications and more flitted through my anxiety riddled mind as I started my engine again.

2.5: Can you hear me now?

Casa de Brooks looked just like any other house on the suburban street. A classic example of the colonial style, it boasted a columned entrance that framed a red door. Brick steps led to a short porch that marked its stylistic diversion away from the Victorian era. Large bushes on either side of the windows allowed for proper coverage while spying into the living room. When I peered inside, I found exactly what I expected to see. Three Furies and two prone boys, the latter with blood seeping from their ears.

The three 'women' in the window had fathomless black eyes and wide mouths filled with sharp, pointed teeth. Their bodies, barely humanoid, looked frail with strips of decaying flesh hanging from spindly bones. A set of huge bat-like wings hung around their shoulders. The sound of their chatter hummed against the windowpanes. Their voices cawed like birds of prey. Even though I was still outside, I shuddered.

Slipping the quartz and aquamarine medallion over my head, I held on to the last few moments of blissful silence. I tried the door, and it sprang open. At first, the Furies were too stunned to react. I guess the presence of two Smyth boys was enough to make them think they had gotten the job done. Wrong. I rolled to the side and slashed open the binding around Harris' hands. He immediately covered his ears. In one motion I pulled the medallion off and placed it over his head. I had to pry his hands away from his face to get it down around his collarbone.

In the few seconds it took me to unbind Harris, all three of the sisters surrounded us. Standing wing to wing they extended each appendage out. Curving their scaled, black skin like a windswept umbrella they blocked any hope of escape. The toes of their clawed, talon-like feet tapped a rhythm to each other as if sending a code through the vibration. In unison they opened their mouths and began to scream. Harris flinched before he realized he couldn't hear them anymore. Unfortunately, Link and I could, though the former appeared resolutely passed out.

I fought the urge to cover my ears and pushed the shotgun into Harris' hands. He looked down at the weapon, bewildered. There was no time to focus on how annoying his incompetence was.

Unlike anything you could imagine, the sound the Furies made chilled me to the bone. The cry was a mix of the screams, dying moans, and vengeful thoughts of everyone you have ever harmed in your whole life. For a Smyth it can be deadly. I've killed a lot of baddies in my day. The first trickle of blood ran down my neck from my ear.

The skeletal hands of the Fury furthest from me stretched a new piece of rope and twisted it in an elegant knot. The intention of the new binding became clear as she pulled the loop loose ready to ensnare the neck of the closest victim. She reached out, her mouth still extended in the cacophony of her song. As she snatched hold of Harris' shirt her hand clamped straight down on the medallion. A high-pitched squeal of pain clashed against the monstrous symphony. Smoke wafted up from the place where the gemstones had scorched her flesh. She backed away folding her bat flaps protectively around her middle. The other two drew closer, their wings shaking making the cries reverberate in pulsating agony.

Before I lost my wits and potentially my sanity, I gripped my dagger by the hilt. Staggering as I tried to stand, I used the momentum of my lumbering form to sink the weapon into the throat of the nearest Fury. From where the blade stuck into her neck a spiderweb of black, necrotic, poison coated her skin. She fell to the floor, dead and blissfully silent. Seeing their sister collapse, the other two expressed their grief in a horrific keening. I looked over at Link; he appeared to be still unconscious. Then Harris, who apparently didn't know how to fire a gun.

"SHOOT THEM!" I screamed. I couldn't hear my voice over the sounds coming out of the Furies, so I had no idea how impactful my words were.

Harris shook his head, no doubt clearing the cobwebs that took up most of the empty space inside his thoughts. He fired one round at the uninjured Fury and missed blasting the crown molding instead. Through the shrapnel of splintered wood, it stalked toward him. The long, blade-like bones at its wingtips stabbed splintering the oak floor and pulled free seamlessly. Harris backed away. Falling to the ground, he scooted further from his pursuer. The rubber sole of his boots scrambled for purchase along the grooves in the wood.

Crawling toward the dead Fury I tried to retrieve my knife. I felt, rather than heard, the other sister march my way. My heartbeat hard against my ribcage, jumping at the vibrations of her heavy foot falls. My knife, lodged firmly into the dead creature's spine, wouldn't give way. My head felt too heavy to attempt to leverage it out. I didn't think I would have the strength to use the blade again, even if I could manage it. Luckily, the next two shots that Harris fired hit their marks. I turned just in time to be met with a foaming, blood facial as the creature coughed and spluttered its last breaths.

Then the room resolved into silence. Silence except for the ringing in my ears.

Finally, I managed to wiggle the knife from the Fury's throat and rolled over on my back. The pressure in my ears made the room spin in a tilt-a-whirl of vertigo. Closing my eyes, I tried to yawn and equalize my ear drums. I felt urgent hands at my shoulders shaking me. Harris tried to lift be up, but I batted him away weakly. His lips moved saying something, but I couldn't hear him. At least not yet. I sat up on my own and felt my ears pop painfully. A light ringing still muffled my hearing, but I could vaguely make out what Harris wanted.

With his neck coated in drying blood Harris sat in front of me, winded. "Are you okay?"

Looking up at his concerned face I really wanted to remark with sarcasm. Instead, I admitted, "About the same as you, I expect. How's Link?"

"He's fine, I think. I put that necklace on him just in case." Harris leaned back pulling at his earlobes as if he too were still trying to hear properly.

The necklace wouldn't do Link any good now that the Furies were gone. That was a moot point, so I didn't mention it. It couldn't do him any harm either. I decided to address a more important matter. "What made you think that you could just swoop in and take over my investigation? Did you even bother to do any research? And why is Link here? Is he training or something? I know he isn't a registered Smyth. Are you just that piss-poor of a caretaker that you decided to bring him along for the ride?"

Harris' expression tightened, "As a matter of fact he *is* in training. Also, what the hell is this about 'your investigation' you don't own every street in Salem. I can look into things around here too. *I* am a licensed Smyth."

I wrenched the Remington from his hands and got to my knees, so I was level with his face. The comment about the license stung. The only reason I didn't have mine yet was because of their stupid age rule. Harris at just barely over 17-years-old could officially use the Smyth's server and claim hunts. "I logged this investigation."

"With your daddy's number," Harris' dismissive tone made me want to punch him but that wasn't a productive use of my remaining strength.

"It's mine. Unlike someone, I know how to follow the rules."

"Except you're not the Hamilton assigned to this case."

"Hamilton's protect Salem," I snapped. "Katie came to me for help. Not you. Not novice-boy over there taking his cat nap."

"Who's Katie?" Harris got up on his knees too, glaring at me. His height advantage was apparently not all in the legs.

I'd had enough. So, I flicked him hard on the forehead and he drew back from me a little stunned. "You barged in here without a single clue what you were doing and nearly got yourself and your nephew killed. Why don't you trot off back to wherever the hell you are staying and keep out of my way." Harsh, maybe, but he deserved it. I mean in hindsight I probably didn't need to be such a ... well, you know.

"I'm not leaving." I could see in his expression that he was just stubborn enough to stick true to his word. I rolled my eyes and took a deep breath.

"Fine," I said through gritted teeth. "Do you know what we are dealing with up there?" I wasn't interested in going into another fight with him unprepared.

"Yeah, Faustian deal, right?" Uncrossing his arms, he got to his feet. He offered me a hand up and my head was still woozy enough for me to accept it. I nodded but found that messed with my ear chemistry too and quickly desisted.

I pulled my backpack off my shoulders and examined the contents. "There are no special tricks to getting someone out of a Faustian deal. You trade your soul; you owe your soul."

"I know that too," Harris' agitation hissed out. "I'm not an idiot."

Wordlessly, I gestured open palmed to the prone boy on the ground. Harris ran his fingers through his chestnut curls in exasperation.

"Saving Willow Brooks is beyond anyone's capabilities. Crossroad demons, aka our Faustian friends are hard to catch unless someone has already sold them something." I pulled out a sachet, a plastic, neon water gun and a silver cross. "The baggie has salt and bone dust." Harris gave me a blank look, "Demons can't cross into a space surrounded by this stuff."

With dawning comprehension smothered in false bravado, he scoffed, "Right, I knew that. I take it the water gun has holy water in it then?"

"Now you're using your noodle, Monroe." I handed him the plastic weapon and stashed the sachet in my back pocket. "What did you bring to the party?"

He held up a small leather book: the Bible. The words on the binding were in Latin. I pulled a similar book from my bag and tucked the cross into my other pocket. "Well, shall we?"

I made for the stairs, but Harris grabbed my arm, "Faust demons don't usually bring Furies along for the ride."

"'Ours is not to wonder why,'" I quoted. *The Charge of the Light Brigade* felt like a fitting poem for the situation. Willow wanted to raise a dead soldier. Given the Fury bodyguards we were facing a much more powerful demon than we were originally prepared for.

Cracking his neck and steeling himself he finished the quote, "'Ours is but to do or die.'"

2.6: Be careful what you wish for.

Leaving Link snoring on the floor, Harris and I made our way to the second story. We proceeded with caution; our footsteps muffled in the carpeted climb. I wondered if the demon knew we were coming for it after hearing the commotion downstairs.

The voice of a woman, I assumed was Willow, fumbled over the foreign words in her chant. On the landing, I caught the first whiff of pungent sulfur, a demons' eau de cologne. As we drew nearer the undertone of a deeper voice came from beyond the open door to the master bedroom. A new, foul smell wafted down the hallway. Having spent a good deal of time around a funeral home, I was well acquainted with the odor of formaldehyde. I put my hand over my mouth in revulsion as we pushed the door open further to reveal the scene.

Mathew Brooks was the picture of heroism. Decked out in his dress blues, the white hat and belt offset the red trimmed suit. His lips and eyes were glued shut giving him the illusion of being asleep. The jacket of his suit lay open at either side of his body. A hole, where his heart had been, was scooped clean. The skin, neatly folded over the side of his ribcage, had a thin layer of yellow fat clinging to it.

Willow had the stolen heart of the young shop girl in both of her hands as she chanted. Still beating, it pumped blood from an unknown source which streaked down her arms. The demon stood behind her concentrating on something near her lower back. A wet sort of ripping sound rent the air. The volume of Willow's words rose in a crescendo as she fought the urge to break her recital and cry out. The demon held up a paper-thin piece of Willow's own skin. The drips of blood at the corners mirrored the letters on the contract.

"That's nasty." The blood drained from Harris' face. I elbowed him to make him shut up, but the damage was done.

Disconcertingly, the demon smiled as it looked up at us. Its face was thickly bearded. The plumed facial hair crinkled out impressively reaching the width of its shoulders then tapered down nearly to its navel. In its black suit and black button-down shirt, it looked almost like an average person. The eyes gave it away as otherworldly. Over large and seemingly lidless they stared out black as if they had no iris at all. It nodded to Willow, who lowered the heart into her son's chest and the skin magically folded over sealing neatly. The demon began to glow, the white light trimmed black at the edges.

Harris fumbled with the pages of his Bible searching for the right verse. Mine, neatly tabbed for easy use, opened directly to the proper spot. The demon eyed us with increasing disdain but seemed taken aback by our lack of fluidity.

I smiled, embarrassedly and shoved my own Bible into Harris' hands, "Dude, seriously?" I placed the marked section of "The Lord's Prayer" into Harris' trembling palms. Haltingly, he began to read. Rescuing a slip of paper from between some of the other pages, I got started on the Latin translation of "The Calling to Saint Michael the Archangel."

The self-satisfied smile slid from the demon's face to be replaced by a scowl. Floating toward us, it moved faster and more gracefully than I could imagine. I lost the thread of my words and stumbled over the next lines. Latin typically immobilized demons.

Seemingly unaffected, Super-beard got close enough to throat-punch me. Gagging, I fell to the floor. It made to move toward Harris, but I kicked it in the shins. It tripped but with that same blinding speed, it turned over then scuttled across the ground in creepy, rapid, jerking movements.

Inches from my face it snarled, "Older than you were prepared for, huntress?"

Harris grabbed it by the collar and received a shove in the sternum for his efforts. He fell back against the wall, stunned. The demon returned its attention to me. Its nose brushed up against the skin of my neck as it sniffed me. I felt a trickle of what I could only assume was drool, drip down my collar bone.

"Body fluids to yourself, please," I said. Then I rammed my knee up between its legs. I don't care if you're a man, woman, or hell beast a knee to the pelvis was painful. It rolled away clutching the space between its legs.

Getting up, I saw Willow doing CPR on her son. She had ripped open his lips to blow air into his mouth. When she pulled away the jagged skin stuck in odd clumps to either side of the opening.

Retreating, I crawled over to Harris. Then I sprinkled the contents of the sachet in a circle around us. "That should keep us safe," I hoped. Harris kept up his chanting but shrugged his shoulders.

Rising to its feet, the demon stalked toward us almost lazily. "I am not an average demon," it proclaimed. Changing its voice, the words came out sultry and alluring, the sounds pronounced in the back of its throat. The dark-edged glow pulsed with power around him. "I am the Lord Mephistopheles."

Harris gulped and the light around Mephisto grew brighter in the moment of silence. I stood up squaring my shoulders trying to look braver than I felt. "Keep reading Harris. As much as it would be an honor to be killed by *the* Mephistopheles, I'm not planning on dying today." The demon seemed to enjoy the complement.

"Don't worry, marked one. I am not permitted to kill you." Mephisto took another step forward, his eyes twinkling in challenge. The Latin clearly slowed him down but not much. "The boy, however, has no such protection."

"I don't know what that means but it's nice to know I'm not on the menu. Gonna have to agree to disagree about the boy, though." I flipped the loose paper I had been reading the prayer from over.

The demon sucked in a breath through his teeth, snarling and inched closer.

I grimaced in mock sympathy. "Let's talk about killing us later. Soldier boy feels like the more pressing problem don't you think?"

To illustrate my point, Willow began pounding on her son's chest wailing, "Bring him back! You promised me!"

Striving for a casual remonstration, I continued, "You see, Lord M, raising the dead is frowned upon in this century. We don't have those convenient grave bells to blame for why, Mr. Brooks over there, might have been mistakenly embalmed."

"You are bold, huntress. I like this." Mephisto's German accent grew more obvious. With a snap of his fingers Willow's voice vanished. Her mouth moved but the sound was gone. "The warrior will rise in due course. I must first dispatch with the hunter chanting in that terrible heathen's tongue."

Contrary to Mephisto's threat he didn't approach the bone/salt circle any further but the confidence in his glare didn't bode well. I pulled the silver cross from my back pocket before addressing Harris, "How's your German?"

Breaking his looped Latin, he turned to me and said, "Non-existent."

Unburdened by the chanting, Mephisto lunged toward us. Tactically, that was not my best move. I grabbed the silver cross from my back pocket by its shorter top point and jabbed the longer end into his lordships over large eyeball. Staggering back and clutching his face we saw smoke coming out from between his fingers. I shoved the eyeball-gooped cross into Harris' hands. "I'll chant, you squirt. When he looks weak enough press as much of that cross onto his flesh as possible."

He pulled the water gun from his back pocket. I smoothed out my loose paper and began to chant amateurly in German. Immediately, Mephisto approached, reaching long, sharp nails out at us. At the sound of the prayer in his native language his whole being began to shudder. Harris squirted away soaking the demon's clothes and patches of skin all of which began to smoke.

Mephisto staggered back leaning against the dresser across from Willow's bed. Exiting our protective circle Harris used the last of his holy-water ammo then chucked the gun at the demon's head for good measure which pinged off harmlessly. Before Harris could apply the silver cross, the demon struck, hitting him in the face. Mephisto breathed heavily, skin smoking, and visibly shaking without stop. He grabbed the Willow-flesh contract and tucked it safely into the front pocket of his suit. Glaring at us, both eyes suddenly bright red, he gave us one last withering stare of contempt. Then, in a flash of light, he disappeared.

2.7: Please don't raise the dead, it's gross.

Willow abandoned the CPR and laid across her son's deflated chest. With the demon gone the promise of the young man's resurrection went with him. I honestly didn't know what that meant for the contract. The bloody rectangle on the dresser indicated that the document had not been merely an illusion.

Reaching out a tentative hand, I gripped the sobbing woman's shoulder. I had no sympathy for her after what she had done to the shop girl. I imagine that she needed the heart because her son's must have been damaged in some way. Not even demons can put Humpty Dumpty back together if some of the parts are missing.

Willow looked up at me, pale faced with red blotches on her cheeks and at the tip of her nose. Her eyes were over bright and manic. She clutched her son's coat and shook him. "It didn't work. Why would he just leave if it didn't work?"

I didn't have a proper answer for that, so I said, "Self-preservation, probably."

That's usually high on a demon's list of motivators. Willow flung her arms around me. The tacky sensation of the not quite dried blood from her hands brushed against the back of my neck. Frozen in place, my arms hung awkwardly at my sides. She wasn't attacking so I couldn't in good conscious fling her off.

Turning away from me, she caressed the sagging flesh of her dead son. I shot an uncomfortable look at Harris. Massaging the point on his cheek where Mephisto had struck him, he gave me a noncommittal shrug. Typical boy, leaving all the hard decisions up to me. Brass tacks: we had a murderer, a dead soldier, three rotting Furies and sleeping beauty downstairs. The time had come for reinforcements.

I pulled my cell from my back pocket and thumbed through the contacts. Dad would have come in an instant, but Uncle Wes would give me less grief about the ditch day.

"Hello tardy girl." Wes' voice was gruff but not without a hint of amusement. "I take it you just couldn't wait to interview Ms. Brooks."

My lips lifted in a sheepish smile. "Something like that."

"This emergent or can I finish my sandwich?" The sound of crinkling wax paper made my stomach rumble.

I turned to the dresser where the contract had been. Something bothered me about all this, but I couldn't quite put my finger on it. "Well, all the threats are neutralized but..." I bit my lip trying to draw the problem out of my brain. Willow had a point. The contract was clearly signed and confirmed. The demon owed his part of the bargain. He took off with the collection slip for her soul after all.

Serious now, Wes coaxed, "But what, Mia?"

I stared, unseeingly, into the ornate mirror attached to the top of the dresser. "Do you think a demon as powerful as Mephisto could raise the dead? If he couldn't then he wouldn't have made the bargain, right?"

"Did you just say Mephisto? As in THE Mephistopheles?" Wes' voice was urgent.

Before I could answer, I thought I saw Matthew's hand twitch in the reflection. His skin was still pale. A snapping of unused joints popped as the fingers of the dead soldier curled and clawed into the bedspread. I dropped the phone.

All our eyes focused on the first signs of resurrection. Willow and Harris seemed transfixed by the jerking spasms in Matthew's hands. They didn't see a set of milky, dull eyes open with mindless purpose. Approaching slowly, I pulled the Remington off my shoulder. I tried to keep my voice calm but stuttered as I warned, "Willow, I-I think you might want to step back."

Foolishly, the woman disregarded me. She placed both her palms lovingly on her son's face. Apparently, the dead eyes didn't cause her any trepidation. She leaned closer planting a kiss on his cheek. His hand reached up and clamped down on the hair on the back of Willow's head. Before I could raise the gun, he fastened his teeth on her throat, ripping out her jugular. I squeezed the trigger in reflex, not really aiming. When the gun shot sunk into his abdomen, he didn't even flinch. Kinda insulting if you ask me. At least he dropped his mother to the floor. Stunned, she didn't even try to staunch the flow of blood that was spurting out of her neck. He sat up, mouth hanging wide in a bloody gape.

Harris backed away from the bed. "Dude, you have to aim for the head. How do you not know that?" Zombie Matt cocked his head to either side jerkily. More pops and cracks loosened his stiff neck.

"Of course, I know that. I couldn't get a clear shot without blasting mommy apart as well." True enough as far as he was concerned.

"Fat lot of good that's doing her now." The front of Willow's shirt was soaked in blood. Her chest rose and fell slowly, and her eyes drooped. The last remaining triumphant smile played at her lips as her eyes faded into oblivion. There was no help for it. We couldn't get to her if we tried.

Matt lurched forward falling to his knees at the end of the bed. Panicking, Harris backed away and pulled out a six-inch blade from his boot. Looking at it morosely he muttered, "Stupid tiny knife."

Taking pity on him I tossed Harris the Remington, "Make it count we only have one shell left."

Unclipping the garrot from my belt I stretched it between my hands. I didn't think I really needed the gun owing to my higher ground advantage as Matt lay on the floor. Only then, our stiff legged friend got to his feet, taking one small step for zombies in my direction. Harris was bigger and had the gun, but I guess I did shoot the soldier after all.

Unfortunately, it turns out that Mathew Brooks was a good 6'2" in life and powerfully built. My much shorter frame couldn't hope to reach his meaty head. I tried to kick out his legs, but he clamped his hands around my arms and pinned me to the wall. His gross foul breath came closer as he lifted me easily off the ground. That's when half his face disintegrated and spattered across my cheek. Ew. Just so very ew.

I got dropped. Ankle and floor did not make friends. The ringing in my ears dazed me. The smell of singed hair didn't dissipate as I lay on the ground away from soldier half-a-face which led me to believe the offending locks were my own. Harris made to fire again, presumably forgetting that I just told him he had ONE SHOT. The zombie formally known as Lance Corporal Brooks advanced toward the new threat.

My garrote had fallen, and I couldn't see where it had gotten to. Fortunately, the Marine came equipped with his ceremonial sword. Limping toward him I grabbed the hilt of the blade, and I pulled it from his belt like it was Excalibur. Then I swung it as hard as I could toward his neck.

It was not so easy to decapitate a person. You may be thinking, 'but you did it so smoothly with Mrs. Chambers.' True but ghouls are just wearing human skin suits. Their bone structure is completely different. Sort of flexible so that they can crawl on in. Crawl into where? You don't want to know.

Standing from the ground trying to reach up to the head of a fully grown man who was damn near a whole foot taller than me made for sloppy work and a lot of swings. After the frenzy of whacks to his neck I was left holding the sword aloft covered in very potent fluids. Matthew's body fell, head rolling to his mother's feet. Harris had to unclench my fingers from around the blade to wrest it from my hands.

Running to the bathroom, I unloaded the contents of my stomach into the toilet. I'm only human, guys. Turning on the faucet, I cupped my hand beneath the stream and looked down into the muddy pool of blood and dirt in my palm. Knowing my face couldn't appear much better I chose not to examine it in the mirror. Instead, I cleaned myself up as thoroughly as possible then made my way back to Harris.

In the hallway, Harris sat with his back to the bedroom door. Glancing inside, I saw Willow dead only a few feet from where her son's headless body had fallen. I slid down the wall, the edge of Mathew's meticulously polished shoe just visible from the doorway. A heavy pang of guilt for killing the man fell to the pit of my newly empty stomach. Though he wasn't exactly alive, it felt wrong to desecrate his body like that after everything he had sacrificed for our country.

Harris handed me my cell phone and I sent a text to Uncle Wes letting him know I was still alive. I felt bad for his sandwich. He probably didn't get to finish it after listening to me get my butt kicked. As the adrenaline faded, my ankle throbbed painfully.

I must have winced because Harris nodded to the offending appendage, "You alright?"

"It's just a sprain I think." My ankle was the least painful part of me at the moment. I preferred the clean-cut monsters: djinn, hell beasts, poltergeists. A young man and his grief-stricken mother dead in the room behind me hit too close to home.

Something of this must have registered on my face. Harris looked down weighing his words, "You did what you had to do."

I scrunched my nose pushing back the sensation of tears, "Doesn't suck any less though."

Changing the subject Harris pondered, "She's not going to go all zombie on us, is she?"

I shivered slightly and brought my knees up to my chest. "No. Matt was made by craptastic magic. The contagious ones are necromancer minions." I got the sense that he already knew that, but I appreciated the attempt to take my mind off what I had done.

Mutely, he reached out his hand and placed it on the floor between us. I took it, not sure why. He held my hand till the others arrived and strangely it made me feel better. There was something broken in him too. He might not have delivered the death blow, but I don't think shooting Matthew sat well with him either. For a few minutes I appreciated the company of a fellow Smyth. Someone who understood the full cost of what we were tasked to do.

2.8: It takes a toll.

Rule # 3: To everything its place.

3.1: For my final meal I'll take lasagna.

With my eyes closed and a cup of coffee steaming around my face I was only vaguely aware of my father's presence in the kitchen. As I put down my mug, a crimson envelope slid toward me bumping the back of my fingers.

The letter was on our traditional family stationery sealed with wax and our signate. We usually reserved it for serious matters. "What's this?"

"An invitation." My dad busied himself pouring coffee into his own mug. I turned the envelope over and read: Harrison and Lincoln Monroe.

"Wow, pretty formal for an inquisition or are we lining up a firing squad as well?" I hoped it was just the boys who were going to get an earful for butting into my investigation. Not my own comeuppance for skipping school.

"Let them know that Molly will be making lasagna."

Molly's lasagna was epic. However, the process usually boded some big family discussion and thus I associated it with ill omens. "Save me a slice?"

"Don't worry, Mia. You'll be getting your fair share." The glint of challenge danced in dad's eyes as he smiled.

Damn, I really hoped that I had gotten off scot-free. "Come on, it was my hunt..."

"Better hurry up." Dad pointed to the clock on the wall. "Don't want to be late for school."

When I say that I spent the entire school day with anxiety racing through my veins I'm not exaggerating. By the end of 7th period my nails had been unceremoniously bitten down to the quick. Plus, I think I gained muscle mass from the constant shaking of my leg. I delivered the letter to Harris with a half-hearted condolence.

When I made it back home, I registered the intoxicating smell of marinara and melting cheese. Molly pulled out a fresh batch of homemade garlic butter rolls when I slipped into the kitchen. I snatched one off the piping hot baking tray before her oven-mitt encapsulated hand could try to deflect me. The minor burns to my fingertips were so worth it as I pulled the bread apart and steam flew upward in wisps.

"Thief." Molly banged the rest of the tray on the counter.

"Can you really blame me." I held the bread out, tantalizingly.

She swatted me away from the rest. Lifting the delicate stem of a wine glass she sipped the excellent vintage no doubt from our own wine cellar. At twenty-one years old, Molly enjoyed showing off the advantages of her adult status. It gave her a sinister pleasure, in my opinion, to rub it in.

Playing with another roll that I artfully snagged without her knowing, I eyed the dishes in the sink. "Did you make your own ricotta?"

Molly gave me an apologetic smile. "Yes. And homemade pasta too."

I groaned. The fresher the ingredients the more serious the conversation. "I won't be hunting till I'm seventeen, will I?"

"It's not as bad as that Amelia," but Molly avoided my eyes by peeking into the oven to check on her masterpiece.

"Oh sure, just full name worthy. I guess I should be glad I didn't get middle or last named too. Then I'm sure I'd be shipped off to Antarctica to search for the lone Yeti on the whole dang continent. For all eternity!"

"Don't be so dramatic. Dad would never let you go out of state and end up just getting a GED."

"HA!" My triumphant expository was dulled somewhat by the hysteria.

Molly dropped the pretense. "I don't know what the punishment will be. I just know he was very specific about the menu..."

"... And you know what that means," we said together then laughed in unison. I stopped and took a deep calming breath.

"It just means he's serious." Molly hugged me, which gave me prime access to the platter of rolls. As she pulled away, I popped another into my mouth.

"Can you make the salad, Mi?" Molly rolled her eyes. "I don't have time now that I need to make another batch of rolls."

I tried to respond but the words didn't make it past my third pilfered roll. Honestly though, what did she expect? They were so freaking good fresh from the oven. By the time I dressed the salad the doorbell rang. I heard my dad greeting our guests in the hall then leading them to the dinner table.

"Show time." I toyed with the salad tongs trying to delay. Molly slid her arm around my waist and gave me a bracing squeeze. Salad in hand I went to face the consequences.

3.2: Could I get a stay of execution?

The Monroe boys stood awkwardly beside the long banquet table that dominated the dining room. My dad looked perfectly at ease, pouring glasses with water and a special one with whiskey neat. He handed out the water and sat down with his glass smiling.

To avoid looking him in the eye, I pulled the plates from a 200-year-old hutch in the corner. Harris lifted the dishes from my hands seeming just as nervous as me. I let him. Doing something felt better than sitting down waiting for the sentencing. My father didn't seem angry. He knew what our punishment would be, and seemed pleased with the level of vindictiveness it would have.

I took my place and Molly sat opposite giving me a weak smile. I tried to pass the salad to Link, but he was staring at the art and memorabilia around the room. He gawked intently at the oil painting that dominated the wall roughly the size of a set of double doors. The man in the portrait wore a light gray suit with a white frilled collar. His ungloved hand rested on a stack of papers. A three-pot inkwell sat nearby atop the green writing desk.

After Link piled a good portion of the salad onto his plate, he stuffed a healthy measure into his mouth. He seemed so eager to ask questions that he quite forgot to swallow. "Is that a replica,"

Link choked, his words muffled behind lettuce. "Sorry, replica of the John Trumbull portrait of Alexander Hamilton?"

"Nope," my dad replied, succinctly. Molly and I snickered at each other. Link's confusion was endearing.

"I could have sworn it was, sorry." Link turned back to his salad. As he played with the croutons, I could almost see the cogs in his brain turning. I sympathized. It can be frustrating when you are sure you know the answer, and someone pulls the rug out from under you.

"No need to apologize, son. You see it's an heirloom. The one at the Met is the replica. This here is the original." My dad took a sip from his glass.

Link laughed out loud, no I will not LOL, learn to read. The sound was quickly stifled as he turned to me, "He's serious?"

"Yup," I cut my words off not trusting myself to speak too much and attract more of my father's attention.

Molly patted Link's hand gently. "Lots of those famous portraits are just replicas in the museums. I mean no one in their right mind is going to let the Mona Lisa get destroyed cause some underpaid security guard didn't follow protocol." Link's mouth fell open in an astonished 'O' shape. "Don't worry." Molly continued, "Mia will bring you up to speed, she lives and breathes this stuff."

"What?" I compulsorily exclaimed. Since when was I being volunteered to teach the clueless kid. My sister's gaze darted toward my dad like she'd just said something she shouldn't have.

Dad rubbed his temple as if trying to stave off a headache. "Molly, darling, can you please plate up a few slices of that lasagna. It smells delicious, sweetheart." She nodded, her cheeks a delicate shade of rose and darkening by the second.

I examined my father's face, set in determination. I didn't do partnerships let alone take on trainees. I didn't want or need extra help. My father's expression of raised eyebrows was a challenge. It said, 'try me.'

When the door to the kitchen swung shut, I stood up and glared at my dad. "You have got to be kidding me, right? I am not playing babysitter to a trainee."

"Oh, yes you are." Dad sipped his whiskey and put it down with a gentleness that seemed at odds with the fire in his eyes. "This week alone you have managed to skip class twice. Once to clean up an unauthorized execution."

I cut him off. "What was I supposed to do, just let Will Forester get eaten between 5th and 6th period? Or better yet just leave her headless body there for her Advanced Algebra class to find?" Sarcasm and exasperation made my tone more sullen than I typically liked.

My father, for all his grace merely smiled at me, in a very patronizing way I might add. "The second time, you ran off to save these two." He gestured to the Monroe boys with a possibly intentional middle finger while the others kept a firm hold on his glass.

I sat back down but pushed my chair away from the table in agitation. I wouldn't have needed to ditch if it weren't for tweedle-danger and tweedle-dumbass over there. Mrs. Chambers was potentially forgivable. There wasn't a ton of time to call in reinforcements. The boys, however, …

My dad just stared; waiting for me, as always, to come to the right conclusion. I knew the correct answer. I could have called any number of qualified Smyths to rescue the Monroe's. "It was my case." My voice was low and sulky.

"And…," dad gestured for me to go on.

"And I should have asked for help." Fine, whatever, he's right. Big surprise.

"Great," Dad clapped his hands lightly and rubbed them together, getting down to business. His expression, though light, made me shiver. "From now on you won't need to call for back up unless something needs to be done during school hours. That goes for all of you. You won't need backup because you will all be working together."

For the first time Harris popped his head up from his eye contact avoiding position. "Wait, what? Like all of us? Link too?" Something weird passed between him and my dad. Harris looked wary.

Dad's eyes flashed in warning. "Between you and Mia, I think you have enough experience to properly teach Link. I know John said he didn't want Link to be a Smyth. I think you can agree that doesn't make a ton of sense now that your brother is gone. He sent you to me for a reason. Link isn't safe anymore. He needs to be trained, plain and simple."

This last bit was intriguing enough for me to forget that I was mad about the whole situation. Why wouldn't Link be safe now that his dad was gone? How would training to be a Smyth help? Beyond the obvious that there are monsters, beasts, and other worldly things all over the place; what specifically could be coming just for him? Not to mention if I wasn't supposed to be near him then why make me his trainer?

Dad crossed his arms over his chest looking imposing enough not to be questioned. "Listen, start working together. If you stick to Hamilton territory, you'll be fine, but the kid can't be kept in a safe haven forever. I've already set them up in the apartment over the bar and if you boys work the dish pit now and then I'll kick something in for groceries. I know you said you'd quit school to get a job, Harris, but if you're going to be here you follow my rules."

Molly poked her head into the room. With a gesture of encouragement from my dad she wheeled in a serving cart piled with beautifully plated lasagna. Despite my preoccupation with unanswered questions, I couldn't help but enjoy my dinner.

When we were finished my dad helped Molly clear the table and set to his post dinner ritual of dishes. The cook never cleans up in our house. Molly kissed me on the top of my head and went upstairs to her room.

I sat in silence with the Monroe boys for a long while. I was trying my best to come to terms with the hated word, *partner.* Just thinking of it made me want to gag. A partner was one thing but then to saddle me with a trainee at the same time was cruel and unusual punishment. There was no way out but through, as usual.

Breaking my thoughts, Harris started speaking in a ridiculously loud stage whisper. "He can't force us to do this. He can't watch us all the time."

Not bothering to keep my voice down I said, "Yes, actually, he can." What poor naïve Harrison Monroe didn't realize was that for a well-respected man like Mitchel Hamilton, eyes were always looking out on his affairs. There was a large bar full of spies, the school janitor, not to mention Uncle Wes.

"Here is what we are going to do," I commanded. "Tomorrow morning the both of you can meet me here. This is probably the best place to start training. Let's make it 10am, I like to sleep in on the weekends." As a teenager, it's exhausting to rage with hormones all the time. Harris looked ready to argue but Link cut him off and agreed. I walked them to the door.

After, I made my way to the kitchen and grabbed a towel. As dad washed, I dried. I didn't know if he would answer but I had to ask what shifted his opinion of Link. "First I was never to see the kid again, now he's my trainee?"

Dad dropped the fork he was cleaning, and it clattered against the porcelain of the sink bottom. He picked up a plate instead. "You'll make a good teacher."

"That doesn't come anywhere near answering my question." I rescued the plate from his hands. He had started scrubbing it too vigorously.

"Some things are unavoidable." He looked almost sad. I wish I could say the cryptic thing bothered me but that was dad's way. You got used to it. His expression said that the subject was closed.

Just one more question burned in my mind. For months I had been helping with the investigation of a spectacular apocalyptic event set to occur on the third Friday-the-thirteenth this year. D-day was nigh.

Piling the dinner plates neatly I broke the silence, "So...Florida?" There were only a handful of times he allowed me to be his full partner over the years and this was set to be one of them. With my newfound twin shackles of Monroe and Monroe I was afraid the arrangement had changed. One look at my father's face told me that my fears were not baseless.

"Come on. I've been researching this event for months dad!"

"It's just an apocalypse Mia." He handed me a new plate. "There will be another one any time now."

"You promised," I muttered, under my breath. Loud enough for him to hear but quiet enough for him to ignore.

He didn't though. "I know, kiddo. You've done excellent work, but you know how important your education is to me. You broke the rules and reckless games have consequences."

"Dad, they don't have a clue what they're doing. Going into things with no research, not knowing what they are facing. To think that Harris is responsible for Link is laughable. He's not even two years older than us for God's sake."

Dishes finished dad dried off his hands. "I agree with you. That's why they need your help."

"Don't try to butter me up now Hamilton. I know a handcuff when I see one."

"I know it doesn't make sense right now, why I push so hard for you to finish school. I'm sure that it feels like 90% of your relevant education is done on hunting trips. One day you might not have the luxury of being at your physical best." The essence of regret resounded in his voice as if he found himself rounding that corner.

I appraised my father. Tall, lean, and lightly muscled he couldn't be anywhere near ready to hang his hat. His beard had only recently begun to change from its dark brown to a peppered chin of white mixed in. The hair at his temples had grown light as well. The skin around his eyes remained crinkled even after he ceased to smile or glare as the occasion warranted. His eyes still had the intensity of a trained and deadly killer. For all his unwavering seriousness I knew deep down he worried for me.

"Okay dad." There was no point in arguing. This was his final word on the subject. I gave him a hug and went off to my room to prepare for the following day.

3.3: Don't nerd out too hard, Princess.

Every ounce of my being did not want to wake up the next day. I spent the better half of the night preparing some materials for Link to study with. Unconsciously, I began to plan out lessons and think of ways to get him some field training. The OCD bit of my brain kinda liked all the details. The 'wake up and deal with idiotic questions' part of me did not.

By the time the doorbell rang I was ready, dressed in jeans and my dad's Black Sabbath t-shirt. I had artfully torn the bottom half of the shirt off so that it fell just below my rib cage. Opening the door, I readied myself to give them a snarky remark about their lateness, but Link shoved a large coffee cup under my nose.

"We would have been on time but *mister thoughtful* here said we ought to bring coffee as a sign of thanks," Harris complained. I gave them both a withering look.

"Coffee and donuts." Link produced the pink box and opened it so I could inventory the variety. I selected a chocolate glazed number and gestured with it to imply they should follow along. As he looked over the box Link met my eyes, but thankfully, no strange tingling happened.

I led them through the maze of staircases and narrow hallways toward the library. Link looked ready to pause at every doorway to examine their intricately carved frames. Instead, he settled himself by asking questions. "This place is amazing. When was it built? Are there carvings everywhere? Have the Hamilton's always lived here? Your dad said that portrait last night was an heirloom. Are you guys actually related to Alexander Hamilton?"

"That was a lot, Link." I chuckled. Looking back, I saw the flush of embarrassment in his cheeks. "From the top then. The manor was built in 1900 by my Hamilton ancestors so it boasts an impressive array of secrets. It was given every possible protection against demons and monsters at the time and successive generations have added to it as needed."

"Even the bathrooms?" Link walked right into Harris as he was looking everywhere but down at his own feet.

Harris shoved him back lightly. "Pay attention."

"I am. House built in 1900, no demons or monsters allowed," Link summarized.

"Exactly." He might just turn out to be a good student after all. "The bathrooms are one of the most important places to have protection. No one wants to be attacked during any activity that happens in there." I winked at Harris who grinned sheepishly for a moment before looking away. I'm not above a little inuendo.

We reached a panel of wall that was decorated in a floor to ceiling portrait of a woman. Her hair was parted aggressively down the middle and plastered to her head. I shuddered to think what that hair gel must have been made of back then. The ringlets of curls descending across her shoulder were the same dark mahogany as my sister and me.

"As to whether I am really related to A. Ham. This is Phillipa, granddaughter of John Church Hamilton, fourth son of Mr. Ten Dollar bill and my great, great, great ... something ... aunt."

"Wow," Link whispered.

"Okay guys, watch this." I pressed a nine-pointed star that was carved on either side of the painting, right about in the same spot you'd expect a light switch to be. The door split Philippa's face down the middle opening into a room beyond.

Link let out an audible sigh of wonder as he entered. Bookshelves adorned by oak ladders on casters dominated every available surface of the walls. The center of the room had a table. Made from the vertical center cut, of a rowan tree that was sanded and lacquered it had filigreed metal legs. After a moment of stunned silence Link raced over to the nearest shelf and plucked an aging volume from the hoard. He opened it lovingly. I waited for him to break out into song or something as he looked ready to twirl and make friends with local woodland creatures.

Above him a book, or should I say tome, flew unassisted from the shelves and whacked Link across the back of his head. I winced. I should have warned him. The overlarge nose and pinched pursing lips of Great Aunt Philippa appeared floating in the air; hand clasped around the encyclopedia of ancient Egypt. Link looked up at her semi-corporeal form and his face drained of color. He scampered away and bravely hid behind me.

"Link meet Aunt Philippa. Pippa this is Link and Harris Monroe." I tried not to laugh. Pippa's manic red ringed eyes were such a stark difference from the primly powdered and flattering image of the portrait.

"Put that book back boy!" Pippa shouted. Her voice sounded like she spoke through a mouth coated in sandpaper.

"Now, now, Pip. They are guests and we need to get Link here trained up." I took a sip of my coffee.

"Is that a beverage in MY LIBRARY!" Pippa screamed.

"What? No," I lied putting the cup behind my back and forcing a look of false innocence.

"AND FOOD!"

I peered down at my donut and sighed. "Listen Pip, if you don't calm down, I'm going to have to banish you to the attic again. We don't want that right?"

Blotches of red coated her face as she raged. She glared at me; her eyes consumed in blackness, the sockets stretching, swirling dark. Her teeth elongated coming to sharp menacing points in a jaw that unhinged and split the ghostly flesh at her cheeks. Flying down, her fingernails grew thick talons, arms growing like tree branches to reach toward me and sink into my flesh.

Both Harris and Link backed rapidly toward the open door, but I didn't flinch. I pulled a talisman from around my neck and gripped it tightly. A blinding white light emanated from my chest and blasted poor Pippa backward knocking her into the wall of books sending some cascading to the floor.

She got up hovering lightly over the ground and breathing heavily. I kept my hand on the necklace. "Are we done Pip? I have work to do."

"Vile girl. Unnatural heathen," Pippa hissed but her face returned to its humanoid form.

"At a girl." My great aunt faded into the bookshelf muttering angrily. I laughed and returned to the boys. They were both one foot out the door looking at me like I was an alien or something. This training stuff was going to take some getting used to.

3.4: Living under a rock.

I coaxed the boys back in and promised them they could still eat their donuts. "Twenty points if you can guess what sort of creature Aunt Pippa has become?"

Harris looked stony, one hand on a concealed knife. I kinda respected the fact that he didn't go anywhere unarmed. Link shook, clutching the book he had originally grabbed to his chest. He squeaked something completely inaudible then cleared his throat, "Poltergeist."

"Good," I was honestly impressed. Not every newbie can tell a poltergeist from a common ghost. "Tell me how you got there?"

Looking to Harris for help Link swallowed. "Um, she could move things?"

Before I could say anything, Harris sat at the table in the room. "Most ghosts can move stuff, Linky."

Finally calming down Link also sat, thinking hard. "She could transform. She was, like, kinda solid too."

"Excellent." I tossed Link a pink notebook with a white cartoon kitten on the front. "Write it down. This is the start of your own monster journal. The most important thing Smyths can do is write down their experiences. If we each share what we find it's easier to know what to do when we come across something similar."

Studiously, Link began to write. "What do my points do?"

Taken aback I just sat down beside him. "Nothing it was just; you know … a joke." Somewhere in the back of my mind I heard the crash of a drum and symbol as my humor fell flat.

Link snorted in delayed amusement. Pausing in his notes, he pointed to my medallion, "What did you do to her?"

Releasing the clasp, I slid the charm off my neck and handed it to Link. "It's a deceptively strong little thing. Concentrates your aura." From the outside it looked like a simple triangle about the size of a silver dollar. "Each of the sides are made with a different material, metal, wood, and stone. The center has a droplet of water behind two thin pieces of glass."

In Link's hands the center turned bright violet. "Woah, what does that mean?"

I smiled at the childlike curiosity in Link's delivery. Looking over at Harris, I saw him giving Link the same indulgent expression.

"Purple is the color of intuition," Harris answered.

"Why is my color so different?" Link pondered still examining the glowing triangle.

"We all experience different colors." I pulled a thin book from a shelf and opened it to the page on chakra and aura. Link looked ready to copy the whole book into his notes, but I stayed his hand. "It's just for reference. I learned how to project my aura with the help of this charm. I used the color, white, for purification. On lesser threats like Aunt Pippa, it's helpful. That part you can write down." Link tried to hand the necklace back, "No you keep it. I have other ones."

"How do you choose your color? Where does the aura come from?" Link was back to rapid fire questions again.

I sighed. "The aura is kinda like your soul. It's tethered to your body but as with astral projection, dream walking and aura blasts (like what I did to Aunt Pippa) it can go places the human form can't."

"Woah, how do you dream walk?" Link's eyes were so wide I started to be afraid they were going to pop out of his head.

"Honestly, I've never done it cause ... cringe, you know?" Harris nodded emphatically. I was half curious what secrets were behind that thick skull of his. The other half...yeah, no thanks. "From what I've read you get to the astral plane, (that I can do) then you dive on in, I guess."

Link scribbled notes on my not-so-great explanation of dream walking. "So, notes help tell other Smyths about what we did. How do we share our information? I mean how many of you are there?" He looked from me to Harris.

I stopped dead then turned and stared at the older boy. He avoided my gaze. How does a kid live with two fully qualified Smyths and not know that? "It's a league, Link. That star on your notebook, the one carved in the hallway out there represents the magical congregation. Three seats for each of the magical communities' most influential members. It's a massive order that spans the globe."

"Wow," Link sat back astonished.

"Are you telling me that your dad never talked to you about any of this?" It seemed inconceivable to me that he could be brought along to monster hunts and not ask questions. Especially, since he seemed to love to ask them.

Harris butted in again, his voice tense with irritation, "Like your dad said, John didn't want him trained as a Smyth."

"Then why drag him along on hunts?" I folded my arms; his attitude was annoying. It wasn't my fault we were having this conversation. I didn't want to train Link. When my father says something needs to be done, I trust him.

While the two of us were glaring at each other Link stood up. "I wanted to go," he said to me. "And I want to learn," he addressed Harris.

"Well, I guess that settles that." I was still extremely wary of all the secrecy but for the life of me I couldn't see the forest through the trees. One of Pippa's idioms but it seemed to fit no matter how old-fashioned it was.

"Sweet! So, Smiths." Link headed a fresh page of his notebook with the title.

Glancing down I corrected, "Smyth with a Y not an I."

"Oh, right" Link vigorously erased his mistake. Then he looked up at me, pencil poised ready to record my every word.

Before he could jump into the billions of questions bubbling on his tongue Harris mercifully took the first stab at explaining it all. "Think Freemasons only we know how to keep our organization underground. Back in the day the town blacksmith was something of the protector for any given region."

"They made the weapons, so they knew how to hunt the hell beasts," I added.

"Right, so the tradition got passed down father to son … or daughter," Harris nodded in deference to me. I smiled, winningly.

As Link's attention divided between me and Harris, he didn't notice the graphite scribble he was making on the page. "And they got someone like Alexander Hamilton on their side?"

Harris chimed in, "It must be nice…"

"I swear Harrison, you start to sing and I'm going to have to hurt you." I shook my head and smiled trying to play off the irritation.

"What if I were rapping?" The falsely innocent grin on Harris' face almost melted my annoyance.

"That too. Now shush." I turned back to Link who was fervently repairing the damage his lack of attention had done to his notes. "It wasn't just Hamilton it was all the founding fathers. James Monroe included." I gestured to Harris and Link, descendants of the fifth president of the United States of America.

"No way, I didn't know we were related to *that* Monroe." The revelations just kept on coming for Link.

I took a sip of my coffee. It was going from lukewarm to cold and I scowled. "Yep, that's how we've managed to keep it quiet."

"Are you saying the whole government is in on the 'monsters are real' secret?" Link's mouth looked like it was permanently fixed in slack jawed amazement.

"Not the whole thing but enough," Harris confirmed.

"Why don't more people know if it's so widespread?" Link's whole world seemed turned upside down. Don't give me crap. Now the whole darn play was stuck in my head. Thanks a lot Harris.

Before Link's head could explode, I decided to conclude this introduction of Smyth lore 101. "I think it was John Mayer who said it best: 'when they own the information, they can bend it all they want.'"

3.5: Gotta have that cover story.

It took me some time, but I found the perfect first hunt for the young Lincoln Monroe. He was proving to be a very dutiful student. He spent a great deal of time in our library going over its many volumes and listening to the advice of Aunt Pippa. She came to like the boy owing mostly to his self-deprecation and flattery. He warmed up to her since she didn't detonate in another scary poltergeist attack.

I met up with Demi outside the school Thursday morning after finding our first target. The benefit of waiting till the weekend was that Link got a chance to follow Rule # 2 and do his research. Demi's well-practiced eyes, ever observant, saw my annoyance at being bound by my father's rules. She placed her hand, shaped in the letter Y, against her chin, her eyebrows creased down. "What's wrong?"

Both hands in the letter O position I shook them side to side. "Nothing." I took out the file that contained the details for Link's first hunt. It was partly from the Smyth database with a few of my own notes. I handed it over to Demi and sat down beside her. "It's good," I signed, "I found something for Link to sink his newbie teeth into."

Demi flipped one handedly through the contents. "I see."

I tapped her on the shoulder so she could watch my next sign, "Do you want to come with us? I got an Air BnB, but I don't want to spend the whole weekend with a bunch of dumb boys."

"Yeah, sounds fun."

A hairy arm reached over the two of us and plucked the file out of Demi's hands. "What do we have here?" Harris pulled the first page from the plastic sleeve.

Demi signed a few choice swear words and insults that I didn't bother to translate. Instead, I snatched back the file admonishing, "Rude. Ask much?"

"So, you finally found something for Linky?" Harris leaned forward trying to read the information on the outside of the file.

"Obviously," I rolled my eyes. Arrogance was only attractive in small quantities. "With no help from you I might add. This is supposed to be a *team* effort."

"Ouch, I'm wounded." Harris pulled an apple from his pocket and polished it on his shirt which was either dirty or 'rustic' either way it didn't look sanitary. "I feed the kid, tuck him in at night..."

"TMI," Demi signed. I agreed.

Link came up behind Harris, "Where'd you get the apple? I thought we didn't have any food in the house." Sheepishly, Harris handed over the fruit and shot me a wink as if to prove his point.

I gave the file to Link. "Good news, I found you your first hunt." Link's fingers tightened on the file to the point where the tips turned pale from blood loss. "Chill out kid, I picked an easy one," as far as I could tell. My hunches on what I was up against were usually pretty accurate.

"It's just a couple of suspicious cow deaths on a dairy farm in Leominster. It's a little over an hour from here. I marked the investigation out as a training exercise so we shouldn't be competing with any other hunters. The disembowelment of a few cows can be allowed to carry on so that someone wet behind the ears can get their shot." I tugged Link's ear lightly. The touch sent shivers up my arms. My strange connection with Link was growing more manageable with the prolonged exposure. I still didn't have any answers why it occurred at all.

Harris brushed his hair out of his face leaving a wave over his forehead that was very cute. Casually handsome. Such a problem. "Okay, let's go."

Link tried to look like he was not about to throw up. "Nope." I put my foot down. Literally, because it had pins and needles from being crossed over my other leg for so long. "The whole reason I got landed with you two was because I skipped school. Dead cows are NOT an emergency. That's why I picked it. Link has tonight to do his research. Tomorrow, AFTER school we will head to the Crescent Dairy Farm."

Harris gave me a look that said, 'if you say so.' I did. If I was ever going to get back in my father's good graces, I had to get Lincoln Monroe trained up as quick as humanly possible.

Just as I said, we departed after seventh period on Friday. I drove, naturally. My car was plenty big enough to accommodate us and the myriad of weapons Link decided he needed, just in case. I let him bring whatever he wanted. If he preferred to be over-prepared that was better than Harris who apparently went into his investigation's guns blazing. Demi and I packed light with a simple backpack a piece and of course my favorite Damascus steel knife.

With my hands on the wheels and the freeway underneath us I turned down the music for the first time. "Alright, what's the plan?" I looked at Link in my rearview mirror. The research he was thumbing through scattered on the floor.

"What?" He tried to retrieve the papers.

Keeping my voice even I said, "The plan, Link. Where are we going first?"

He looked confused. "The dairy farm, right? Croissant?"

"Crescent," I corrected, praying for patience.

"Right, Crescent Dairy Farm, in Leominster, Massachusetts." He recited and smiled as if proud he remembered.

My fingers tightened on the steering wheel. Was this a joke to him? Demi looked pointedly out the window in the front passenger seat. Catching my expression in the rear-view mirror Harris intervened. Finally. "Look man when you start a hunt you need to have some kind of reason you are questioning the people involved. Like, remember when your dad was on that case of the Drekavac? He posed as an insurance agent to talk to the parents of the little boy. That way he could get some answers about the kid's death and see the extent of the haunting of his mom and dad."

"Oh," Link realized, "so, I need a cover story." Harris clapped him on the shoulder proudly. He gave me a 'see we're not as dumb as you think,' look.

"Only you're a little young to pass yourself off as an insurance agent," I added.

"Right." Link stayed quiet for a long time.

I probably could have bailed him out a few miles ago, but I waited till I could see sweat beading on his forehead. I tapped the glovebox in front of Demi, and she understood. She pulled the camera from inside and held it up.

"You're a reporter for the school newspaper," I offered.

Link reluctantly took it. "You came up with that quick."

"It's an easy standby to have around. I keep this camera in the car all the time, though, in a pinch I could just use my cell. The bulkier version makes me look more 'official.' Use it if you like. Or else you have another thirty minutes to come up with something better. Just remember you will always need a reason to be poking your nose into sketchy stuff."

3.6: Confidence and Pickled Eggs.

The dairy farm was a bust. Though, I did enjoy the over acting from young master Lincoln. He snapped photos like he was Peter Parker pretending not to be Spiderman. I drove us to the Air BnB in nearby Action, Massachusetts, thus, chosen because I liked the name of the town. I mean if all I got to do was make the arrangements, I needed to have a little fun.

Link slumped onto the couch. He turned on the news and sat watching it. I suspected he wasn't exactly spellbound by the reports of Mr. Politician and his bid for a second term. Demi and I dished up the takeout that we grabbed on our way to the house and handed Link a plate. Harris could make his own.

Using my expert dexterity, I grabbed a large piece of orange chicken with my chop sticks and deposited it into my mouth. The restaurant was highly rated. Amidst the research a person does for a proper investigation the local cuisine must be included. To be honest that was more or less a Mia specific rule. I didn't leave that up to Link, though. I was not into eating whatever lazy fare a teenage boy considered worthwhile.

Demi watched the news report intently. She caught my attention and made the 'V' shape with her fingers pointing them from her eyes toward the screen, "Look." The reporters had shifted topics and were now babbling on about some pet adoption event scheduled for the following morning. The scroll at the bottom of the screen read: "The carcasses of several wild animals were found in the fields of Idylwilde Farms." I reached over and grabbed the remote from Link's unresisting hand. I hit pause, thankful that the house had a DVR.

"Found you a new lead, kiddo." I patted his cheek, affectionately. There were no shivers this time, but I was beginning to wonder about my willingness to keep touching him. It seemed almost involuntary.

The next day we went out to Idylwilde Farms. The most striking feature of the property was a grocery store that was stocked with every farm to table item you could imagine. It had the produce section of my sister's culinary dreams. Link looked ready to resume his gumshoe camera boy routine, but I told him to act casual. This was a business with a lot of locals who were probably already talking about the strange goings on. Honestly, we could have stood admiring the gourds for an hour or so and heard all the town gossip. But Link needed to be in the driver's seat of this investigation and time was of the essence. We had to be back in class Monday morning.

Link filled up a basket with three bananas and a jar of pickled eggs. I didn't even know such a thing existed, but he was eager to get to the checkout stand. I stood back with Demi examining the homemade chocolate bars. A thin, young woman gave me a dirty look, scoffing at the chocolate in my hand. Curvy girl prejudice. I gave her unflinching eye-contact till she embarrassedly began to mind her own business.

Meanwhile, Harrison, the derelict, flirted with the girl at the butcher counter. Mutely, Link put his selections next to the register for the man in overalls to ring up. Beside them a cute, little-old-lady chatted animatedly with a young female cashier.

The older woman fiddled in her purse for exact change. "I can't believe some wild beast killed all those poor animals near your farm Kaycee."

"Neither can we, isn't that right Papa?" Kaycee addressed the man ringing up Link.

"Never seen anything like it." The older man was having trouble with the point-of-sale system. He didn't realize that the bananas didn't have a barcode. He kept trying to scan every inch of them to no avail. "Scared off Lucy Galvin. Had to cover for her today." He turned to Link with an apologetic smile. "Sorry kid, I'm not used to this stuff," the man gestured to the computer.

Link was silent so long that Papa Overalls gave him a concerned look. I walked over, adding my chocolate bar to the counter and kicked him in the shins. "Ow, I mean sorry. No, I mean it's okay. You guys have any idea what did it?"

The older man smiled again. "Nope, animal control came by and took the bodies. I mean those coyotes could have been killed by anything, you know. Lots of predators for them but that black bear was massive. At least six hundred pounds."

Link began to studder. His mouth seemed caught on the B of black bear. I kicked him again. This time instead of getting back to his questions he glared at me and said in a shrill voice, "Black Bear?!"

Demi retreated further into the store hiding behind the giant shelf of assorted jams. Harris turned around, the girl at the butcher counter deep in blush. I smiled at him then turned to Papa Overalls. "Sorry sir, my friend has a bear, um, phobia." I grimaced, embarrassed.

After his daughter helped him ring up our bananas and eggs, we left trying unsuccessfully to go unnoticed. Being incognito was sort of a tenant of Smyth life. Apparently one that I needed to instill in Link.

Once we made it to the car, Link regained his voice. "A bear!" he shouted in that same shrill, carrying tone.

"Chill Link, the bear is dead," I tried to console him.

"What killed it isn't," Link's voice went up an octave.

Harris unhelpfully shrugged like; *he has a point.* I ignored him. Bracing my hands on Link's forearms, I gripped him tightly. It was something my father used to do with me to help me center myself. A firm grip can really help reduce anxiety. "Tell me what you know?"

I took two long exaggerated breaths and unconsciously Link joined me. There was an easy rhythm between us. It was so Zen that even Demi and Harris started breathing in unison.

"The beast has a taste for meat." Link recited; his eyes closed. I squeezed his arms in encouragement. "It can take out large creatures but doesn't seem interested in people."

"Good, keep going." The longer I held onto his arms the more secure he grew. There was a faint aura of lightness that surrounded him, though I had to be imagining it.

"The cows were burned as well as eaten." Confidence was beginning to seep back into his words.

"Right. So, what next?"

Link's blue eyes snapped open and rested on mine. The look was so intense I found it hard to let him go. I detached myself but only after a lot of mental prying.

Standing solo, Link said, "We need to see where the animals were found. We need to know if they were set on fire too."

3.7: Fangs or Fire.

Everyone loves a good barbeque, but the smell in the field was not appetizing. The bear and several coyotes had indeed been burned prior to eating. The scorch marks in the grass made it perfectly evident. We went back to the rental house to regroup. Link pulled out a laptop and set to work, hopefully, concluding his research. I didn't need to narrow it down. I knew what we were up against.

No, I'm not going to tell you. It would spoil the surprise.

Link let us know that we would head back to Idylwilde Farm after closing time. I didn't argue, he had a solid plan. Night was a natural time for creatures long since deemed mythological.

No one spoke on the drive to the farm. Even Demi's hands remained in her lap. Occasionally, Harris tried to catch my eye in the rear-view mirror. I didn't meet them. He may only suspect what we were facing, but I knew. I didn't want to make mommy worry about little Lincoln. I wouldn't let anything happen to Harrison's charge.

The lights of the farm were out. We pulled into the empty parking lot. I had put the noise dampening charm on my princess anyway, just in case. Gliding into a spot beside the handicap designations I put the car in park. Even after hours it felt wrong to occupy one of the blue marked spaces.

According to Link we would head toward the fields and track the beast as best we could. As with the best laid plans a detour switched our route. The door of the store was open. I take that back: not open, torn down. Strips of wood were scattered like matchsticks in front. I nudged Link with my toe.

"Will you stop that?!" Link hissed.

I held my hands up in surrender. I liked that the kid had finally snapped back at me. Showed some chutzpah. Link looked ready to apologize, but I smiled reassuringly. From the trunk of my car, he loaded himself up with weapons: a silver knife, a gun, pockets full of potions and for some reason a broadsword I wasn't sure he could lift over his head. He took a deep breath and led the way inside. We all followed, Demi in the rear. Not exactly a Smyth and not quite a witch either, Demi had at least been on enough hunts with me to hold her own.

The smell like that of a wet dog was strong once we made our way inside. Harris stepped up beside Link ready to take the lead, but I tugged the collar of his shirt back and pressed a finger to my lips. It wasn't our fight. We were back up only. Link turned on a flashlight and tiptoed further in. Literally, tiptoed as if he were sneaking out of his room to catch Santa in the act.

From the depths of the aisles a goat bleated. Link froze. His flashlight beam began to quake in his shaking hand. As far as sounds of impending doom went, this one seemed tame to me. But I guessed Link's nerves were on an extremely thin ledge. Though growing impatient, I chose not to nudge him again. Ironically, the roar, like that from a lion, got Link moving. He wasn't creeping forward either. A purposeful stride pushed him forward like he was ready for the mystery of it all to be over.

Link's flashlight lit upon the creature. The serpent's eyes contracted in the light becoming mere slits of razor thin pupal. A forked tongue slithered out scenting the air. The massive head, roughly the size of a cantaloupe, had horned spikes on the end of its nose. Its neck blended smoothly from grey and black scales to coarse golden fur at the back end of the beast. Sticking out along the spine the head and forelegs of a goat reared back like a stallion bucking its rider. The goat's soulless eyes stared in apparent dissatisfaction at the lion that headed the creature's front. The shovel-sized, sandpaper tongue of the lion lapped up a puddle of soy milk. I wondered if its choice was in deference to its goat companion. Or perhaps the lion simply enjoyed alternative dairy products.

A breathless, squeaking sound reached a pitch that drew all eyes. At first, I looked at the viper headed tail only to see it staring fixedly at Link. The snake coiled back aiming to strike. Before it could, I wrapped an arm around Link's middle and pulled him behind a shelf of miscellaneous ingredients. The sign above the clearance items read: "Try Fusion. Make life interesting." I thought privately that Link wouldn't agree with that statement.

"A chimera!" Link's eyes were wide as saucers. A growl of agitation came from around the corner.

"Are you crazy?" Harris added. I ignored him. Demi agreed with the boys in sign, but I chose not to translate.

I turned to Link calmly. "What kind?" He looked at me incredulously confused. "You did your research." I clapped Link on the shoulder, a proud mama. "Chimera is correct, but each type has a different method of being neutralized. What kind is that one?"

Link's eyes bulged. I could relate. Though difficult to think under pressure, it was a necessary skill to obtain. "Grecian, because of the goat." The animal in question let out another loud bleat and a plume of fire shot toward the exposed beams above. Luckily, they were properly lacquered and didn't immediately catch fire. A few more shots, though, and they might.

"Good. How do we stop it?" I could almost read the word *retreat* in the glaze of his eyes. "Come on, Link. You can do this. Rule #1; when in doubt..."

"Myth it out," Link finished. "Okay, Bellerophon killed the chimera. He had a Pegasus and arrows and a big ass spear. I have this." He tried to lift the broadsword and as I suspected he couldn't handle the weight. It clattered to the floor and the chimera let out a room rumbling roar.

Demi rested easily, cross legged on the ground and started reading a culinary magazine that she had snagged from the front registers. The vibrations of the heavy animal's feet didn't seem to faze her. Over our long friendship she learned to trust the process.

"How about a Monroe family rule," Harris offered. "K.I.S.S.." For a half second, I thought the two were talking about some incestrious methodology I didn't want to know anything about. Then I realized it was an acronym. Keep It Simple, Stupid.

"What part of this is simple," Link squeaked.

"Listen to Harris," I offered, and the elder Monroe let out a triumphant, 'ha.' "You have fangs or fire."

"How am I supposed to deal with either," Link cried.

"Harris, darling, give the boy a leg up, he needs a Pegasus." Both boys stared at me like I was insane. I looked to the ceiling in exasperation. Did I need to hold their hands every step of the way? I pointed to the top shelves. Harris still seemed bewildered, but Link finally got it.

3.8: Damn you, Tiger King.

Without a word Link stepped onto Harris' shoulders and climbed pushing boxes of breadcrumbs and microwave rice to the floor. Harris grumbled as Link's sneaker departed company with his face. I appreciated that the kid jumped into action. Unfortunately, he just demonstrated that his chosen 'spear' wasn't going to work since he couldn't get it more than two inches off the ground.

Running toward the front, I grabbed a basket and dumped a large portion of apples into it as well as several butternut squash. Coming back, I handed the basket to Harris. "Little Red Riding Hood forgot grandma's goodies." He obligingly reached up and gave them to his nephew.

Link picked up an apple and looked down at me confused. I mimed tossing an object overhand. Harris very convincingly played the role of goat and caught the invisible fruit in exaggeratedly displayed teeth.

"Oh, I get it," Link said, louder than I would have advised.

This exclamation was enough to get the goat's attention. It let out a blood curdling scream as it turned on Link, but he placated the beast by tossing a fresh apple into its mouth. With a soft, staccato 'blah' the goat waited for another apple.

I rounded the corner of the shelves. The goat had thin whisps of smoke curling up from its nostrils, but it seemed decently preoccupied. I figured it was unlikely to breathe fire again. While Link distracted it, I set up the next tool the kid would need. Not the fire breathing kid but the boy. Oh, you know what I meant.

The serpent tail rested lazily coiling in on itself. As I bolted past, it stuck a forked tongue out almost lazily but didn't move to strike. It looked a little ill in my opinion. In the back of the shop, I grabbed a wooden broom. Snapping my fingers, the shaft split in two. I didn't like to use my telekinesis that much but occasionally a time saver was needed. The broom cracked leaving a spear shaped wooden dowel. Over at the butcher counter I stabbed several honey-baked hams making a lovely kabab.

I came back to where Link was tossing the goat apples. Harris had his hands half extended upward, typical helicopter parent. I planted the end of my spear on the ground and leaned down to check out the recipe on the page Demi was examining. The dish of lamb over a Mediterranean olive and feta couscous sounded delicious. I'd have to get Molly a subscription to that magazine.

Standing beside my staff of perpetually salty, cured meat, I marveled at how easily Link rolled with the changes. With the goat eagerly anticipating the next launch of fresh produce, Link chucked the butternut squash at its head. The straight cud grinding teeth snapped the squash from the air, but the rounded bottom stuck in its over extended jaw.

Link looked down at me as the lion roared. Apparently, there must be some shared nerve endings that alerted the head to the misfortune of its Bovidae companion. The serpent tale slithered around the corner of the aisle and Demi signed a frantic warning then hurried out of the way. Not knowing specifically what Demi was saying Link got the gist and scrambled down the shelves. He jumped over the serpent tail as it struck out at Harris. The older Monroe rolled out of the way and grabbed the broadsword. Jarringly, Harris smacked the weapon into the serpent's very solid fangs. The impact seemed to disorient the snake and it shook its head trying to rid itself from the vibrations of metal on… well... tooth.

Without questioning it, Link grabbed the ham tipped, DIY, spear from my hands. Like a natural he thrust it, unflinchingly into the Lion's mouth. The chimera gagged and heaved like a cat hacking up a hair ball. He pulled out his silver knife and made toward the beast. While I admired the cutthroat nature Link displayed, the chimera wasn't the type of creature that needed to be killed for the sake of mankind.

Grabbing Link by the elbow, I waited while the adrenaline faded from his eyes. "Rule # 3; To everything its place. Not every creature is a threat to people. Those that are, we dispose of, but it's not the chimera's fault that it's in the wrong place at the wrong time."

"So, what do we do? It can't live here in the grocery store." Link looked warily at the hacking lion, dazed serpent, and spluttering goat.

I pulled out my cell phone and began to dial Brian Grimes the local Smyth zoologist. As the phone rang, I began to explain. "Chimeras are not native to the US. Been really bad over the last few years after Netflix premiered Tiger King. Now we have a whole host of Joe Exotic wannabees trying to raise natural and supernatural big cats."

Brian picked up and I put him on speaker phone. "Mia?"

"Hey, my trainee bagged that chimera." I smiled at Link, proud of the kid.

"A chimera hunt for a newbie?" I could hear the laughter in Brian's voice. "You're one tough trainer." The validation that this creature was indeed more complicated than a new trainee should be able to handle made Link look incredulously at Harris. Honestly, if they were going to put all the choices in my hands, they got what they paid for. If it were me, I would have loved to get something this exciting for my first time.

I gave Brian the address and exchanged a few more pleasantries before hanging up. As the lion head kept trying to hack up the ham skewer the snake end regurgitated a whole coyote. The gelatinous sack of curled up canine smelled worse than the lion's fur, so we all retreated outside to wait for the zoological team.

"Are you telling me this Brian guy could have taken care of that thing this whole time?" Link shook his head.

"Yeah, so could I and about a dozen other Smyths. You needed the practice. Next time, I probably shouldn't help so much." Link glared at me cupping a frozen bag of peas to a burn on his forearm that I hadn't noticed before. "You did really well. That wasn't easy," I admitted. Link nodded. I smacked my lips together, awkwardly. I wasn't used to sentiment.

A puzzled look came over Harris' face. "Did you say Joe Exotic?"

"Oh yeah," I replied. "Carol Baskin had a couple of chimeras too."

Demi signed, "Crazy white people." I translated. Despite our visible connection to the category mentioned Link and I joined in with Demi and Harris as they were overtaken by laughter. Once we all started, we couldn't stop. It was one of those problems with extreme adrenaline levels when the high comes down all your left with is a strong sense of hysteria.

Rule # 4: "In union, there is strength" – Aesop.

4.1: My Sweet Silent Sixteen.

My work with the Monroe boys was going smoothly as September faded into October. By the end of the month, we successfully investigated a Satyr turning love interests into shrubs as well as a very confused Piper that kept the local squirrels from their winter prep duties. I felt very confident in our arrangement till the morning of my 16th birthday.

I woke to a puff of glittery dust suffocating me. Once I'd coughed half my lung out, I cleared the clouded air with a wave of my hand. My sister sat on my bedside looking at me, regretfully.

"What the hell, Moll?"

"Happy Birthday, Mi." She looked almost sad. That didn't bode well.

"I was hoping not to suffocate thirty seconds into the day but, hell, everyone likes a challenge," I wheezed.

"It's only 24 hours, I promise."

"What is?"

I rubbed my fingers down my cheek and pulled the gray, sparkling particles away from my face. I recognized a few ingredients. One larger bit held a portion of a seed pod in the shape of a skull. Snapdragon, the flower of deception. "What did you do?"

Instead of answering Molly got up and raced for the door. I didn't bother trying to get dressed. I padded barefoot into the hallway and chased her down the stairs. I jumped the last few steps trying to catch up, but she was too quick for me. Only a half pace behind her, I slipped into the kitchen before the door closed.

My dad looked up and smiled at Molly, but he didn't even acknowledge my presence. Sure, it had been only like three whole seconds since I walked into the room, I didn't expect confetti to fall from the ceiling or anything. Would have been nice but whatever. What irritated me aside from my dust facial was that he didn't even look in my direction.

"Is it done?" Dad addressed Molly.

She peered at me sympathetically and nodded. "She's actually right here."

"Oh, excellent. Happy Birthday Mia!" Only he was looking in the completely wrong direction. I glanced over my shoulder in case I had some sort of doppelganger impersonating me but nope.

I turned mutinously to Molly, "He can't see me, can he?"

"No. No he can't."

"Or hear me?" She shook her head. Something she said before registered to me, *24hrs.* In my silence a serious amount of rage was boiling to the surface. I reached out to grab the back of her ponytail and my clawed hand slipped right through her skull. Not in a gory brain matter exploding way but right through as if I didn't even exist. She merely shuddered as if struck by a cool breeze.

Lacking the capacity to beat my sister to death I yelled at her instead, "Are you trying to tell me not only am I INVISIBLE but I'm INCORPOREAL TOO!!!" She shrank against the noise and gave me an apologetic grimace.

My dad said my name several times before I heard him over the onslaught of curse words, I hurled at my sister. She nodded to him when I was finally quiet. "Don't be angry with Molly. This was my idea."

Bctrayal.

Seriously, of all days he had to pick my birthday. Not that I was a huge celebrator. Having a Halloween birthday makes your special day take a backseat to everyone else's candy mania.

Molly kept looking between me and dad, waiting for me to explode. Yelling at him wouldn't do any good but I was way too mad to simply accept this and roll over like a good girl.

Dad tried for a placating tone as he began, "Listen Mia, I know this doesn't seem fair. You've done a couple of trips with Harris and Link. While you clearly know how to teach, you haven't done so well collaborating with your *partner*." He emphasized the last word trying to remind me that it wasn't the Mia show.

My arms were still crossed, but my expression must have softened. Molly no longer looked ready to bolt. My dad went on with a bite of his usual sternness, "Harris usually doesn't even know what you guys are going to be investigating. I'd bet he doesn't know what you are doing tonight."

True, but only because I didn't trust Harris. He seemed all too eager to give away insider information to Link. The answers needed to be won the hard way not gifted on a silver platter.

"The only person apart from Molly and people sensitive to the veil ..." my dad began.

"Am I dead?" I barked at Molly, "I better not be dead Moll or so help me I will drag you down with me."

"You're not dead, stupid," she rolled her eyes. "Dad was trying to tell you something important. See why we had to put the mute button on your ass. You can't even shut up when no one can hear you."

"I'll show you where to put that mute button," I growled.

"Very mature," she grumbled.

"Are you two done?" Dad was used to these spats. Siblings have to fight. We both nodded in answer though I reflected he couldn't see me doing it. "The only other person who can see you is Harris."

Great. Happy Birthday Mia. Communicate or else.

4.2: None for me thanks, I don't have a functioning jaw.

A cascade of golden-brown syrup poured generously over a warm buttery stack of pancakes. The cook at the diner had even added sprinkles to the batter for that extra festive touch. The fork slid into the pillowy layers cutting away a portion. Link raised the bite to his open mouth and sighed in appreciation. Show off.

I sat across from him with my chin resting on my open palm. Being incorporeal I couldn't eat anything. I wasn't hungry but pancakes weren't about that. They were simple delicious ecstasy.

Link couldn't see the indecent way I was watching him eat but Harris could, and he cleared his throat. "Did you bring the file for the hunt tonight?"

I looked at him incredulously. "What do you think?" Then I passed my hands through the table, my flesh falling through the wood as easily as if it was water.

Link looked up brightly, his pancakes half devoured. "Harris, can you tell her happy birthday for me? I almost forgot we are birthday buddies."

"Harris, can you remind Link that I can hear him. Also let's not do the birthday party bit."

"She says Happy Birthday to you too."

"Thanks Mia," Link crooned, bursting into a natural smile.

I was not in the mood for sunshine and puppies. Wandering around my city barefoot in Molly's hand me down pink pajamas with penguins on the bottom gave me a very surly outlook. I couldn't even put on a bra. A fact Harris had clearly already noticed. He continued to observe this every few minutes or so.

"Can you at least tell us what we are investigating?" Harris took a sip of coffee that steamed up around his face in a loving caress. Coffee, another thing I couldn't have.

Fine dad, here we go just as you ordered. "Turner's Seafood."

"Isn't that a restaurant?" mused Harris.

"Huh?" Link mumbled through a mouth full of pancakes.

"Nothing Linky." Harris waved him off. Such was their relationship that Link didn't appear offended, he just took the dismissal in stride.

"You can't do that," I gestured to Link's bowed head. "These investigations are his opportunity to train. Judging by my father's evil plan I suspect that the lesson is more than just you and I communicating. You need to teach him, not protect him."

"Fine give me the low down and I'll translate."

"Okay, the restaurant is also known as the Lyceum. Before that, it belonged to Bridget Bishop, the first woman hung in the Salem witch trials. She was basically offed for daring to act however and wear whatever she wanted." Harris scoffed. Link looked ready to interrupt. He didn't know I was speaking so I guess I couldn't exactly call it that.

Harris held out a hand and again Link backed down. Realizing what he was doing he flinched, "I see what you mean about that."

"It's a work in progress, Monroe. Anyway, the restaurant has had reports of hauntings for ages. That's not why it went on the top of my birthday wish list. Last Halloween a group of 'paranormal investigators' decided to do a séance to get the ghosts talking. The problem is that when amateurs dip their toes into the dark arts, sometimes, they get their hands on the real deal. Over the last year ghost sightings have gone up exponentially. Not to mention the sudden difficulty retaining staff and reports of physical attacks. It's the place to be tonight when the veil comes down."

Unconsciously mimicking Harris, Link looked in my general direction and nodded along. This prompted me to add, "The end."

Harris seemed startled. I think he forgot that he had to take the lead giving Link his instructions. "Oh, right." He turned toward his nephew. "The restaurant is haunted."

"Cool, sounds fun." Link leaned back full and completely at ease. You had to hand it to boys, they were simple creatures. The lack of details didn't matter much to them.

Harris turned back to me, munching on a piece of salty, crunchy, succulent bacon. If I could have drooled, I would have. "What's next?"

Frustrated, I looked around the room for Captain Obvious. Being that it was only us and the waitress idly filling the coffee maker I settled for another meditation moment. "That's up to him, Harris."

"Oh, right," he snapped his fingers and pointed at me. "Rule 7 Do your research."

"Number two," Link and I said in unison.

Harris laughed. "You two are nerds." He crammed the last of the bacon in his mouth, dropped a very crappy tip on the table and said, "Off to the book lair, then."

4.3: Silent and sleepy don't mix.

To Link's credit he filled in the blanks in Harris' 'explanation' wonderfully. He found the articles on last year's séance. Pieced together the reports of physical attacks and basically showed me that I've been coddling him too much. The wisdom of my silence started to seep in. Thanks a ton, dad.

I had already arranged to have a private 'Halloween experience' at Turner's Seafood after closing. When we arrived, however, we ran into a pair of uninvited guests. A short bespectacled man held a camcorder roughly the size of a football and filmed his companion. The other man that rested against the door frame looked familiar. His ginger hair turned russet in the shadows as he leaned in talking softly to the night manager. The woman, probably in her early 40's, took the attention with mocking amusement.

"This guy bothering you?" Harris stepped up puffing out his chest. You had to hand it to him, the alpha male routine did have its merits.

"No. I was just explaining to Mr. Reaper that we have a private event tonight." The woman stood with a hand on her hip expertly blocking the entrance.

Reaper straightened and turned to Harris. Then I remembered where I'd seen him before. I came up next to my only outlet for information. "That's Daniel Reaper, he has his own YouTube channel 'Reapers Guide to Death.' He's the one who held the séance last year."

"He a Smyth?" Harris forgot to lower his voice.

"No, I'm Dan, Daniel Reaper."

Both men stood flexing slightly, staring each other down. Link stepped forward, slipped easily between Harris and Mr. Reaper, and held out his hand to the night manager. "Hey, I'm Link. Amelia Hamilton set up our tour tonight."

I passed a hand through Harris' shoulder, and he shivered. "Focus on the manager. Her name is Trish. We don't have time for wannabe ghost hunters." Harris opened his mouth to respond to me, but I doused him with my icy touch again. "Stop talking to me. You look crazy."

Harris shook his head and put his dazzling smile to work, charming Trish. I'd paid a pretty penny to get us in there, but a little extra flirtation couldn't hurt, I guess. "Mia couldn't make it, but she sent us along. I'm Harris and this is Link."

Trish gave him an indulgent smile. "Mia put you two on the guest list. You're free to go on in." Dan and his camera man made to join us, but she held out a hand, "Not you Mr. Reaper. You had your shot last year."

"Listen, I'm meeting a friend around here in a bit. If I could just get a quick clip that would be awesome." He gestured back to his camera friend. "My video of this place went viral less than a day after I posted it." That was true, even I had hit the like button on that one.

"Sorry man, that's not going to happen." Harris stood beside Trish in the doorway.

"Look kid, I'm sure you and Scrappy over there have a lot to Scooby do in there but a follow up video could earn me big bucks in adverts." Usually, I put fake ghost chasers up there with Jersey Shore boys but this one came with my favorite flavor of mockery.

Thankfully, Trish ended the testosterone show down. "I worked a twelve-hour shift and for some unholy reason I open tomorrow. You two, here," she handed Harris the key. "You," she poked Dan in the chest. "Clear out or I will call the cops."

Dan held his hands up in surrender and moved to the middle of the street to film his update with the restaurant in the background. Trish left and Harris locked the door behind her. Despite my current worldly state, I felt giddy. I loved ghost season.

Harris and Link's feet sent the sound of creaking wood blaring through the place like an alarm bell. Even if I could have walked properly over the planks, I usually had a light tread. Evidently, noise control didn't factor in either boy's mind.

The large, curved windows facing the street bathed the bar in a dim orange light. Harris twisted the bottles on the shelf reading the labels. "We could drink whatever we wanted."

"I doubt that would help you find the ghost," Link said before I could. The level of sarcasm in his voice made me proud. I might be rubbing off on him after all. We weaved through the high-top tables set beside a lukewarm fireplace. The coals crackling softly gave the only other light to the room.

I avoided all the pointed table edges until I remembered I didn't need to. After that I gloried in walking straight through the solid objects. I was further delighted to find the action made Harris visibly uneasy.

Too busy watching me, he caught his foot on an awkwardly positioned chair leg. As he stumbled, he cursed. "Is all this darkness strictly necessary?"

"Yes," Link whispered. "Quiet would help too."

"Ghosts thrive at the witching hour, AKA midnight. The more shadows the better," I added for Harris' benefit only. My trainee clearly had a handle on things.

"I say we head upstairs." Link clicked on his flashlight casting the beam at the wide wooden steps. "That's where the other group did the séance."

"Sounds like a solid plan to me," Harris agreed.

As an unlikely gentleman Harris gestured for me to follow Link first. The protocol for this chivalrous action made me pause. If I accepted, was I expected to curtsy? I decided not to make the joke and proceeded up the stairs. Because of my hesitation, Link made it to the top landing by the time Harris donned the first step.

Link paused looking at something Harris and I couldn't see. "Whoa, who are you?"

The figure above was shadowed but solid. The words sounded in a rhyming cadence as if someone were casting an incantation. Then a gust of wind passed through me and slammed into Harris. He tripped and fell flat on his back knocking his head on the hardwood. When I looked at the landing, Link was gone.

My first thought was *Crap.* Followed by, *Oh, hell no.* I charged up the stairs and into the upper dining room. My eyes, well-adjusted to the dark, searched the space but it was empty. Not even a stray blonde hair could be found. Then I looked into the mirror and did a double take.

Link was there, alright. Just barely getting up off the floor. I took a quick glance behind me to make sure it wasn't just a reflection but there was nothing. Just a host stand with extra silverware and to-go boxes. Above him stood a girl probably not much older than I. She didn't look like a ghost, but it was hard to tell. I vaguely recognized her from the photos of the séance.

Mirrors were tricky things. People had damn good reasons to cover them in the house of the dead. As I was a novice at being dead-ish I didn't know how to get in. Link couldn't be allowed to handle this threat alone. There was training and then there were suicide missions. I wasn't about to waste all the time I had spent with him.

My shoulder suddenly felt bathed in ice. As I had become ill accustomed to having a body with sensations like that I jumped like a startled cat. My 180-degree spin in midair put me face to face with a woman dressed in the peasant gowns of the late1600's. She shimmered at the edges, glowing faintly. When she spoke, it sounded like an echo but without the preemptive original words hanging in the air. "She must be warned."

"What? Who? Warned about what?" Why did ghosts always leave out the important details.

Tragically, she pointed to the young woman in the mirror. By that I mean the vindictive little kidnapper not my own reflection. They seemed to resemble each other though not exact copies. "Mama mustn't go. Death waits at the end."

"Preaching to the wrong choir, sister. I got death coming out of my yin/yang right now."

She cocked her head, confused. Even if I wanted to give someone a warning only those with two feet in the grave and the zonked-out boy downstairs could hear me. Not to mention I still hadn't the faintest idea how to get into the mirror realm. Something of that last thought must have crossed my face because she took my hand and placed it on the mirror. Instantly my fingers began to melt into the surface.

"Okay, wow. I'll try to tell her about the death and stuff. I need to go get that boy downstairs he's kinda my … translator." She smiled at me warmly. "Thanks."

"Rebecca," she put her hand on her heart.

"Thanks, Rebecca."

Before she could say another word, a scythe struck down into her chest around her neck and yanked her back. In the dark a pair of glowing yellow eyes lit beneath a classic buckled puritan's hat. The ghost man was holding my new friend suspended off the floor. I blinked and they both disappeared. Snarling, I clenched my teeth, "Ooh, I'll be back for you mister."

As there was nothing I could do about the ghost drama I turned and raced downstairs to Harris, still unconscious on the floor. Placing both hands on his face I hoped that the sudden cold of my touch would be enough to shake him awake. Fail. I tried shouting his name. No dice. Sitting back, I steeled myself for the only other option at my disposal. I needed to dream walk him.

As I once told Link, I've never tried it before. I did know the theory. First, get to the astral plane. Bonus, I was already there. Second, get close to the subject. Check two. I took a moment to center my thoughts. I couldn't go in panicked. Then I placed my face directly above his which seemed like the most likely way to join with his dreams. As our foreheads touched, I felt myself tumble down the rabbit hole.

4.4: Sweet dreams are best unseen.

If you ever get the opportunity to creep into a teenage boy's dream, don't. Nothing good happens in that subconscious.

In the dream, I found myself standing beside Harris. The slightly scrawny, piss poor beard-shaver that I was accustomed to, suddenly, had body builder muscles. Two belts of ammunition were strapped crisscross on his chest. His mocha skin glistened in small beads of sweat that trickled down pecks I wasn't sure he really had under the ratty t-shirts that he favored in real life. A red bandana held back his chestnut curls. My Rambo loving friend crouched down and shoulder-rolled across the narrow alley we were in. I sighed in exasperation and walked after him. We didn't have time to play warzone. With his dramatic summersault across the alley over, he came to kneel beside another man. The older soldier held an assault rifle and peered around a dumpster.

John Monroe looked the same as when I'd met him four years ago. Close cropped, ash blonde hair with a small crown of balding just over his ears. A cigarette teetered precariously between his lips as he addressed Harris. "I told you never to let them be together." John had tears in his eyes despite the remonstration.

"You didn't tell me this would happen." Regardless of Harris' physically domineering image he spoke like the scared teenage boy that he was.

A blast from somewhere beyond the dumpster shook the ground. John reached out and grabbed Harris by the throat. "Grow up Harrison!" I scooted back a little, shocked. I didn't think John would speak to his brother like that, but what did I know, I'd only met the man once.

"You can't leave it all on me. I'm not ready." Harris whined.

"I don't have much of a choice. We both know I won't make it out of this." Tiredly, John slumped and lit his cigarette with trembling hands. "Go on kid. Take a look."

Harris stood up peaking around the dumpster. I looked too. The air in the street beyond was murky with dust and debris. A mossy green glow cast down from high above swirling darker as it retreated amidst the smoke. Misshapen lumps littered the sidewalks. When I examined them closely, I saw that they were bodies. Then an unearthly scream came from the light source.

After the sound quit reverberating through my brain, John stood up and gripped Harris by the shoulder. "The girl is dangerous." John spat out his cigarette and stamped out the embers. "Don't let her take him down." He pushed Harris forward. "Get out there and fight."

I followed closely behind Harris as he positioned himself below the green glow. A gust of wind blew upward as if a small dust-devil were clearing the air between us and the light. The mist evaporated enough so that two forms could be detected holding hands in the air. A fair-haired man and a raven-haired woman. Both with jet black eyes.

Though too far above us to tell for sure, the woman looked disturbingly like me. She smiled a wide, white grin, held out a hand toward the ground and the concrete began to shake again.

A horrendous boom beat loudly against my eardrums. A chunk of glass roughly the size of a refrigerator skidded toward my toes. I jumped back before remembering that it wasn't real. With a loud snap from the woman's fingertips the glass broke into millions of razor-sharp splinters. They rose in the air and turned their points toward Harris.

Rambo-boy made to run but his legs moved in exaggeratedly long steps. The panic in his face flooded with frustration as his body refused to listen to his desire. Before the tiny blades could cut him into pieces, darkness enveloped us.

Suddenly, Harris and I were inside my library at home. The rapid shift in location gave me a momentary sense of vertigo. Link sat at the table with his nose in a book. He looked so much younger than I had grown used to seeing him, maybe seven or eight-years-old. It must have been the way Harris saw him in his minds-eye. No wonder he treated Link like a child. He never got over the time that his nephew was just a little boy in a dangerous world.

Harris browsed the shelves with more interest than I had ever noticed before. That aloof exterior must have been just part of the mystique he tried to put forward, I guessed. At heart, he was curious. When another version of me walked into the room he seemed to expand: his arms filled out with thick muscles, and he grew a good three inches taller.

The other Mia had an overly seductive voice and massive breasts. Naturally, both Harris and I had our eyes locked on the pair of E or F cups. I'm not flat chested by any stretch of the imagination but this girl was practically Barbie proportioned. A wonder that she didn't fall over under the weight. Though disgusted with his mental alterations of my bust I was pleased to see that Harris' fantasy Mia didn't have any magical slimming through the hips and thighs. My thick curves didn't detract from his idea of beauty.

"I've been waiting for the moment when I would finally get you alone," the husky voiced Mia said. I looked around and saw that Link had disappeared. Convenient.

"Have you?" Harris tried for coyness with little success, at least in my opinion.

"I've wanted you since the first time we met." Her voice was as gravelly as a cat's purr. Harris only managed a grunt deep in his throat. Sexy Mia laughed and shook out her long dark hair letting the light catch the mahogany strands.

With a vixen-like gleam in her eyes, Sexy Mia teased the hem of her shirt up over her stomach. I realized that she wasn't wearing a bra. Rapidly, I stepped between Sexy Mia and Harris. He looked down, shrinking to his normal height; still a good foot taller than me. I must have been a sight; messy hair, pajamas, and the usual agitation etched on my face.

Putting on my best school master routine I put my hands on my hips, "Time to wake up, Mr. Monroe."

He cocked his head to the side, confused. This was not at all how this fantasy was supposed to go. That led me to believe he'd had it before. Ick. Harris smiled then and tucked a loose strand of hair behind my ear. Surprised I had an ear capable of being touched, I could almost feel Sexy Mia disappearing behind me.

"You look good, Hamilton," he smiled. Not even a trace of irony in his voice. The way he used my surname caught me off guard. I called him Monroe all the time, but I didn't realize it had become a term of endearment. The tenderness of his fingers as they traced the curve of my earlobe sent shivers down my spine and made the hair rise on my arms. I looked down expecting myself to have transformed into his fantasy. Nope, still me.

I grabbed his hand as it made its way down my jaw line. I pressed it firmly to my cheek not trusting myself to let go. I hadn't expected the essence of romance in his attention. To see me as a physically pleasing object was one thing. Me, with no makeup and my natural bust size shouldn't have been a thing to rouse his affections. I couldn't afford to play in this scenario with him. Link was in danger. I did the only thing that came naturally. I slapped him.

Harris looked momentarily stunned. An all-consuming blackness erased everything from my vision. Then a gust of what felt like wind chucked me so forcefully from his subconscious I nearly blacked out. If that was possible. Could ghosts faint? Whatever, not important.

Harris shot straight up. "What happened?"

"I don't know. Something knocked you down the stairs. It took Link. I saw him in the mirror."

"Like *inside* the mirror?" demanded Harris. The life of a Smyth was just strange enough that neither of us were terribly surprised.

"Yeah."

"Damn it."

I agreed again. Harris took the stairs two at a time and I followed as quickly as I could. This shifting from being a real girl and a wisp wasn't easy to manipulate. On the landing I found Harris staring into the mirror. Now bound to a pole of some kind, Link struggled.

"What do we do," Harris pleaded.

"We have to break him out." I tried to hide my helplessness.

"If we break the mirror he could be stuck in there and we'd have no way to reach him." Harris ran his fingers through his hair pulling on the ends.

"I could go in alone, but you'd have no way to help, and Link can't see me. He might be able to on the other side, but I don't know for sure." I was comfortable heading into the mirror realm but not so confident that I could pull off saving someone when my chances of being seen were slim to none.

"I need another option, Mia," Harris began examining the mirrors edges looking for a flaw. The girl who kidnapped Link looked out at us confused. I suspected she couldn't see me either, so it was just Harris standing out here talking to himself.

"I can try to drag you in. I think that girl took Link over the threshold maybe I can do it too."

Harris looked at me and that same sweet affection danced in his hazel eyes. Then he held out his hand. Concentrating, I grabbed it willing myself to be solid. When I finally felt something more like a psychic connection than a physical one, I pushed my way through the mirror.

4.5: I really hate game shows.

The mirror realm seemed more than happy to admit two new victims into its depths. Traveling through the glass felt like pushing against a strong wind without the biting breeze. A force resisted my movement, but it had no texture to the way it squeezed around me. When the sensation finally stopped a booming voice announced our presence, or at least my companion's.

"Let's welcome our newest contestant, Harrison Monroe." The man who spoke had sleek dark black hair gelled up in a tall bouffant. Dangerously lean, with deep hallows beneath his rouged cheeks, he still sported full lips. Bright green eyes sparkled though he wasn't looking at anyone in particular. The announcer man waited while the sound of applause came from the abyss of the room.

Looking around for the source of the noise I noted that every surface was covered in a mosaic of reflective glass. Though standing stoically in the center of the room giving his own image a rakish smile, our host's reflections clapped enthusiastically. When he shifted his attention back to the cue cards in his hands, his eyes periodically darted around the room catching each angle of his likeness.

The man placed the cue cards in his front lapel pocket and straightened a sparkling silver bowtie that perfectly accented his moonbeam gray suit. "Harrison is a guardian with a dark secret." Woah, what did he mean by that? I tried to catch Harris' eye, but the boy looked pointedly away. "And I'm your host, Prince N! Welcome to Name! That! Incantation!" Prince N said each of the last three words with an excited, punchy verve.

Harris suddenly stood behind a clear glass or lucite podium. So did the other contestant, the girl who kidnapped Link. She had some kind of buzzer in her hand as if ready to ring in to answer a question. It seemed at least for the time being that I was still invisible to everyone but Harris. I guessed the girl wasn't a ghost after all. Probably a witch if she could cross into the mirror realm. Though that fact wasn't nearly as important as to why she hijacked Link in the first place.

"Here's what we are playing for folks." Prince N gestured to Link, bound and gagged to the post. "The soul of this fine young virgin." I cringed with second-hand embarrassment. Link made a muffled moan of protest and Prince N patted him on the shoulder. "Virgin souls have a myriad of magical uses. Curry favor with the god or goddess of your choosing. Sacrifice for fame or power. Not to mention they fetch a great price on the underworld black market."

Link let out a high-pitched squeak and Harris gripped his podium tightly. "In order to win our fabulous prize," Prince N continued, "you must correctly name the Incantations! I will give you the ingredients needed for the spell, and you must identify its purpose. For each correctly identified spell I will award you ten points. The player with the most points at the end of the game WINS! Are all our contestants ready to play Name! That! Incantation!?"

The reflected images of Prince N all clapped and smiled at their source. The girl held up her buzzer in anticipation. Harris picked his up and glanced at me. I just shrugged. I didn't see any other options.

"Excellent," Prince N began. "Let's start with question number one." He pulled a card from the pocket of his suit, or rather a thin piece of mirror. From behind all we could see was our own faces. I shifted over toward him to try and get a look at the clue. Prince N tilted the card so that all I could see was a vague outline of letters on a mirrored surface. I couldn't tell if the move to block me was intentional or not.

Something in the back of my mind jumped up like a brownnoser trying to get the extra credit point. I couldn't seem to hear what it was saying. I knew who this guy was from something I'd read but accessing the memory proved elusive.

Reading from the card the prince continued, "What spell requires rainwater, fresh basil and candles?"

I raised my hand. The other girl buzzed in. Harris gave me a half quizzical look and snorted. Then he bit his lip to stop the expression. No one else knew I was there. Lowering my hand, my cheeks flushed.

"Those are the three main ingredients for a cord cutting spell," the girl responded. Looking at her I couldn't escape the feeling that I knew her and not just from the pictures of the séance. I wondered if it was from town or school. She had brown hair tied back in a neat ponytail and focused brown eyes. She had an intensity about her that was slightly unnerving.

"That's correct!" the prince boomed. Behind him a glass altar rose from the floor. The light of the candles danced in all the reflections. There were three different colored candles; red, white and blue. Water sloshed lightly in the clear bowl and the dazzling green of the basil leaves brought a solidity to the surface. "Ten points to Bridget."

I looked the girl over. It couldn't just be a coincidence. The mysterious stranger who kidnapped Link sported the same name as the restaurants most famous ghostly inhabitant. She didn't look like a colonial lady, though. In fact, she had ripped jeans and a faded t-shirt with a snowy white owl that read "Still waiting for my acceptance letter."

Bridget produced a poppet made of varied strips of fabric. Judging by the colors and patterns I figured it was created with swatches from her own clothes. Making her way to the altar she submerged the doll in the water. Once soaked she pulled a basil leaf from the plant and placed it across the body of the poppet. She then proceeded to drip the wax from each color of the candles onto the leaf to seal it to the poppet's fabric. As she followed these steps, she chanted a phrase in what sounded like Gaelic. It was odd to use the Highlander's tongue for spell work but not necessarily unheard of. I didn't understand much of what she said, but I did catch the words 'uair' for time and 'anam' for soul.

Out of the corner of his mouth Harris whispered, "What is she doing?"

"The water, wax and basil are all part of the cord cutting ritual. Usually used to get rid of negative energies. Pretty basic," I whispered back then realized I didn't need to. "The poppet and Gaelic...I don't know... looks like hoodoo."

"Question two; name the incantation for identity concealment." Prince N wiggled his eyebrows up and down in an exaggerated gesture of tantalizing mystery.

"BUZZ IN!" I shouted.

"What! Why? I don't know that answer." Harris was barely concealing his words as he addressed me.

"But I do." I rung my hands frustrated with their futility.

Bridget buzzed in instead. She gave the answer, got her points, and cast a blessing on a burlap bag that she plopped her poppet into. Bully for you Bridget. The ghostly applause rang through the room bouncing like a racket ball off the mirrored surfaces. Out of the corner of my eye I thought I saw a young woman running in the distance behind the clapping images of Prince N, but I didn't have time for any other oddities.

The prince's smile glittered. If this was a setup, as I suspected, it was going great; well, great for them. "Question 3: The blood of the innocent is the primary ingredient needed to open a portal. What is the incantation for this ritual?"

Strangely, Bridget was silent. She made a rather obvious play at pretending she was thinking about the answer. In her hesitation, Harris buzzed in, "Aperi viam temporis." Latin for 'open the way of time.'

"Correct," the prince crossed the room and picked up the bagged poppet from the altar. Producing a silver dagger, he slashed out at Link opening a gash along his bound forearm. Blood spurted immediately, landing across the little doll's encasement. Link strained against his bindings, the veins in his throat standing out as he silently screamed.

Beside me Harris swore and tried to move but his feet were rooted to the floor behind his podium. I was free to roam but all that did was give me a better view of the blood spreading out on the floor ringing the reflective ground in a circle of droplets. When they connected in a shape the size of a manhole the mirror darkened to the point that I wasn't sure if it was still solid ground.

Prince N didn't seem fazed by the sudden change in atmosphere as he awarded Harris his obligatory ten points. He produced another card. Another question. Another trap. "Question 4: The flesh of the oppressor is a sacrifice required to navigate temporal portals. What is the appropriate spell used after collecting this ingredient?"

Harris dispensed with the subterfuge and looked directly at me. "Its 'sacrificium viscera' if that helps?" I didn't know what else to tell him. We needed the points to save Link.

"He's already bleeding. Now you want me to take a pound of flesh?" Harris hissed out.

I sighed and searched the room for something else we could do. All I found was Bridget preoccupied with a hangnail and Prince N making kissy faces at his reflection. The blood flowing freely from Link's arm was beginning to make him pale. "I honestly don't think we have any other options."

Harris gritted his teeth, buzzed in, and repeated the Latin words. The prince moved with incredible speed slicing the lobe of Harris' left ear clean off. The new Van Gogh screamed clasping his hands to the wound.

Momentarily stunned, I quite forgot I didn't really exist in the traditional sense of the word. I ran for the prince as he bent to pick up the severed lobe. I didn't have a solid plan, but I couldn't stand by anymore. Prince N turned with a suddenness that scared me. Unnaturally fast. He grabbed me by my neck, choking me. Taken off guard by the fact that I didn't realize I had a neck capable of grabbing let alone dying by asphyxiation, I didn't even struggle.

The prince didn't seem to be able to meet my eyes even as I started to squirm under his firm grip. That's when his full name popped into my head. I tucked my chin into the webbing between his thumb and index finger. That's a pro tip if you don't want to die of asphyxiation. With a small space allowed for air I said, "Obscurus Enthymema." Latin for: "hide the mirrors."

4.6: Tip toe through the centuries.

Every reflective surface dimmed behind a mystical smoke. That got the prince's attention. His *full* attention. The jovial face and dancing eyes fixed on me with murderous intensity. He really was stunningly handsome but the deep need in his expression dampened his features. I struggled for air that I wasn't aware I actually needed. Burrowing further into his stretched hand I managed to gasp enough to croak out his name, "Narcissus."

He dropped me as if my skin had suddenly electrified. Names have power. Behind me Bridget retrieved the piece of Harris' flesh and dropped it into the blood-ringed pit in the center of the room. A howl rose from the depths.

There are two common portals, the first were psychic ones. For the second: if you guessed demon portal, you win this mangy hell hound. The beast clawed its way out of the hole with six-inch talons ringed at the paw by gangrenous nail beds. It had the body and snout of a wolf but a frame closer to that of a bear. The fur matted across its back bristled as it opened a mouth full of razor-sharp fangs and growled.

Link was closest to the beast, but it seemed to have gained a taste for Harris' flesh and stalked toward him. The older Monroe backed away slowly, "Nice dog. Good boy. Pretty devil beast." The hellhound snorted, puffing an acrid cloud of doggie breath in Harris' face. By the paling of his cheeks the smell must have been horrendous.

I had other problems. Devoid of reflective surfaces, Narcissus focused solely on me. I remembered belatedly that the prince was known to be a skilled hunter. He grabbed his dagger in his hand like a stalker in a horror film.

Bridget seemed to decide that the unmasking of our host meant that she won by default. She grabbed the bag containing the cursed poppet and slashed open Link's bonds with a knife she had concealed around her ankle. Link made a great show of sagging against his post looking drained and weak. She bent down to grab his arm and drag him to the center of the room. As she got close to his face, he headbutted her and she staggered back holding her rapidly bruising cheek.

The hellhound leapt at Harris, but Link scrambled over and pulled him away at the last second. Being non-corporeal I wasn't exactly sure what would happen if Narcissus stabbed me. As a rule, I tried not to get stabbed.

I dodged another attack using the podiums to keep Narcissus at bay. Then spotted Bridget at the side of the pit. The poppet was sliced in half, the bag disappearing into the void on the floor. She held one piece of the doll in each hand. In profile she stirred older memories. Memories of another girl I'd only ever read about. Bridget Bishop. I thought about Rebecca's warning, but my translator was currently hiding from a drooling beast. Link let out a little squeal of terror as the hound swiped viciously. Luckly, it was far enough away that it only snatched his pant leg.

"I'm sorry I had to involve you all." Bridget looked at me for the first time and smiled sadly. All the action stopped. The hellhound paused to scratch vigorously at a spot behind its ear. Even Narcissus turned to watch though the girl was near the mirrored altar so it's possible he just got distracted.

Bridget took off her shirt to reveal a corset of embroidered lace. Harris and Link did a double take at the disrobing woman. "I tried to get that pointless influencer, Reaper, to join me but you didn't let him in the building." She took off her pants and a pair of billowy bloomers remained. "Probably for the best. I doubt he or that hapless camera guy would have qualified for the category of 'blood of the innocent.' No time to chit-chat though. I'm gonna change things. Catch me in your history books." Then Bridget leapt into the hole.

The edges pulsated. The hellhound perked up, pausing in its groaning pleasure of finding the right itchy spot. Sniffing the air, it growled. It bounded back to the demon portal then it barked and jumped inside. I couldn't exactly say why, but I suspected it was supposed to be a guard dog that just failed to protect its territory. Part of me felt concerned for Bridget's safety but on the other hand she did orchestrate this event that maimed my colleagues.

Before I could register the bazar notion that the real Bridget Bishop was a time traveler, I felt a solid force drive painfully into my shoulder. I looked down at the area and found a fist on top of my clavicle. It released the hilt of the dagger stuck straight down.

Stumbling backward I caught the look of triumph in Narcissus' eyes. He stood straight and gave an ironic bow. The growing darkness of unconsciousness popped black bubbles across my vision. My spell to hide the mirrors dispersed slowly and Narcissus returned to gazing at his own reflection. He struggled trying to clean the walls with his sleeve, the image wasn't as clear as he obviously wished.

Just then, Link threw him a translucent bottle with his uninjured arm and Narcissus snatched it out of the air. I didn't realize the kid was packing potions. The prince gratefully looked into its unclouded surface. "There he is. The most beautiful creature in the world."

"Open it," Link suggested. "It smells as good as it looks."

Narcissus gloried at the idea. The uncorked bottle let out a strong scent of vinegar. The prince and I both wrinkled our noses. The pit on the floor contracted as if inhaling and Narcissus stumbled backward. His perfectly shined shoes slipped into its dark depths, and he fell cursing and trying to catch the light along the glass vial.

With the prince returned safely to his private suite in hell, the mirror realm spit us out. Unfortunately, it left the weapon in my shoulder intact. I sat down on the ground hard, trying not to black out. Link eyed the dagger, and I wondered placidly if it looked disembodied. Kneeling beside me, Harris grabbed the hilt. I raised my hands to dissuade him of this notion, but I was weak. The first, most elementary, rule of stab wounds was not to remove the blade. He pulled it forcefully upward and fell back as the motion was not equal to the resistance. My body let loose the object as if it was merely stuck into soft butter.

I could feel the shock flooding my system; my hands trembled, and my head felt as if it was floating away. What I didn't feel was the warm cascade of blood down my chest. I looked to see no indication that the blade had ever connected with my skin. I didn't really have skin after all. I would have probably still passed out if Link didn't whoop with victorious joy.

"I did it! All by myself. Did Mia see that? Damn, I feel like I'm on fire," Link exclaimed. Harris and I looked at him speechless. "Shoot, do you think it counts that I bought the banishing potion? I paid Demi for it." Link's concerns were fleeting, too high on adrenaline he didn't even notice the blood dripping from the slash on his arm. Harris did and started to wrap it with a cloth napkin from the bussing station.

Still reeling Link let Harris doctor him without protest. "I can't wait to tell Demi how good that worked. The only thing that doesn't make sense was that Bridget girl. Who the hell was she? Where did she go?"

"To Salem," Harris answered before I could. He must have picked up what I had noticed. Bridget was making a portal, not to hell but as a passageway to another time. "Salem circa 1692 or before that more likely."

"You mean she was traveling time?" Link looked thunderstruck. "Do you think she can really change things."

Harris and I looked at each other again. A grim expression crossed both of our faces. "I don't think so buddy."

Link turned back to the mirror peering in as if he could still see the game show and not just his own bewildered image. "But why do it then?"

"Everyone has regrets," Harris began. "We all look to the past and pinpoint where it all went wrong but everyone needs to grow up sometime."

The words echoed for me from Harris' dream. I wondered how that conversation with John had really gone. The dream distorted reality enough that specifics were unattainable for me, but the theme was clear. Harris felt that John rested the weight of the world on his shoulders.

"So, if it never works then why do people try?" As usual Link was a dog digging for a bone. Relentlessly oblivious to how the questions were being perceived.

"I don't know if it 'never works,'" Harris responded. "I just know that people who try to fix the past aren't thinking how to improve the future." I didn't know he could be so deep minded.

Harris gingerly touched the edge of his skin where his earlobe had been severed. "Molly can fix that," I gestured. "And him too." Link's napkin was already soaked through.

Harris translated this information to Link. For the first time it was word for word. Finally. Link examined his crudely bandaged arm critically. "Do you think it will still scar if Molly fixes it with magic?"

Harris turned to me and shrugged. I smiled wanly and got to my feet. Then we both turned to the stairs and made our way down.

"Wait guys!" Link called, somehow divining I too had left him behind. "I'm serious. Chicks dig scars, right?"

Side by side Harris and I walked away. My fellow trainer held out a fist and I tapped my incorporeal one against it. The only reaction to the cold that Harris let slip was a slight widening of his eyes. Other than that, we let the fist bump be the end of the night and the beginning of a more cohesive partnership.

4.7: Learning a little Her-story.

Molly did indeed patch up the Monroe boys. Poor Link didn't get his sexy scar but at least Harris got his earlobe back. The next morning when I could finally lay hands on things, I chose not to throttle my sister as was my first inclination. She got a stay of execution for her help. I met her in the kitchen after I made a detour to grab a book from the library.

"You owe me pancakes," I announced when I came in the room.

Molly smirked. "I thought you might say that. Check the microwave."

Following instructions, I found that the pancakes were still steaming. I pulled the plate out and got a fork. Molly got out the whip cream and a small bowl of sliced bananas from the fridge. I'm not a syrup girl. I was touched that she had my favorites ready.

Taking the first bite, my eyes rolled up into my head and I groaned in pleasure. I pointed my fork in Molly's direction. "You, my darling sister, are entirely forgiven."

"I thought that might be the case." Molly turned her head and read the title of the book I brought down, "'Witches of the Salem Trials?'"

I tried to respond but I couldn't. Swallowing hard I said, "Yeah, the witch who kidnapped Link made a time portal." I opened the book, found Bridget's portrait, and turned it toward Molly. "It's a pretty accurate likeness."

Molly looked me in the eyes to tell if I was serious, I shrugged. It all seemed wild to me too. "Did she say why?"

"Something about changing things."

"Damn. I guess she failed."

"I don't know." I turned the book back so I could read the chapter. "If you think about it Bridget Bishop scared the bejesus out of the pious members of the Salem colony. She had three husbands, owned her own property, and spoke her mind."

"I see what you mean." Molly poured me a cup of coffee and I thanked her.

"These days the worst thing to happen to a girl like Bridget might be mockery from internet trolls." I picked up a whip cream coated banana slice and popped it in my mouth.

"Well, in 1692 the punishment for being a self-sufficient woman was death." Molly took a seat next to me and stared down at the portrait. "Imagine if she really could have changed the course of the trials."

"Might have moved women's rights up a few decades." I took a sip of the coffee and sighed morosely. Gender equality still had a long way to go even in our own time. "I should have known it wasn't going to go well for Bridget. I met her daughter. She tried to get me to warn her mother about going into the portal."

"I assume she was a ghost?" Molly flipped idly through the book.

"Yeah. Some other ghost came by and grabbed her by the shoulder with a scythe."

"I can get my coven on that. Banishing evil spirits isn't nearly interesting enough for the great Mia Hamilton." Molly swayed into me and bummed my shoulder. I smiled at her. She may be annoying, but she knew me well.

I closed the book on Bridget Bishop. There was no sense worrying over the past when the future was still being written and there were pancakes that needed to be eaten.

Rule # 5: Be a jack-of-all-trades and a master of as many as possible.

5.1: It takes two to tango; literally.

The mirrors in the dance studio felt sinister for the first time in my life. After the ghost hunt at the Lyceum, I regarded my reflection as something nefarious. Still, it was necessary to be surrounded by mirrors when learning to dance. Proper angles matter.

The bell at the top of the door rang as Harris and Link came inside. Demi sat at a counter in the front of the studio with her feet up and her arms behind her head.

Link signed, "Hello, how are you?"

Despite Demi's usual emo moodiness, she smiled and tapped her thumb on her chest in an open palm gesture. "I'm fine." I liked Link for trying. His vocabulary was in its infancy, but he gave it his best shot. I hoped he was up to the task I had for him.

"This place is great," Link's eyes darted around the room. "How did you find it?"

"It belongs to Demi's mom. She used to be a ballerina but now she mostly hosts classes for cute toddlers." I signed my words for Demi's benefit.

"Damn Hamilton. I don't think I have ever seen you in a dress," appraised Harris.

I actively tried not to cover myself up. My dress was black with a basic boatneck leotard and a skirt that slit up to mid-thigh on either side. It was a calculated look designed specifically for the dance I had in mind.

"Subsection of rule number two: 'research means learning what to wear and what weapons to bring.'" Link recited. He only had enough ASL to hold up two fingers.

"Why are we training here?" Harris looked around. "I figured we would be teaching him basic martial arts."

"Ever watch a Jacky Chan movie?" I subconsciously straightened my skirt. "It takes a lot of choreography to synchronize those moves. Even professional football players study ballet. This brings us to Rule number 5: Its best to be a jack-of-all-trades but as a hunter you should be a master of as many as possible." Link pulled out his notebook, but I waved it away. "No, this is going to be a hands-on lesson. Harris, can you tango?"

"Who me?" He looked around the room searching for another volunteer.

"Pretty sure you are the only Harris present," I responded. He looked distinctly uncomfortable. "Come on Monroe, you're not actually trying to tell me that John didn't make you learn ballroom dancing?"

Harris took off his jacket. "Be gentle, I haven't tried this in like three years."

I smirked; amused by his discomfort. "Dance is all about communication. To my father's credit we got a nice strong lesson on that during Halloween. This kind of communication though is nonverbal." I addressed Link who looked like he would love to take notes on the subject.

I pulled the tiny stereo remote from my boob pocket. Yes, I said boob pocket. Ballroom dresses don't come with places to put things. If you don't know what I'm talking about in general, then you've clearly never met a girl. Turning on the music, I put the remote back where I had found it. Consequently, I had to snap my fingers under Harris' nose to keep him on track.

He placed a firm hand at my back and took my offered right keeping his arms bent in a passable version of holding his posture. Color me impressed. In time with the music, he urged me backward with a slight shift of his arms. Slow, slow, quick, quick, slide. Our knees were bent slightly, our bodies close, but not touching as his feet moved one planted between my own. We went around the room like this focusing on the first most characteristic piece of the tango.

"Do you see Linky?" began Harris. "She knows when the next move will begin by the slightest change in the way I hold my body." He switched it up suddenly shifting to a corte, dance lingo for moving backward. I followed his lead easily and did my best to maintain my own center line. "See what I mean?"

Link nodded emphatically. I smiled at Harris and beckoned Demi over to dance with Link. He looked a little concerned. "Don't worry, Demi can feel the beat in the floor. That's why she isn't wearing shoes." He glanced down to confirm my assertion. "Plus, the tango is about body language which is basically Demi's best form of communication." She signed something to me quickly and I smiled. "Right, second only to her expert use of the withering stare."

Link did reasonably well with Demi. He only stepped on her toes twice. My friend was a good partner for any beginner. She picked up on cues that not everyone noticed. By the time the song was done he had mostly mastered the first crucial steps. I restarted the song and offered him my hand. Demi relinquished him with a sardonic bow.

The moment Link's fingers touched mine a buzzing sort of vibration began lightly beneath my skin. I found myself incapable of taking my eyes off his baby blues. He held me with the posture of an expert, not the clumsy self-doubt he'd shown with Demi.

Moving me backward in the way we had shown him, he added in a few progressive rocks dipping us back and forth in time with the music. He spun me forward coming up behind me and placing his hands at my waist. I felt the tip of his nose travel up my neck and his lips teasing at my throat. Spinning me back around he walked us down the room, hands clasped forward in a promenade. As the music reached the end of the song, he dipped me dangerously close to the floor.

Looking at him there was something different in his expression. Confident, self-assured. Not the kid I'd gotten to know for the last few months. Pulling me up, he let go. He bowed briefly then looked confused.

"Wait...," Link returned to his usual slouch shouldered stance. "Aren't we going to dance?"

"You just did," Harris looked at me with concern.

"You did great," I added. I couldn't help it, I totally avoided making eye contact. "Looks like you've mastered that one. I guess I'll have to find something harder next." The Jekyll and Hyde routine creeped me out.

Mollified, Link pulled on his jacket and made his way outside. Demi followed him out. She relished the role of ASL teacher. I'd bet by the time Harris joined him Link would know the signs for everything in the parking lot.

Feeling a bit off center, I sat down to remove my heels. "I didn't know you could be so graceful," complemented Harris from above me.

"What are you trying to say? I'm not merely a blunt force object."

"I didn't mean that." Harris shuffled his feet, hesitantly. "It's just that I think you're doing a really great job with Link and, well, I appreciate it."

"Thanks," I bit my lip unsure how to ask what was on my mind. "At the restaurant when you got knocked out, I had to dream walk you..."

Harris stiffened, "Oh no, then you saw..."

I blushed, "That and other things." Harris' eyes darted around in panic trying to remember what else I might have seen. "The part with John... Did he tell you Link shouldn't be near me?" I studied his face but all he did was gulp.

The bell above the door chimed again. Link came rushing in with a blast of cold air. "Check it out," he made the sign for car, parking lot and the phrase 'I like you.' That last one made me smile despite the tense conversation with Harris. When Demi and I said goodbye to the boys I elbowed her in the ribs, and she gave me a wink.

Going home I reflected on the dance lesson. Link was a completely different person when dancing with me. So much so that I wasn't sure it was really him at all. If we had been in any other place I would have wondered if the kid had been possessed or something. Darwin Studio was warded against such things. Demons love to dance. And sing. There is an inherent magic in both. The first humans danced to pray for successful hunts. Sang songs to ease their loved ones into the afterlife. Tangent, sorry.

What troubled me most wasn't that the connection between Link and I had seemingly caused this abrupt change in his demeanor, it was that it had happened before. If it could occur again what was the purpose of it? What if there was a next time?

5.2: Hey Murphy, can you take the night off?

The yard outside the main entrance of the school was coated in a fresh powder of snow. I liked it like that. Undisturbed, no slushy footprints marked at the corners with muddy brown edges. I got there early just to see it undefiled. Naturally, the first person to approach me clomped right on through. He kicked up a clump that fell in the exact wrong spot, so it slid down my boot soaking a portion of my sock.

"Hey Mia," Link's perpetually sunny disposition made it difficult to hold a grudge, but my foot was cold. "Guess what I just did?" Playing twenty questions with a teenage boy wasn't on my bucket list, particularly not when I hadn't finished my coffee. I just stared till he continued; in sign language no less, "I asked Demi to the Winter Formal."

He shocked me out of my grumpiness. "No way? Did she say yes?" I didn't mean it to come out disbelieving, but I could tell it had.

"As a matter of fact, she did." Link puffed out his chest with pride.

"Good for you. I bet you guys will have a great time."

"You mean, *we*, right? We will have a great time. Didn't Harris ask you yet?"

"What?" I spluttered, laughing. I couldn't tell if he was serious at first then I remembered who I was talking to. Link didn't have an ounce of deception in his body. "No, he hasn't"

Looking concerned he examined my face. "Does that mean you'd say no?"

I considered that. "I don't know. I've never been to a school dance."

Link shuffled his feet. "Look can you pretend I didn't tell you. Harris would be pissed if he knew. Anyway, I know Demi would feel more comfortable with you there. My ASL is still pretty sketch."

"I'll think about it," I agreed, though the notion made me feel odd. On one hand, there was definitely something brewing between me and Harris. On the other, I couldn't help but worry that Link had put him up to it.

Luckily, boys aren't often subtle creatures, so I didn't have a lot of time to ruminate on the subject. Passing the admin office after my first few lessons, I stopped to chat with the school secretary. Pro tip: if you want to know everything about a school campus get in good with the secretary. They have all the juicy gossip.

"Who's retiring?" I pointed to the cheap paper congratulatory decorations.

"Mrs. Sterling. It's her last week but she's still going to chaperone the dance." Ms. Robins clacked her three-inch acrylic nails against the keyboard. The mere fact that she could type legibly with those claws was impressive. Girlfriend could actually go 120 words per minute.

"That's good. She's about as sympathetic as stucco." Everyone who had ever been sent to Mrs. Sterling as long as I'd attended always ended up leaving in tears. It was an unguarded secret that she abjectly hated teenagers. "Have you met her replacement?"

With a conspiratorial raise of her eyebrows, Robins beckoned me forward. "Actually yes. He's this recent college grad. The kid is hands down less than a decade older than you guys."

"Is he cute?" I twirled the fake flower topped pen on the counter.

Reaching over me a large hand plucked the pen from my fingers. "Who me? I mean I'd prefer hot, but I'll take cute." Harris bonked me on the nose with the flower. He was holding it in his left hand, I don't think I noticed till now that he was a lefty. I pushed him away playfully and said goodbye to Ms. Robins.

Harris and I took off down the hall together and headed for lunch. "You know, Linky asked your friend Demi to the formal?" I gave a perfunctory 'uh, huh.' Putting his hands in his pockets he tried to look relaxed. "Well, I figure the kid could use a chaperone." Seeing that I wasn't going to help him get there he continued, "and a translator. That's where you come in. So maybe we go together and help out and stuff."

"Okay," I agreed as he muttered something that sounded like 'only if you want to.' "I'll be wearing red. It's a formal, so get a tie to match. My dad can help if you need advice."

Clearing his throat to regain his composure he said, "Yeah, great, awesome." I walked away not wanting him to see my smile. There was something distinctly endearing about him, and I couldn't help but like him a little bit more.

***

The night of the dance Demi came over to get ready. She chose a black, fitted strapless bodice. The sparkles in the fabric gleamed against her bronze skin. Her long, matching, gaucho pants gave the illusion she was wearing a full skirt which was only dispelled when she walked. She tried to play it cool, but I could tell she was excited for the date. Demi usually dated girls but being Pan, aka pansexual, she followed a different set of rules when it came to who she liked.

It was one of my favorite things about her. Love for the sake of love. Attraction without limit.

I had her zip me up in my skintight red dress. I might not come across as a girl with a fondness for sparkles, but I've always related to Jessica Rabbit. Curves in all the right places. The split in my dress only went to my knee, mostly to keep my father from having a heart attack.

When I made my way downstairs, I found my dad helping fix Harris' tie. Looking at the boys from the landing I couldn't help but feel like this was more fun than I had anticipated. Demi came down behind me and by the look on Link's face she was the bell of the ball.

Link presented her with a corsage that had a green silk rose amidst the white of baby's breath. "I thought this might go good with the color in your hair." He forgot to sign but she was sufficiently good at lip reading to get the drift. Especially as he tucked a lock of green tipped hair behind her ear. "Oh, shoot sorry, Mia can you translate?"

Demi tweaked his tie to get his attention then signed, "I understood you." She held out her wrist for Link to decorate. Slipping her hand under his proffered arm, he led her outside.

"Be home by midnight Cinderella." My dad kissed me on the cheek.

"Will do," I responded with a wink.

Harris didn't offer his arm, but he did hold the door open for me. "I didn't get you a corsage cause like I tried to tell Linky their so old school. But riding in style is classic." He gestured down to the street where a deluxe sports car had been stretched three times its original size. The suicide doors were open invitingly. It was nearly the same shade of red as my dress.

I ran my fingers along the sleek curves of the hood. "Nice one, Monroe."

He held out his hand to help me get into the limo. "Ready for our first normal outing, m'lady?"

I laughed lightly which was a mistake. I should have known then that it was an ill omen to test fate. It's not a rule because it's basic but you should always expect the unexpected. As Murphy's law would remind us; 'anything that *can* go wrong, will go wrong.'

5.3: Our school councilor needs therapy.

Arriving at Hamilton Hall we stepped out to join the throng of well-dressed teenagers. The three-story building made from red brick had white framed windows and dark green shudders. While named after my ancestor it wasn't built by my family but architect Samuel McIntire. I can't take credit for everything in this town. Our party waited in line outside. Though I sported a thick winter coat, my legs were freezing; a fact exacerbated by the slow-moving queue.

The hold up turned out to be the ASB's insistence that directly after flashing your ticket you were forced to take your picture. When I got close enough to see, I found Kiera Weinhard slipping back in front of the camera after every couple passed to retake her photo. Insisting on the right angle she was also asking if the lights could be dimmed then brightened then dimmed again.

We took our photos and proceeded into the hall. It was super dark. Colored lights shown from the second-story balcony and shot across the floor in circles. A DJ blasted today's most popular out-played singles. Most people milled about on the outskirts of the dance floor, but a few were grinding obscenely. The chaperones circled around like vultures plucking couples aside and instructing them to keep their bodies at least a few inches apart.

Coach Underwood stood guard over the punch bowl. I pitied the fool who tried to spike it. I thought I would see Mrs. Sterling but she didn't seem to have joined the birds of prey around the dance floor yet. Just as I started to crane my neck around the room, I spotted her teased gray curls glistening near the DJ. Her skin was coated in liver spots and wrinkles. Sunken eyes peered over the crowd as she grabbed the microphone which let out a high-pitched screech.

"In honor of my retirement I have arranged for a special experience for you students." Creepily, the 's's' in her words hissed out of her like a snake. She handed the DJ a record then whispered a message to him. When she turned back to us all and smiled, she looked positively insane.

The DJ played the record in what sounded to me like reverse. I turned to Harris questioningly when suddenly the house lights went on full blast blinding me. Damn, green eyes and bright lights don't mix. A good thirty seconds went by before I could blink the flashes out of my vision. When I could see again, Harris was no longer beside me. The odd skipping noises coming from the speakers echoed around the room.

I found Harris and the rest of the students standing in front of an impressive row of carnival games that hadn't been there before. A bemused look crossed Harris' face, "I didn't realize it was this big from the outside."

"That's because it's not," I responded. What I was looking at was approximately a football field full of booths. Flashing lights and booming voiced attendants beckoned my classmates like moths to a flame.

Demi caught my eye, confused, and signed "What the hell?"

"Stupid magic again," I signed in response.

I rolled my head around cracking my neck. Time to get to work. Fact number one: she and I didn't have the same dopey look on our faces as the rest of the hall's occupants. Including Harris and Link. Okay, so we had something the others didn't.

My fingers immediately went to the back of my ear where a tiny tattoo of the Chinese character for listening rested. Despite my age I had several small protective inky charms. The character was a symbol comprised of 5 different elements: hearing, seeing, mind and heart. In the center, like a strike between the two sides, was the character for focus. Though honestly this was the first time I'd received the benefit of the charm which was nice since it hurt like hell when I got it. Obviously, Demi, being deaf couldn't hear the record.

Simple questions sometimes get simple solutions. I walked over to the DJ and reached over to shut down the machine. A yellow nailed claw grabbed my wrist. "Too late, Ms. Hamilton." Mrs. Sterling's face looked like a badly covered fondant cake complete with ridges in odd places and cracks. The skin moved smoothing out in places as if worms writhed beneath the surface. "I'm surprised you showed up here. This sort of soiree is not really your cup of tea, is it?"

"Didn't peg it for yours either," I shook off her bony grip. The record began to skip but the DJ had floated trance-like toward the games. She let go of my arm and delicately grabbed the disc, placing it back in its protective sleeve.

"I used to have to sing this wretched song. Those performances were not nearly as effective as all this." She patted the speakers lovingly. "I can reach a much larger audience. I must say it is nice vinyl came back in style. I was afraid I was going to have to make a digital copy. These last few generations have been exceptionally greedy with technology. Altering devices every five years as if half a decade is any measure of longevity."

I'd heard other old-timers talk like this about today's youth. Something about the way she spoke gave me the impression she wasn't just referring to the last 80 years or so. A collective noise of disappointment came from the crowd of spellbound kids behind me. I turned around to see Will Forester shaking his head in defeat.

With a sigh of relief Mrs. Sterling sat down on a comfy-looking bench near the wall. My high-heel clad feet begged me to join her. As a rule, I try not to get too chummy with hell-spawn. Watching her I noticed she was growing less wrinkly, and her hair was thickening. Whatever magic she had invoked had clearly taken effect.

Demi tapped me on the shoulder and pointed to Kiera Weinhard. She was playing a balloon dart game very, very poorly. Worse than that, she had suddenly sprouted a lot of grey hair. That record wasn't just witchcraft, it was sorcery. For those of you playing at home that means it's worse… way worse.

Transfixed by what I was seeing I didn't even turn around to speak to Mrs. Sterling. "Want to make a deal?"

"I believe I have everything I need. Things are already so much better." Her voice had gone from the brittle quaver of age to a bright clip.

I turned and looked her straight in the eyes. The rest of her slowly smoothing face was distracting. "This spell is powerful but with power comes limitations. I'd guess you only have an hour at most to collect years." She nodded, unconcerned. "You'll get your youth and maybe a little extra time, but you'll be back at this in a century or so."

She stretched her newly un-arthritic fingers. "A century is a long time dear."

"Not for you." It was a guess but the grimace on her face told me I was right. The flashing lights and loud salesmen-quality pleas to 'Step right up' boomed through the space. Sterling winced at the volume of cheers and sighs of disappointment. "What's with the carnival anyway."

"A child's version of gambling. If I've learned anything this past decade its that 'age-appropriate' is extremely important to you mortals." Sterling tugged on her ear trying to encourage her morphing skin to pull taut. "When I worked the textile factories children as young as seven could roll dice and out fox the most skilled adult. Though, to be frank, it was a lot harder to fool those young hoodlums. Weighted dice didn't have the same brightly alluring effect as all this." She gestured to the row of booths.

"So, it's just a contract. Play the game, win the cheap mass produced stuffy. In exchange for the chance to take home the 'prize' they pay in time not money." I summarized.

"Very good, Ms. Hamilton." Sterling crossed her legs. Her exposed knee no longer looked swollen and crooked. The skin was perfectly pink, and the bones were straight. "Now sit back and enjoy the show. The house always wins but you have to love these poor fools for trying. By the end of the hour most of them will be dead but I am sure you will be able to enjoy the last few days of life with a select lucky few."

"Make me a deal." I casually removed my heels.

"Why?" Sterling examined her newly healthy nails and straight fingers.

"If my team can beat all those games before the hour is up, you lose all the years you've collected so far. If we can't, you can have all our years. Every last one of us in this hall." I tried not to sound too desperate.

"You're just as cunning as ever. I remember you from your life before. In fact, it was one of your disciples who gave me this spell." Okay, so apparently the youth music wasn't working on her brain. She sounded ready to play so I didn't say anything. "Alright Ms.

Hamilton, but why not raise the stakes. When you lose, and you will lose, I want your souls too."

I was already gambling everyone's lives, the souls felt like an afterthought to me. "Deal."

5.4: I try not to un-alive my classmates.

Coach Underwood had his hands clenched on the drinks table. His eyes darted from the punch bowl to the games with dizzying rapidity. He had clearly received the message to go gamble his life away, but he was duty bound to monitor the beverage station. I had to hand it to the man, physically resisting a spell that strong must take a lot of will power.

"Yo, Coach!" I skidded the last few feet to the table since I had dispensed with my heels near the DJ. He had a hard time looking at me between his obsessive need to scan the drink station and his preoccupation with the carnival booths on the opposite side of the room. "Do you mind if I steal this Sharpie?"

"As a matter of fact, I do mind, Ms. Hamilton. Without proper labeling we could have an outbreak of covid or worse mono. Do you want to explain to your first kiss why you might give them herpes?" The coach absentmindedly poured me a cup. "Now make sure you put your name on that legibly."

Once handed the pen, I took off. "Thanks Coach!" If an encoded sorceress' message didn't make him leave his post my thievery couldn't do it either. Or so I hoped. Looking back, I found I was right. I handed the pen to Demi and signed the plan.

We tracked down the Monroe boys and as carefully as she could she traced the symbol from the back of my ear onto their skin. Owing to the fat tip of the pen and the moving target of boys, the character took up most of the side of their necks. Luckily it worked. They didn't look in too bad of shape either. Harris had an interesting patch of gray on each of his trimmed sideburns and Link had cute little laugh lines around his eyes.

"What the hell just happened?" Harris made to rub the side of his neck, but I caught his hands before he could smear the ink.

"We don't have a lot of time so let me skip to the end. If we don't beat each of these games before this hour is up, everyone here dies." I tried not to sound melodramatic, but the situation didn't allow for it.

Beside me Demi signed the bit about our souls too. Given Link's new ASL skill level he unfortunately got the message. "Wait, we die, AND she gets our souls?"

Outraged, Harris turned on me, but we didn't have time for arguments. I held my hand up to keep him from asking more questions. "Listen we have a little over 30 minutes to win these games we need a strategy."

"Sub section of rule 5, 'play to your strengths'," Link recited.

"Exactly," I began. Looking around I noted five different types of booths. "Okay we have darts, basketball, duck hunt, milk bottle toss and high striker. Who feels good about one of those?"

Demi waved to get our attention then mimed putting a ball in the hoop which wasn't specifically the correct sign, but we all got her drift. Harris looked at her short stature with skepticism. Before he could protest, I stepped in, "Trust me, she can do this."

The line for the basketball booth was long and populated by our varsity team. The jock at the front of the line held the ball expertly on the palm of his hand, bent his knees and in one smooth upward motion released the ball from the tips of his fingers. It flew into the air and banged on top of the rim of the hoop circling a few times before sinking through the net. I didn't really know the kid by name, but his skills gave me hope for this season's team of Witches. Yep, our mascot is the Witch, feel free to laugh.

The attendant of the booth had the classic flat brimmed straw hat and a red and white striped vest over a basic white polo shirt. Red curly hair escaped from under the brim of the hat and a spattering of dark freckles congregated on his nose and cheekbones. His expression however was bored to the point of falling asleep standing up.

"Well done." The attendant said in his monotone voice. He could have given Ben Stein a run for his money if he had tried out for the economics teacher role in *Ferris Bueller*. "Now for the lightening round."

The attendant pressed a button on the wall that housed the basketball hoop. More lights flashed and the hoop began to follow a path along the wall as if it was on its own rollercoaster ride. It sped up and slowed down along this track in seemingly random places making it near impossible to predict where to send the ball so that it sank into the net. The jock took the ball from the attendant and assumed the expert stance of a professional. He did his best to time his release and came close to sinking the shot, but the hoop moved jerkily which caused the ball to bounce aggressively off the rim and fly directly back into the boy's face, promptly knocking him on his ass.

Before I could suggest that we regroup and discuss the clearly homicidal game Demi stepped over the boy's body. She retrieved the ball and knocked on the front lip of the booth to get the attendants attention. He slowly turned and pressed the button on the wall. The hoop returned to its center and stationary position.

Harris helped the rest of the jocks lift their buddy out of the way. The former kid now looked like he was pushing forty. Demi stepped up and though she was a good foot smaller than the jock her form was just as, if not more, flawless than Mr. Varsity. She made the first shot easily. The fanfare from the booth caused the attendant to jump. Moments before, he had his eyes closed and his mouth hung loosely open, a thin strip of drool making its way down his chin.

The sleepwalker hit the button again and the hoop took off in random patterns across the wall. Demi got the ball and watched the pattern of the hoop intently. She made several false starts, dipping her knees and letting the ball drift to the tips of her fingers before pulling it back in. Link's heart couldn't take the tension. He placed both hands over his eyes and peered out from between his fingers. I'm pretty sure I started holding my breath at one point.

For a moment it felt like the whole room went silent as Demi tensed and released. All we heard was the swish of the ball falling squarely through the net. Demi held her fists in the air, and I wrapped my arms around her middle lifting her up slightly. Lights flashed announcing her winning status.

When we calmed down long enough to notice, the forlorn booth attendant got our attention and handed Demi a cheap stuffed bear. She snuggled it looking pleased. All down the elongated room the basketball booths went dark. A collective sound of disappointment filled the air, but the spellbound crowd moved on to other games. The dude who had supervised Demi's victory mysteriously disappeared.

"One down four to go." I took a deep breath. More nervous than I cared to admit, I turned to the boys, "Either of you have a good throwing arm?"

"I got this," Harris replied. I gave him a curious glance. "John taught me. My childhood wasn't all demon hunting." That caught me off guard. Even though he didn't mean it as a slight I found myself reflecting. There was hardly a day in my past that I could remember doing something as normal with my dad as throwing a ball.

We all made our way up to the booth. The attendant had the same freckled face and blank look as the basketball guy. He handed Harris a container with three softballs. Across the short expanse six heavy milk bottles were stacked in a deceptively precarious pyramid. It occurred to me belatedly that these types of games are notoriously rigged. What, at first glance, appears to be the simple task of knocking down these empty bottles turns out to be much more difficult. The bottles might just as well be made of concrete for all their sturdiness.

Harris took off his suit jacket and handed it to me. As he rolled up the sleeves of his white button down, I got a good look at his powerful forearms. He plucked the first ball from the basket supplied to him, aimed, and released. The collision of the ball and the jugs made a sound like that of a fender bender, but Harris managed to dislodge all but one bottle. He shot me one of his patented confident smiles and blasted the last bottle against the back tent wall. Again, the lights of the booth flashed and died.

I craned my neck over the crowd to relocate Mrs. Sterling. She stood at the end of the aisle of games glaring at me. Her creepy eyes looked almost yellow in the dim light.

Turning away from her, I moved to the balloon dart station. “Okay Monroe, my turn.”

Harris crossed his arms over his chest. “You sure you can handle that?”

I may have been nervous about Sorceress Lamp-eyes back there, but I knew my own strengths. “Please. Watch me.” Five darts in the basket and I was only permitted to miss one. The balloon dart game was all about the surface tension of the balloon. The fuller the balloon the more likely to pop. The board in front of me had tiny brightly colored nubs of nearly flaccid rubber.

I lifted the heavy tipped dart balancing it and found the perfect grip point. The cold ridged metal felt good beneath my fingertips. I raised my hand up just beside my ear, cocked back, and released. The balloon popped with a very satisfying snapping sound. So did the following three targets.

Turning around triumphant, I tossed the final dart over my shoulder and heard the poor man with my prize bear say placidly, "Ow." Oops. On the bright side I didn't think he was a real person. More like a magical place holder.

Harris looked impressed and amused by my final dart's location. "Where'd did you learn to throw like that?"

I took the pink bear that I won and handed it to Harris. "Not a lot to do at a bar when you can't drink," I shrugged. "Plus, it's not that much different from throwing knives."

"If you say so."

Link walked over with his phone out, trusty Google on the homepage. "I figured out the high strike. All we have to do is..."

Glancing at Harris' watch, I noticed that we were coming up on 15 minutes left. "Great Link. Let's do more show and less tell."

The high strike looked like a scale for a giant. Blue faded letters marked each foot above head height with messages. The lowest levels made disparaging remarks on the hammer wielders' strengths. 'Is that all you got?' 'My hamster could do better.' The middle condescendingly encouraged another try.

In true Link style he couldn't help but narrate. "Okay, what I read online was that you take the hammer like this," he lifted the rubber tipped clown device above his head. For a split second my mind played me a scene where Link lost his grip and knocked himself out. Stupid anxiety.

Reality was much better. Keeping his body straight as an arrow he said, "You make as much downward momentum as possible." Letting the hammer fall he pushed down with all his might. The meter spiked ringing the bell at the top. The attendant forked over the obligatory bear and Link gave it to Demi. She rubbed her face along the soft fur of her prizes. What fun we were having.

The last lit booth shone eerily through the dark room. The hoard of newly middle-aged students gathered around it mesmerized. None of them approached. It was waiting for us. Even so, we had to push our way through the crowd to get close. What had once been a gallery of cardboard cutouts of ducks with targets on their bodies was now an open field behind a counter. It looked like something out of virtual reality which made me wonder just how real it actually was.

"Don't worry sweetheart, I got this," Harris tried.

"Cute, milk boy. There is a lot more skill in shooting than tossing a ball." I meant it to be playful but some of my resentment for his closer-to-normal upbringing came through.

"I'm a good shot, Mia. You sure you want to leave this to chance?" It was a challenge, and I knew it.

Link muttered something trying to get our attention, but I didn't have the patience for it. My blood was boiling. "Can it Linky, the grownups are talking."

Harris got close to me, fuming. "Don't talk to him like that. Just cause you're afraid I'm gonna..." We both received a sharp blow to the head. Demi stepped back, signing rapidly about what a bunch of idiots we were and how we were wasting time. Then she pointed to the booth. Two shot guns sat side by side. We got what we asked for, a competition.

5.5: Fairs fair at the fair.

I tucked the comb of the shot gun under my arm. I checked the sight and cleared the barrel. For a carnival prop it was sturdy. Glancing over at Harris, I saw his face set in determination.

In a bored sort of way, the booth attendant gave us the rules. "You must each hit five birds to avoid eternal damnation. The player who gets the most birds within the minute timer wins this fabulous prize." He held up another small bear.

"Bet." I pulled the gun up and cocked my head to the side to aim.

At first the woods ahead of us were silent. Then I caught the tiniest rustle of bushes. A glint of bottle green shown amongst the darker leaves. I fired and an explosion of duck feathers plumed up. On the counter in front of me the number one flashed on a screen that I didn't notice before.

"First point to Hamilton, take that Harris." In response my competitor felled two ducks that flew up in fright from my shot.

"Two to one, kiddo," he teased.

Oh no. It was on. We both continued to shoot, keeping our numbers toe to toe. The ground of the virtual forest was littered with duck genocide. The minute timer ticked down the last ten seconds. A tingling on the back of my neck told me I was being watched. Not just the crowd of spellbound teenagers, either. Not even Demi and Link. Somebody powerful and pissed.

Forgoing my win, for the record I was three ducks ahead, I spun around and aimed at Mrs. Sterling. Far too close for comfort the end of the gun practically touched her nose. Behind me Harris whooped briefly in triumph then realized we had bigger problems.

Sterling looked terrible. Her skin had reverted to its wrinkled, hanging quality. Her hair somehow even thinner had completely bald patches covered in moles. "You cheated." Her voice was cold, deep, and full of magic.

I hesitated. Link stepped up beside me and rested a hand on my shoulder in solidarity. I stood up straighter, confidence and power flooding my system. Sterling seemed to be trying to push her words into reality. Even Demi looked abashed. I don't know if it was the tattoo or my natural inclination, but I could almost see where the magic and the truth were separated.

I got in Sterling's face, unafraid. "No, we didn't."

Quicker than I would have expected for such a frail older gal, she reached out and seized Link by the wrist pulling his cellphone forward. "Technology, a cheat for the things you have not the knowledge of. Like stealing the answers from the paper of another pupil." She ran one gnarled finger over the offending object's cracked screen. Then her eyes locked on mine, and she snarled, "Plagiarism."

I lowered the gun and set it on the booth. I was pretty sure the duck hunting bullets wouldn't do me any good with this lady anyway. I paused a moment trying to think how to explain that the internet was not a cheat but a research tool. I guessed we only had ten minutes or so to save all our lives. Not nearly enough time to argue with a woman clearly set in her ways.

I gambled that if her face had reverted back to ancient times her spell must not have agreed with her. She still exuded enough power to pulverize a good deal of the fine students of Salem High though. "Fine. Replace the game. Give us another," I agreed.

A very evil smile emerged on her lips. She let go of Link and snapped her fingers. Suddenly, instead of a football field of booths, we all stood at the base of a mountain. On the bright side the crest only went up three stories high. I assumed the parameters of the spell were limited by the building's height. On the downside it looked to be a 5.12 on the Yosemite Decimal System which basically meant it was for expert climbers only. This was no easy grip rock wall. There were no safety harnesses.

"Nine more minutes Ms. Hamilton. Get to the top and ring the bell. Or you could just make peace with the god or goddess of your choosing." Mrs. Sterling laughed like the joke had some essence of irony to it. I didn't get it but I'm sure if you live for centuries on end, you're bound to develop some mental illnesses.

Turning toward Harris, I said, "Hand me your knife."

Harris glanced around furtively looking for an authority figure to bust him. "What? I wouldn't bring a weapon to the dance."

I knit my eyebrows. "Don't be cute. If I had any place in this ridiculous thing," I fidgeted with my dress pulling up the straps, "I would have hidden a whole arsenal."

Harris pulled out the knife from the back of his slacks, offered me the hilt and whispered. "How's this going to help?"

Taking the serrated portion, I tore the slit at my knee clean up to my hip. "I swear Monroe if you try to look up my dress it's the last thing you'll ever do." For good measure I cut the flowing fabric till it resembled a mini skirt. I pushed the extra material and knife into Harris' arms.

There wasn't time to track a proper path. Sometimes you can examine the rock for the easiest climb. I had to wing it. Picking up a handful of dirt, I rubbed my sweating fingers in the particulates. With a clap to dislodge any excessive dust I found my first hand-hold and began to ascend.

I had climbed walls in a gym with proper gear many times. What I missed most at the moment wasn't my harness but my shoes. My toes protested immediately to the rough surface of the barely shelved footholds. Finding the next likely place to put my hands and feet came like second nature. After you climb for a while, you learn that relying on the strength of your arms was the quickest way to tire out. While it may seem impossible in such precarious places the position of your feet matters the most. Even the tiniest grip on the side of my foot carried all the strength I needed to make it to the next higher point.

As I reached the summit, I noticed the evil sorceress had placed the bell up a literal chimney. I had climbed these types of spaces before. It was in some ways easier than the grade I had just come up. The problem was that my hands were shaking, my fingers were rigid from holding cramped and desperate to tiny crevices. My feet were blistered and bleeding from minor slips and scrapes.

"Three more minutes, Mia," Link shouted up at me, helpfully.

"Crap," I whispered. I didn't have the strength to make any more noise.

I positioned my body for the new assent. Scaling a chimney was all about tension. I put my back to one side then placed my feet against the opposite wall. I scissored my legs bending at the knee keeping my soles on the wall one above the other. My hands pressed flat at my sides against the surface at my back. In inches, I pushed with my palms and thighs climbing like some travesty of a zipper. In the end I was so tired that I was afraid to move my hands over my head. I didn't want to use my powers for fear of being called out for cheating again.

"You can do this Mi," Harris shouted. He didn't sound scared. He truly believed in me. I don't think he doubted for a second that we were going to win this challenge. A bolstering thought.

I reached up and with the merest graze of my fingertips the bell let out a light chime. I slammed my hand down trying to regain my grip, but I couldn't do it anymore. I slipped sideways, my legs letting loose. There was a part of my brain that wanted to try to reach out to regain some kind of grip. The problem was that my hands had become stone claws and my legs noodles. Not literally but it damn well felt like it. As I fell my brain registered one concept. I won. I'm the winner. Suck on that Sterling.

5.6: He's a keeper if the Real Housewives don't scare him off.

Exhausted, I was halfway down the mountain when I realized I was being lowered slowly by a safety harness. I didn't think I had it on going up. No, I was fairly certain I didn't.

At the bottom Harris caught me. He cradled me in his arms. "Can you stand?" I shook my head weakly.

Around us my classmates began coming out of their trance-like state. The mountain I had climbed was replaced by the hall's second floor balcony. There wasn't a trace of carnival booths, prematurely aged teens, or Mrs. Sterling at all. Magic set everything back to normal.

The DJ broke the silence with a record sped up to sync with the bass heavy beat track. Our little group made for the coat check. I didn't think I could dance on my noodle legs, nor did I have any inclination to try.

We passed the drink table and Coach Underwood shouted, "Hamilton! You're out. That dress is way above the appropriate knee length."

Great, slut shamed for saving his life. "Don't worry, we're leaving." Harris hefted me up and glared at the coach.

"You're welcome, by the way," I added.

When we got home, Harris carried me to the front door even though I felt better. My father cheerfully answered, "Didn't expect you all back so soon. Was it 'lame.'" He caught a good look at me between his finger quotes.

"Cinderella lost her shoes I'm afraid, sir." Harris came inside and deposited me on the couch. With a presence of mind, I didn't expect he helped me out of my jacket and covered me in a thick blanket. There was a tenderness in the way he tucked the ends of the quilt around my cold, bruised toes. "I'll come check on you tomorrow, okay?" I nodded. The instant my body was transferred to a soft surface and carefully wrapped in warmth my eyes began to droop. I could only vaguely hear Harris explaining my state of dishevelment to my dad.

The next morning, I found that Harris was true to his word. Molly mopped up my minor injuries. A few pulled muscles and a lot of surface scrapes. Even though it was all mild I felt top to bottom like every inch of my skin had been vigorously scrubbed by a loofa. My muscles resisted even the smallest movements. I got a few minutes of relief after ibuprofen doses, but I couldn't pop pills all day. I had a liver to care for too.

Harris came into the living room and smiled at my swag set up. Molly was very good at healing both mind and body. She got me coated in salves and a healthy dose of trashy reality TV. I used my power to levitate a can of Pringles my way. My muscles and skin might protest movement, but my mind was alert and ready to do my bidding.

Fiddling with a small box in his hands, Harris sat in a chair beside me. The silver wrapping caught my eye. "I thought you could use a pick-me-up." He handed me the package.

I delicately pealed back the paper. Normally, I am a tear the thing to shreds kind of girl, but my fingertips weren't having it. Inside, a box opened easily revealing a glittering silver pendant. The curved shapes interlocked three pointed ovals. "A triquetra?"

"Yeah, I made it myself. It's for protection but it's also meant to harness three points from magic in perfect harmony. Since you saved my skin with those Furies, I thought I'd make something for you as a thanks. Your dad let me use the workshop in the basement while you and Link were hitting the books." He paused scanning my face. "Do you like it?"

I looked up at him with a smile that felt more natural than any other that had come before it. "I do. Thank you." I removed the delicate charm from the box and placed its chain across the palm of my hand. "Do you mind?" I held the necklace out to him. He obliged. His fingers grazed the sparse hairs on the back of my neck that fell as I held the rest of my mane out of the way. Goosebumps erupted up my arms. After a few clumsy minutes he managed to secure the clasp.

The cold metal rested easily on my sternum. I ran my fingers over the smooth surface. As with most boys he had exhausted his capacity to express himself emotionally. He squeezed my hand briefly smiling at me. Much to my surprise he sat back in the chair and after a long pause I pushed play on my mindless reality TV show. He stayed for an impressive two whole episodes before saying goodbye. Either he was getting into the show, or he really did like me that much. I tried not to consider that. Harris Monroe came with a luggage cart of baggage. He also came with an unmatched energy that resonated with me more than anyone I'd ever met.

Rule # 6: If you can't beat 'em, bewitch 'em.

6.1: California dreaming.

We only had a few days left of school before winter break which meant that me and my sore muscles were shipped off to class. I met up with Demi in first period and I could tell something was already a miss. Considering these mood swings were usually a direct result of dealing with her mother I chose not to pester her about it till break.

After putting away our books I leaned against the locker and signed, "What's wrong?"

Demi dug in her backpack for a moment and handed me a letter. The front marked it from Cordelia Moss. I hadn't heard that name in months. Demi's ex-girlfriend moved out of state after an explosive break up. Scanning the contents, I sighed. Ms. Moss had run away and joined a cult.

"I dreamed she was being killed as some kind of sacrifice," Demi explained, her hands flying in front of her. "I woke up and mom gave me the letter."

The fact that Cordelia, or Delia for short, joined a cult was not in itself cause for major concern. Groups like that pop up all the time. Hell, there was a whole subsection of Hollywood waiting for the aliens to arrive. Demi's dreams on the other hand should never be ignored.

Demi and the Monroe boys came home with me after school so we could piece together some kind of plan. Though growing very chummy at the dance Demi couldn't seem to look at Link at all. I figured the situation with Delia messed with her head. The girl was the first person my friend ever loved. Teenage romance as a whole always leaned toward the overdramatic and in the end, jealousy won out between them.

I paired my laptop with the TV in the living room so we could all see the website of Delia's 'resort for like-minded people.' The pictures of the smiling sun-kissed members and gorgeous landscapes blended smoothly behind the directory. Their mission statement was simple and corny: 'To unite all mankind with love.'

I pulled up the activities list hoping for a clear direction on how the enigmatic leader had convinced our young friend to leave home. Scrolling through, I pointed out, "It's all meditation, yoga, basic stuff."

"Wait," interjected Link. "What's Reiki?"

"It's a Japanese alternative medicine. Uses the forces of the universe to heal the body by manipulating energy flow. It can be powerful if the person knows what they are doing," I explained. "Most of the time though, it's some whack job with Tibetan throat music playing out of their iPhone giving you a really crappy massage."

"Maybe Demi should take us through her dream? That might give us some clues," ventured Link.

Demi gave me a look that intimated that she would rather not. I knew why she was reluctant to tell us about the dream. To do so she would end up using the personal sign for Delia's name. C and D signed one letter on each hand and connected in the middle to look like a heart. It was a very personal moniker. Link was right, though, the dream might be our best lead.

One of the things about ASL was that it's not just a combination of gestures. Through facial expressions and body movements it was just as expressive as any other language. When Demi began her story, the motion felt more like a dance. She told us that in the dream she was walking through a field of high grass. When she came upon a clearing, she saw a large circular building with a canvas tent drawn up in a cone, like a short-roofed circus.

There were people all around, but she couldn't see their faces and they moved strangely as if they were in a trance. By a force that Demi didn't fully understand she felt compelled to enter the central building. In dreams, details are often sharp or dim with very few things in the middle. The vivid memories stuck out making traps that glued the mind toward their meaning. In great detail she described the slats of wood that held the tent roof up. The knots interspersed with darkened rot. Creamy faded colors from dark to light as if the wood was painted by a poorly mixed cup of coffee and milk.

In the dream, Delia, dressed in a white gown, lay in the center of the room on a bed of pure white lilies. Demi described the disconcerting fact that the young woman appeared to be at perfect peace as she drowned in a wave of blood that crested and crashed filling the whole room. Demi's final breath came in a gasp that sat her bolt upright in bed before succumbing to the suffocating pool herself.

Dreams were eerie things that when recited seem to cause everyone in hearing distance to want to talk about their own latest nighttime adventure. Demi's didn't have that effect. We all sat for a while not knowing what to say. As the translator I was particularly disturbed by what she told us. I saw more than words in the motions of her hands. I saw fear, worry and sadness.

6.2: Pass the peanuts.

There wasn't much to research. The dream, though disturbing, didn't have a lot of clues. The leader of the 'Higher Self Resort' didn't offer his photo on the site just a brief blurb about his 'credentials.' I didn't consider 'living free of society's expectations for more than 15 years' a legitimate recommendation. Similarly, his 'name,' Falcon Journey, was clearly made-up nonsense.

With my dad's blessing I booked the tickets. The whole squad would fly out to California, as per the return address on the letter. Of course, we left *after* the conclusion of Friday's lessons. With an extra bonus, we got Molly as our chaperone.

The holiday season made the airport the stuff of nightmares. Crammed together in the sardine-can of black retractable stanchions we waited our turn to be processed. One woman ahead of us had her entire suitcase open on the table of the security station. Her shrill voice rang out refusing point blank to dispose of the myriad of makeup and anti-aging products. Per the norm all the TSA agents were on hand to cope with the rabid woman.

When we finally made it to our terminal, our plane was already boarding. This gave me no time to mentally prepare. Seeing my panic Molly smirked. "Who's unlucky enough to have drawn the seat next to Nervous Nellie over here?"

Checking the seat numbers Harris raised his hand. "Why?"

"Oh, you'll see." Molly unsuccessfully suppressed her giggles.

My typical response to this kind of razzing would have come in the form of a scathing comment, but I was too busy worrying about the locations of the emergency exits. Also, I didn't trust myself to open my mouth. The tunnel to the plane closed in on me, suffocating. Stepping up through the door near the cockpit I began to panic. Molly took the window seat, Harris the middle, which left me on the aisle. Demi and Link had the seats in front of us. I immediately buckled my seatbelt then reached up to direct the air onto my sweating face.

"You hurl and I hurl, Hamilton," Harris warned.

Plucking the magazine from the back of Link's chair Molly perused it easily, "Don't worry, Harry, she's more a whiner than an upchuck girl."

"Firstly, 'Harry' is a four-eyes who rides a broom. Its Harris, Harrison, or supreme lord of the hunt to you." I tittered hysterically and Molly rolled her eyes returning to her magazine. Then he addressed me, "Secondly, if flights make you this dramatic than why fly or if you have to why not take a Xanax or something?"

Molly put down her magazine with a smug look that should have been criminal. "I'll answer for clench-jaw over there. Hamilton's don't fly if they can help it. Why do you think I'm here and not dad. There's a reason they stick to their own state. Usually if they need to go a long distance they drive."

"Aren't you a Hamilton too?" Harris clapped back.

"I take after my mother," Molly winked.

"Ew, Mrs. Robinson," I groaned. "Can't do Xanax it makes me loopy."

"For goddess' sake, Mia," Molly began. "It's not like this what's his name: Forest, short-pants, hemp-bracelet is going to be at the airport in San Diego."

Falcon, but she had a point about the rest. The truth was that I didn't like feeling out of control. I didn't like the concept of flying but the thought of flying on drugs somehow sounded worse.

The plane began to taxi toward the tarmac. I bit my lip so hard it bled. Every fiber of my being didn't want to act like a petulant child. The butterflies in my stomach argued for stomping feet and whimpering. We rounded the corner to the fairway and picked up speed. I began to shake violently. Before the wheels left the ground Harris took my hand and pinched the skin between my thumb and my palm firmly. My breathing eased slightly, and I found myself focusing on the firmness of his grip and the coarseness of his skin.

When we leveled out, he let go. "Thank you," I murmured.

"No worries," Harris responded. "Linky used to get anxiety attacks all the time when he was little. Pressure points can be very useful especially since a compression hug isn't really possible right now." I blushed at the concept of Harris hugging me.

I watched Harris with curiosity after that, accepting my offered peanuts graciously. The salty treat helped ease my stomach which still jumped at every small instance of turbulence. The care that he showed me, and Link was reminiscent of how Molly behaved. Though only a year and a few months older than us he was just as parent adjacent as she.

We landed without incident. As per Molly's prediction Falcon Journey wasn't waiting for us at the airport. Instead, an indecent amount of sunshine beamed through the large terminal windows boasting 75 degrees Fahrenheit on the bay and 80 inland. With our winter coats slung over our arms, we faded into the untroubled faces of the flipflop-clad Californians.

6.3: Glamping with hippies.

Downtown San Diego ringed a glisteningly blue bay. From our rental car we saw a port with a strange assortment of ships: a three masted sailing vessel docked near a steamboat and a submarine. Our destination was further inland in a town called San Marcos. Everything in this city seemed to sport a Spanish name hailing from the colonization days. The GPS told us that the trip would take a staggering hour owing to traffic. In Massachusetts an hour's worth of travel might just land you in another state but here on the West Coast this distance was considered normal.

The resort sat in the hills far off the main freeway. Standing out among the low bushes an ancient stone mission dominated the landscape. Beyond that an interesting concrete slab had a large circle of rocks laid out in a maze about ankle high. As we drove, the road changed from the city run asphalt to well-worn dirt. Rounding another corner, we got our first look at a large circular yurt crowned with a semi-circle of white canvas tents resting in the valley.

We parked and walked down to a pop-up tent alongside the road barring the rest of the way. Operated by a stringy young man we watched his boredom evaporate at the sight of us. "Hello travelers, I'm Viking. Do you have a reservation?"

"Yeah," I pulled out my phone to bring up the confirmation email. "It's under Monroe."

"It is?" Harris craned his neck to try and see over my shoulder.

"Yep," Viking agreed. "Got you right here two tents for a four-day spa experience." He reached into a box on the table and pulled out a printed itinerary of the services and events. "You guys came at a great time. We hardly ever get patrons over the holidays. You'll have the place to yourself. Well, your group and our core staff. We all live on the property."

"Really? Why is that?" piped up Link.

"Oh," Viking's eyes shifted away momentarily. "We're a tight group of like-minded souls." That last bit sounded rehearsed, and often.

"Fascinating," Molly cut in. "Can we be taken to our room now?"

"Sure thing." Viking's posture tightened as if preparing for a confrontation. "The resort does have a strict no tech policy. All devices will need to be checked in with me. Your possessions will be taken care of and kept in our standing safe in the main building."

The tension between us all grew exponentially. Taking a teen's phone was tantamount to cutting off one of their arms. Link went first handing out the rectangle of endless use with a mild tremble. We all deposited our phones, laptops, and tablets with the same sense of being mortally wounded.

With the sticky situation behind him and our devices intombed in a box under his arm, Viking led the way to our accommodations. From the road the tents looked simple but up close they were magnificent. Propped up on wooden platforms they each had a porch sporting distressed white painted rocking chairs. Inside was a kitchenette, couch, dining table, ensuite bathroom and two bedrooms. It was nicer than most of the hotels I'd ever stayed at. The warm blues in the fabrics paired well with the mismatched lighter woods of the furniture. An accent wall above the couch burst plentiful with healthy green herbs. In the warm sunshine the shade felt pleasant on my overly untanned skin.

Leaving us to unpack, Viking shuffled back to his position near the road. Harris flopped down on the couch, "Why'd you use my last name?"

"Oh," I turned away on the pretext of checking the contents of the fridge. It was empty. "I never use my real surname for things. I don't like to announce a 'Hamilton is here'. I usually use Demi's but since her crazy ex might see, I didn't want that name out there either. Just in case something shady actually is happening here. Element of surprise, you know." That was all mostly true, but I did get some pleasure at seeing my name next to his. Though, even if I did end up with Harris, I would likely never change my name. I would be a Hamilton for life.

With Molly and Demi busy making the bedrooms homey, aka scattering our possessions, I was left with Harris and Link. The former had his dusty boots on the coffee table, the latter's face was deep in the greenery on the wall. Pondering the life choices that led me to be responsible for these two, I got lost in thought. A knock at the tent flap brought me back to reality.

The man outside was brilliantly tanned everywhere visible except the crinkles at his eyes. The cream linen shirt he wore had twine laced at the top in a loose 'V' shape over his bulging pecks. There lay a sideways cross at the nape of his neck and finely beaded hemp bracelets crisscrossed up his right arm. His face, while not unattractive, had nothing distinctive to adorn it. He did indeed have wide legged pants that only fell to his midcalf, good call Molly.

"I'm Falcon. Welcome to the resort."

6.4: Chakra and awe.

Three minutes of conversation with Falcon Journey and I began to understand the allure. Self-assured, intelligent, and cunning; a dangerous combination. Following behind him we listened to the litany of services the spa offered. Walking past a group of about six people twisting their bodies into pretzel-shapes he lamented that we missed the start of their daily yoga.

When we reached the main circular tent, I was surprised not to find a full circus complete with elephants inside. The wooden platform floor opened in the center to allow for a leaf bare sycamore tree to sprawl out. It was honestly nice to see that something in California acted like winter had come. The top of the tent had large panels of clear plastic to allow the tree its necessary light.

Too mesmerized by the centerpiece I didn't see Delia emerging from a room off to the left. However, I heard her loud and clear. Her shrill cry of delight vibrated enough to catch even Demi's notice. The girl ran up and tackled my friend in a bone crushing hug. After a second of stiff ill ease Demi hugged her back letting go of the past.

"What a wonderful surprise, you know Daffodil then?" remarked Falcon. I snorted and then quickly hid my expression. 'Daffodil', though, seriously how does one keep a straight face.

Noticing me, the newly dubbed flower child gave me a warm smile and another big hug. She was slightly thinner than before, but we ladies usually carry a bit of puppy fat in our early teens. Her rich brown hair was decorated in strands of braided ribbon and milk chocolate-colored eyes brimmed with happy tears. "These ladies are from Salem like me. I wrote to Demi hoping she might come out and see how amazing it is here." The girl's earnest face beamed at us then fell on Falcon with a slavish look of pure adoration.

"In that case I should probably leave you ladies in D's more than capable hands." Falcon picked up the girl's hand and kissed it a little too long to be construed as a casual gesture. She blushed and bowed to him. Getting super judgy, I felt a little bile rise in my throat.

"If you don't mind, I think I have a few things on the grounds that might interest our young men here. We can meet back up for lunch," suggested Falcon.

D showed us the rooms on either side of the main lobby. They featured massage tables, sound therapy, and mud bath among other treatments. Molly seemed eager to sign up for pampering. Being more concerned with checking every available surface of the rooms I zoned her out. I needed to try to get some idea what sort of supernatural threat we were dealing with. Everything was plain, white canvas with small pops of blue floral patterns. From what I could tell it was all normal and more than likely properly done to California business code.

The tour took us to an area filled with differently sized copper bowls and flat black stones stacked inside a steaming bath. D started her sentence for what felt like the hundredth time with, "Falcon says..." I got the feeling that what 'Falcon says' could fill a book, or at least a manifesto. D continued, "... the combination of hot stones and sound therapy can help you open each of your chakras."

D pulled a charm from her flowing dress; on a thin, straight piece of metal were four stone beads. The bottom was red followed by orange, yellow and green. "I've been working on opening up my throat chakra. That's why I sent Demi the letter. Communication is so important but I'm still working on it. Every time we master one, we get a bead.

I stepped forward and delicately examined the charm. The metal was sterling silver with no embellishments. The stones were merely tumbled rocks; nothing of particular significance. I suspected both were purchased in bulk online. No technology, yeah right, hypocrite. The pursuit of opening a person's chakras was a typical practice in these retreat circles. It was, unfortunately, the only thing loosely connected to the paranormal.

"How many chakras are there in total?" I let go of the charm and picked up one of the copper bowls.

"Oh, great question," D brightened. If she didn't stop that, she was going to burst into rays of sunshine. "There are seven. Red is for the root. That's where you ground yourself and it gives you comfort and safety."

Cutting her off I said, "Great, I'm glad you found so much peace here." I didn't need a lecture. The only reason I asked the question was to determine if we were dealing with Buddhism or Hinduism. The Buddhist only have five chakras, Hindu had seven. Not much to start with but better than nothing.

We did indeed meet back up with Falcon and the Monroe's for lunch. Completely red in the face, Link avoided making eye-contact. I wondered if the poor kid was averse to all the heat and sunshine. Not nearly as flushed Harris gave me a sheepish grin. Neither boy looked the worse for wear in the perspiration department, so I second guessed my assumption about the heatstroke.

Before I could ask what happened outside D brought over a tray of artfully plated salads. The bright green romaine leaves sat as a base for a sliced and fanned out avocado, crispy chickpeas, roasted on the vine grape tomatoes and slices of watermelon radish. The lightly drizzled dressing was divine with the combination of ingredients. I sighed with pleasure.

"We have quite a talented staff of cooks," Falcon affirmed, eyeing me lewdly. I shivered and took a seat as far from him as possible. We had our legs dangling over the opening in the floor that enclosed the tree. Interspersed cushions encouraged the seating arrangements.

Harris scooted closer blocking part of me from Falcon's unwavering gaze. He tucked a stray lock of hair around my ear then glared back in the older man's direction. I didn't usually like the whole chivalry thing but given the stare down from Creepy McCreeperson over there it felt nice.

Daffodil finished handing out the salads and sat beside Falcon. "Everything is locally sourced." She plucked a tomato off the vine and popped it into her mouth. "We grow most of it ourselves and the chefs love having the opportunity to cook garden to table."

I wanted to ask if they too had chosen to name themselves after plant life, but the best way forward was in. The in-crowd didn't question the leader's rules, spoken or not. Commence operation: play nice. Peering around Harris' bulk I smiled warmly at Falcon who met my attention with expectant grace.

"I have to say everything here is immaculately done, you must have amazing sponsors," I took another bite of my salad and didn't need to fake a look of appreciation.

"It's mostly donations from our patrons. Our services make us hard to walk away from." Falcon put his hand on D's thigh, and she giggled.

My cheeks twitched as they fought the desire to scowl. "I can see why." Behind me Link gasped. I turned to see Demi's foot retreating from his toes. If I had to guess, he was making some disbelieving face. We needed to regroup. "You know I think we would all love an opportunity to look over the itinerary and decide what activities we want to do next. Do you mind terribly if we pop back off to our tent?"

"Not at all," Falcon said. "It will give you a chance to change and meet us for meditation at dusk."

The event sounded less like an invitation and more like a command. I agreed courteously and gave his muscles a falsely appraising look. His chest swelled at the attention, and he answered my interest with a flex of his pecks. Ignoring my natural inclinations, I looked down and then peered shyly at him from under my lashes. Helpfully, Harris tugged my arm to help me to my feet. Good, a jealous other man would make me more appealing. I managed to keep eye contact all the way out of the building.

6.5: The Oscar goes to ... me.

Harris marched me all the way back to the tent, hand still clamped around my upper arm. Once inside, he gave me a little shove before letting me go. I snickered which was a big mistake, his fragile ego couldn't handle it. Stepping up inches from my face he snorted like a raging bull.

I put placating hands on his chest and edged him back. "Easy there Ferdinand." It felt good to make a snarky joke again. Going those few moments without one felt wrong.

"That guy is a predator, Mia," Harris seethed. "You know where he took me and Link? To a pond where the other girls like to bathe. None of them looked much older than you and they were all nude. Waving like they wanted us to join them. That guy has to be upwards of forty. What the hell does he have that makes you girls fawn over him like he's some kind of god?"

That was an interesting idea, I made a mental note to check into Hindu gods.

"For the record," Molly cut in, "I found him pretty skeevy."

Demi signed, "Me too."

All eyes turned to me. "Of course, I think he's gross. I do appreciate the vote of confidence in my acting skills, but I was barely holding it together. Figuring out what's happening here isn't going to be easy. There are no red flags. So far, I can't detect even one obvious supernatural thing going on, can you?"

"No," taking a deep breath Harris plopped down on the couch. "He purposefully took off his shirt around the girls, but I didn't see any tattoos or markings that might indicate magic. Just a four-leaf clover, under his arm pit of all places."

"Could be something Celtic but the four-leaf thing is basically an American bastardization," reasoned Molly.

"We got nothing from D. She's got a chakra necklace, but it doesn't exactly scream supernatural." I sat across from Harris not trusting his anger had truly abated.

Link collapsed next to me. "So, were flying blind?"

Losing interest in the conversation, Demi wandered into the bedroom. It was harder for her to read lips when multiple people talked rapidly. She returned abruptly; her face as white as the dress she held up. Pointing her free hand to her temple she pulled it away twice making a hook, "The dream."

I rose and crossed to her, wagging my own index finger back and forth I signed, "Where?" Wordlessly, even for ASL she pointed to the bedroom. Inside I found a similar white, cotton dress. A note on top said, 'Required for tonight's ritual.' At least this answered two questions, the first being why the booking site had asked for our measurements. Second, how long we had to prevent Demi's dream from becoming a reality.

By the variation in the stitching the simple dress appeared to be handsewn. The accompanying front clasp bra and underwear, also white, were manufactured and satin in contrast. The frilly lace designs and underwire push up padding was suggestive; someone wanted it seen.

"Harris," I called. "Can you help me bring out my suitcase?"

Obliging, he lugged my largest bag into the living room. "What's in here, bricks?"

"Close. Books," I affirmed. "We're going analog."

Unzipping the top, I tossed the flap back to reveal my bounty. "Did you bring the whole library?" complained Harris, massaging his biceps.

Molly picked up a book and flipped it over to read the back cover. "Don't be ridiculous. Pippa would never allow it."

"The fact that that's even a consideration baffles me." Harris chose a thin pamphlet from the pile and let it fall open in his palm.

Good old Link and his plucky attitude grabbed a book and added, "We've got a few hours till dusk. Let's see what we can find."

As the sun dipped under the hill side, we had to concede that we discovered exactly nothing. Dismissing the boys to their tent to get dressed, we ladies donned our ceremonial outfits. Demi fidgeted with the skirt of her gown uncomfortably. She hadn't worn a dress since she was old enough to tell her mother 'No'. I noted that while the A-line boddice just barely covered the bra it left plenty of cleavage. I pulled each of my ladies up positioning them for maximum boddice heaving perkiness. The flowing skirt did nothing to accentuate the rest of my curves. I'd have to rely on my bust to break down Falcon's defenses.

We made our way over to the boy's tent. The Monroe's emerged wearing matching cotton pants held together with rope and plain white t-shirts. Harris walked up to me and tucked the bra strap under the dress' collar. "Looking good, Hamilton. I just hope you know what you're doing."

I wanted to reply scathingly but getting into character I admitted, "So do I."

Viking, our hall monitor came jogging over to us waving enthusiastically. "Look at you guys. Everything fit alright?" Nodding in agreement I didn't bother pointing out that underwire bras have a tendency to dig into the skin. "You're going to love the meditation moment, it's the best part of the day."

Privately, I felt like the best part would be when I could get back into my jeans and out of this hippy hell. That was a moot point. Instead, I hitched up as dazzling a smile as I could muster and followed the man obediently.

6.6: Link wears his sunglasses at night.

Halfway up the road, with Viking marching ahead, Link's hand grazed mine and he froze. I turned to him to see why. His eyes glowed in a blue ethereal light. As Molly passed me, I snatched her sunglasses off the top of her head.

"Woah there, cyclops," I whispered putting the rhinestone coated frames over his eyes. I looked around to see if anyone had noticed. "Let's not scare the locals."

To be honest the phenomenon frightened me. I hadn't seen his eyes glow since that day with the Wampus cat. The gleam of the light that reflected against his skin died out. He gripped my arm tightly, "Don't leave the group. Stay with the group."

Stopping aways ahead Viking called down, "Are you guys alright?"

I waved and smiled, taking Link's hand off my arm and ushering him along. Staying in the back of our party I bent my head closer to him. "What did you see?"

He avoided my gaze. "Just don't leave the group, okay?" I agreed though my curiosity hadn't been slated.

Viking led us to the round concrete slab ringed with low stones. From the road the pattern appeared to be random but up close it looked like a purposeful path. Candles illuminated the route, flames flickering in the light cool breeze. Nice to know it got colder at some point in the day.

At the center of the circle Falcon sat waiting for us to arrive. His minions all gathered around him on the ground. Viking split us up to be surrounded by the strangers. Eyeing the girls around me I marveled that Harris was right, none appeared much older than Molly. They all had the same adoring expression as D did when gazing at Falcon. The group consisted of maybe two dozen followers and all but five of them were female.

The silence was absolute amongst the crowd. For a solid three minutes or so we all seemed to breathe in unison. The sensation wasn't brought on by magic but the collective human tendency to mirror each other's behavior. Just as I began to feel the awkward sensation that we were breaking some kind of protocol the sound of frogs rose in a chorus. Falcon met my eyes and winked at me knowingly. Frogs ribbit to attract a mate.

"My family, my new friends," he gestured expansively with both arms trying to embrace us all. "We are blessed on this night to sit beneath the stars with our guests and introduce them to the bounty of the universe." Beside me, the girls closed their eyes and raised their hands into the air trying to touch the spirit of the sky.

"Please, my loves, close your eyes." The purr in Falcon's tone had me following without question. "Imagine yourself in a pure white room. There are no furnishings, no art, just walls and floor. Alone with only your thoughts and feelings allow each to embrace you."

He waited and I could hear us all breathing deeply as one. I could see the room in my mind's eye. For some it may have been a cold and daunting place, but I felt at ease. Comforted by the release of the material, the simpleness gave me peace.

Falcon's honeyed tones slipped again into the rhythm of my breathing, "You close your eyes briefly in this room and when you open them the color of the walls has changed." With my eyes already closed, I pictured darkness. When I called on the room again a violent shade of red surrounded me. The color of blood, deep, thick, and primal coated every surface. It almost seemed to move, flowing like in the vitality of the vein or the mortality of a wound.

"A door you didn't see before appears," suggested Falcon. Huh, look at that it did. "You move through the door and out into an open terrain. Coming toward you is an animal."

I stepped out into a forest. Tall pines towering overhead met a canopy of rich greens in shades of light and dark. Crunching softly on the fallen branches a sure-footed wolf stalked toward me. I stiffened; the orange eyes fixed on me with intensity. Larger than the average dog it bent its head low, assessing. I knew that deadly jaw could tear me to shreds but it didn't strike. We stood before each other, hunter, and prey, but I couldn't tell which one I was anymore.

"Your new companion turns to leave, and you follow." Falcon instructed. So, I did. "You come across a body of water."

The wolf paused at the base of a river. Walking forward I nearly fell down the sharp cliff edge. Who knew meditation could get so dicey? My feet tucked safely on the ridge; I looked down. The waterfall cascaded in a foaming mist. The pool at the bottom looked terrifyingly tiny from my vantage point. There was no telling how deep the water was down there. Even here in my own head I was scared that Falcon's next instruction might be to get in.

Of course, that's exactly what he told us to do. I looked back at the wolf. It sat primly at the river's edge staring at me, its head cocked to the side as if wondering if I would really jump. I did. Leaping down, my feet crashed into cool water. The gooseflesh rose on my arms, and I shivered. This physical reaction reminded me that I was not under the surface of a fathoms deep pool of water. I was sitting on cold concrete in the growing night chill of southern

California. Remembering this I took a deep breath that would not suffocate me with water.

"Submerge beneath the surface," encouraged Falcon. Check. "See the way the light dances off the ripples of your presence. Feel the weightlessness pull you to the air above. When you break through, allow the sweet oxygen to lift your spirit." Around me everyone took a deep collective breath. "You may open your eyes."

Not sure if his prowess at leading group meditation, my over-active imagination, or something magical was at play, I opened my eyes feeling lighter. Looking around, everyone but Demi had dreamy, content expressions. She just looked bored, poor thing. I spun both fists around then let my fingers out like I was dramatically dropping something, the sign for 'magic.' Demi shook her head. Still at square one with the 'what the hell is happening here' crusade.

"We will now split into groups for reflection of our journey's," announced Falcon. I smiled at Link, his vision proving helpful. Link didn't seem terribly pleased that Viking was leading him and Harris off in a different direction than the girls though. The swarm of ladies ushered us off back to the main building before I could ask for more details. Trusting his original instructions, I kept to my group.

6.7: Busting through walls, "Oh yeah".

When we got to the main building the girls split into even smaller clusters. Disconcertingly, this separated me from Molly and Demi. I got put in a group with Daffodil and two other girls who seemed equally as new to the resort, which didn't feel opportune. I needed to question people who had been around longer and knew more about what might be happening.

Fortunately, Falcon turned out to be the leader of our session. He came into the room we were segregated in. It happened to be where the massages were done. D sat on the table swinging her feet back and forth off the edge in a child-like way. She beamed at the sight of the leader. He kissed her lightly on both cheeks then helped her down from the table.

Leaving the room at his gesture she returned a few moments later with a platter of food. The appetizer charcuterie consisted of cheese, dried and fresh fruit alongside a biscuit and pickled asparagus. Having been previously impressed with the cuisine I dug in. The combination of the gouda, dried apricot and the slightly still warm biscuit flooded my mouth with desire for another bite.

D busied herself on a counter pouring tiny mugs with a floral smelling tea. I took the cup warily. It wasn't going to be that easy to get me to drink the Kool-Aid. Instead of taking a sip like the rest of them I nibbled on the end of the asparagus. Pleasantly spicey, the tang of vinegar sent me back for respite in the biscuit.

Falcon cleared his throat, putting down his own portion of the meal on a counter. "Our meditation this evening was more than just an exploration of your superconscious. It was actually a psychological assessment of how you perceive yourself, others, life, and death."

Rapt by his delivery, I took a sip of my tea. Then I let the liquid fall out of my mouth realizing what I was doing. I looked around to see if anyone had noticed but only Falcon had his eyes on me.

Looking unconcerned he smiled at me warmly. "Would you like to help me demonstrate how these revelations affect your chakra, Ms. Monroe?" For a moment I wondered who he was talking to, then I remembered that was my code name. Falcon patted the massage table invitingly.

"Oh, no thanks," I dismissed. I'd be keeping my chakra to myself. Then to smooth over my refusal I added, "I really don't like being touched."

Mildly disappointed, Falcon encouraged D onto the table. Laying down face up; her closed eyes and open palms exuded trust. Rubbing his fingers gently between her eyebrows he explained, "This is where your third eye rests; home of your connection to the beyond. It is what controlled your feelings when you first imagined the white room." His tone was soft, low, and soothing like it had been during the meditation. "Were you scared, lonely, wanting? Or brave, humbled, accepting? That room represented how you feel about death."

I reflected on my experience. The white walls gave me a sense of peace and tranquility. There was no fear. Nothing to suggest an unfulfilled purpose. Could death really be as welcoming as it felt in that room?

Falcon's fingers traced up D's forehead and plunged into her hair line. She writhed with pleasure. If she wasn't severely underage, I would have felt they should get a room or at least let me leave this one.

Falcon continued, "When the color changed in the room this was a reflection of how you view yourself. Ruled by the Crown it guards your knowledge, spirituality, and self-realization. Was it a pleasant color like sky blue? Lightly lifting you. The ease of your intentions flitting by in a breeze. Perhaps deep forest green. Grounding you, setting roots."

The bite of cheese in my mouth felt solid as I remembered the red walls. The color of blood; live giving and death releasing. Was that really me? I'd taken my fair share of lives but was it equally so, that I'd given just as many? Did the ones I'd saved outweigh the blood I'd spilt? It disconcerted me that my defining self-vision was an exercise in the primal notion of preservation.

As I contemplated, Falcon's hands smoothed out the tension in D's shoulders and traced her collarbone resting a palm between her breasts. Her contented smile was truly sickening. "Here, at the Heart chakra is where you met your guide," Falcon tapped his fingers against her sternum in a rhythm like a beating heart. "The animal and biome you encountered after leaving the room represents how you feel about others. Was your interaction friendly or confrontational? Are others viewed as companions or predators?"

That gray wolf with its beautiful orange eyes and full feather soft coat floated up in my mind's eye again. How did I really feel about it? I could sense it cocking its head at me again wondering the same thing. If I was honest with myself, I felt a kindred spirit with the stalking canine. Wolves, like most natural predators, weren't wasteful. They killed for need or protection, so did I.

Hands moving again, I watched as Falcon stopped at the girl's lower belly, his fingers resting on the top of her pelvic bone. "The water is ruled by your Sacral chakra. Sexuality and pleasure." My gaze flitted up to Falcon's eyes only to find him undressing me with them. I shrank back and scrunched my shoulders taking another bite of biscuit. I didn't know if it was the unwanted attention or the cooled bread, but it tasted suddenly bitter.

My fear of the waterfall came back to me as Falcon suggestively massaged the girl's inner thighs. I wanted to look away as the man described the different ways the water might make you feel about desire, but I felt like his words were floating me away. The room took on a fuzzy glow like that of a dream. His voice sounded deeper somehow, seductive. I couldn't feel my face any longer. The next time I blinked, my eyes refused to open again. I fell back cracking my head against the wall. It didn't hurt ... yet.

6.8: Just your average mortal.

When I drifted back out of the black of unconsciousness, I registered a few concerning facts. First, my hands were bound in a silky scarf, my body laid flat on a mattress. Second, a large man was hovering over me shirtless and kissing my neck. Third, I felt relaxed and mostly unconcerned about the first two things. Magic didn't do this, drugs did.

I mentally kicked myself for being stupid enough not to realize that the biscuit was probably coated in some sort of substance. I naively ate the whole delicious thing. Whereas I might not have cared so much about the slobber on my neck I did object to the hand reaching between my legs. I squirmed slightly but given my heavy limbs the motion seemed to encourage him rather than repel. I opened my mouth, but my words wouldn't cooperate with my mind. Falcon took the opportunity to plunge his foul tongue in. Moaning weakly, he took this as another 'come-and-get-it' signal.

Though my mind was sluggish I had more control over my thoughts than my physical being. Using the only tool left in my arsenal, I pushed the man back with my telekinesis. He fell off the side of the bed. I was aiming to smack him into the nearest wall, but it would have to do.

Falcon scrambled up and looked down at me with mounting fear. "What the f..." interrupted by the crashing door and sharp blow to his head the man crumbled to the floor at Harris' feet. I rested back on the pillows, a dull ache in my temples beginning to plague me. Deft fingers worked at the knot at my wrists. It felt like it took me an age to twist my neck to see my savior. Demi's face was set in a hard line of disapproval.

Releasing one bound hand she signed, "Why do you have to be so stubborn? You don't have to do everything by yourself." I felt at a distinct disadvantage since my hands were not currently listening to my brain and I couldn't defend myself. "You know what Delia told me? That guy has raped every girl here. Drugs them then makes them feel like they asked for it. That vision I had...we were too late he took her virginity weeks ago. Almost got yours too." She punched me in the shoulder. I couldn't tell how hard because I couldn't feel it.

Harris took her by the arm pulling her away from me. "What the hell did she say?" Molly unbound my other wrist and shrugged.

I couldn't speak, my mouth felt like I'd chewed up chalk. I just let tears well in my eyes. Demi had a point; I was stupid to get myself into that situation. Shaking off Harris' grip my best friend returned, wrapping me in a tight hug and rocking lightly. Pulling away she rubbed her fist in a circle over her heart, "I'm sorry, you scared me. It's not your fault."

"Yes, it is," my words were slurred. "It is my fault."

"Hell no," Harris crossed to the bed and sat beside me adjusting my dress more modestly over my shoulders. "That creep is to blame. The other guys told us... honestly, too many gross things. You don't need to hear it now. You got drugged. They were all snorting Special-K and tried to get me and Link to join them. There's nothing supernatural here just a disgusting man with too many addicts' dependent on his access to the pills."

Crying freely, I tried to squash the guilt. I didn't feel comfortable being a victim. The label scratched against my hardened protective armor. When Molly pulled me into her arms and Link went on a tirade of very tame curses, I felt worse. I had to learn how to be dependent for a change. I still couldn't walk and talking was a chore.

Link's eyes darted between the room and the doorway making sure we weren't going to be interrupted. "If he's just a man, what do we do? Call the police?"

Molly stared down at the prone figure of the shirtless man a look of repulsion on her face, "For starters, yeah. But just because there wasn't a magical cause doesn't mean we can't have a magical solution." Reading Molly's lips Demi nodded slowly, a mischievous smile emerging on her face. "Want to help me with an impotence curse?" Molly held her hand out to Demi. My friend agreed emphatically and gave the man on the floor the finger.

Both boys squeezed their thighs together uncomfortably. "Are we really allowed to do that?" Link pondered squeamishly.

"All part of rule 6," replied Harris before I could form the words in my numb mouth. Impressed that he knew the rules, I let him explain. "If you can't beat them, bewitch them. Humans are protected by Smyth law but in certain circumstances... like if they are dabbling in dark arts or being giant pricks like this guy, a little magic is generally permitted."

"Good," Link kicked the unconscious man in the groin. "He deserves it." I couldn't agree more.

Thankfully, after a few minutes the drugs wore off enough that I could finally hold my head upright on my own. "I wonder what his real name is?" I still felt lightheaded, but I was pleased to hear the question came out of my mouth without slurring.

Harris paced the floor keeping a wary eye on Falcon. "Bertram Bottum."

"Seriously?" My head heavily swiveled to look down at the unconscious man.

"Yeah, the other guys told us. I guess they got a glimpse of his ID once while he signed for some deliveries. I hope the name serves him well in prison." The savage remark felt odd coming from Link. Almost in contrast to his words he wet a piece of cloth in a shallow bowl and wiped down my face. The cold water felt good, and the sense of cleansing helped my general feeling of ickiness pass.

When the two witches came back with a handful of acupuncture needles I had most of my wits back. Without asking, Molly took the knife from Harris' hands. He didn't protest. 'Hell, hath no fury' must have kept him at bay. She grabbed Mr. Bottum's discarded cotton shirt from the floor then swiped the sharpened blade up tearing it in half. With perfect precision she folded the fabric, tying certain ends with thin strips till it resembled a crudely made poppet.

Molly looked down at the doll with loathing then she handed it to Demi. Molly bent and placed the tip of the knife into the webbing between the prostrate man's thumb and index fingers. A small well of dark blood coated the tip and Molly ran the blade from head to groin on the poppet leaving behind a trail of bright red.

"By point of pain I bind your power." Demi played Vanna to Molly's Pat Sajak and jabbed the acupuncture needles into the poppet's nether region, continually. As each needle pierced the fabric Molly repeated her spell. The magic made the air dense, almost electric. My sister finished her spell quickly and the satisfied smile on her lips told me she'd done good work. Who knew taking a man's libido could be so easy?

Harris called the police when I finally got to my feet. In the main room surrounding the sycamore tree, what looked like all the girls of the group waited. They watched me as I stumbled out and Delia rushed forward to aid me.

"It's over." I clutched Delia's hand. "He can't hurt you anymore."

"What did you do." Delia let me go and I swayed.

Molly came behind me and slipped an arm around my waist. "A punishment befitting the crime," she whispered in my ear. Privately, I felt a better punishment would be to hot stone the man to death, but I might have been bitter at the moment. Molly addressed the crowd, "The police are on their way."

Most of the other girls just looked resigned by this news. I guess the cult leader's charms were not sufficient for complete loyalty. It was the younger girls who seemed distraught; Delia included. Many of the others covertly took off not wanting to be caught with the drugs in their system and the misdeeds on their conscience.

No magic potion could make a person see reason. If such a thing existed, we would be putting that stuff in the drinks of all our world leaders. Running off to live with Falcon was a symptom of a much larger concern. If a person was broken enough to accept ritual rape the blame couldn't land solely on the man performing the act. The world failed girls like Delia, teaching them that their only self-worth lay between their legs.

After I refused medical attention when the police arrived, we gave statements and gathered our things. We got a room in a part of San Diego aptly named Hotel Circle. Molly changed our flights so that we would make it home before Christmas day. The extra crowded airport didn't seem as menacing on the return journey knowing I wouldn't need to spend my holiday in 80degree weather. Other people might enjoy the respite from the snow, but I liked my Christmases white.

Demi explained on the flight that Delia texted and let her know she was safe and home. I didn't expect that to last long. Though we stopped the man from harming anyone else we couldn't undo the damage. Reflecting on our experience I couldn't help but feel like of all the monsters and demons we'd faced so far, humans were the worst.

Rule # 7: Make offers that can't be refused.

7.1: Hamilton family round up.

"You are cordially invited to the wedding of Celeste Freya Hamilton to Caelian Alistair McRannoch on January 21st" I read out loud.

"Aw, Cousin Celeste is getting married? How exciting," Molly cooed.

"You get a chance to see Uncle Alex," I looked up at my dad. He let out a derisive noise. The relationship between my father and his siblings was, to put it mildly, strained.

Molly fiddled with the RSVP return note. "We *are* going, right?"

"Definitely," dad replied. "Put us down for two plus ones unless you finally asked out that mechanic?"

Molly flushed. From the look on her face, she didn't think he knew about that. "Nope, I don't need a plus one."

"So, were bringing the Monroe boys?" I guessed.

Dad examined the invitation. "Naturally."

As predicted my conjoined twins agreed to accompany me without much provocation. Another road trip this time with my new real deal driver's license, no magic for me. Molly decided to ride with dad, so it was just me and the boys.

Link chose to pass the time by playing a thrilling round of twenty questions with me. “This Celeste is your Uncle Alex’s daughter, right? Do you have any other uncles or aunts?”

Eyeing him in the rear-view mirror I sighed, “Celeste is Alex’s youngest she’s just a little older than Molly so she’s the closest cousin we have. As for the other Hamilton’s my Grandpa Ben and Grandma Julie had seven boys.”

“Woah,” Link exclaimed. I agreed, that was a lot of testosterone. “So is your dad the oldest?”

“Youngest,” I answered. Harris chuckled, as the baby of our respective families, we all shared a sort of kindred spirit. “Alex is the oldest now but that’s cause my Uncle Benedict Jr passed on from a heart attack about six-years-ago.” Seeing Link’s eager face, I continued. “After Alex came Thomas, he died in childhood from whooping cough. Next was Jackson; killed by a Yeti in Quebec. Henry is an accountant. James is a Smyth too, but he lives in Milwaukee. And then there’s my dad.”

I could still hear the scratching of Link’s pen when he said, “Are your other uncles coming?”

“Not that I know of. Henry doesn’t associate with the family and James won’t leave his dogs behind for that long.” Both things were true, but the reality was that it was more likely that neither wanted to fly out. The flight issue wasn’t just a me and my dad problem.

Harris fiddled with the strings on his hoody, thinking. “Isn’t Alex on the Smyth council?”

“Yeah,” I confirmed.

Link’s face popped up in between the front two seats. “Council?”

I resisted the urge to play whack-a-mole with his face. “It’s the governing body of the Smyths. You know that star on the notebook that I gave you? Remember, it represents the nine members of the congregation. If someone has a complaint, or someone doesn’t follow the rules that’s when the council steps in.”

"Wait, like what rules?" Link was practically climbing into the driver's seat. I nudged him back with my elbow.

"Dude all we've talked about over the last few months have been the rules." I watched the dawning comprehension cross his face in my mirror. "Look, Hamilton rules are a little more specific than the councils, but the gist is the same. Basically, the council makes sure that we don't reveal too much to the regular folks."

"So, police are involved ...," Link began.

"Some but not all," Harris cut in. Then under his breath he added, "That's a mistake I'll never make again." I chuckled lightly. I didn't know the story, but I understood the sentiment.

"Right, noted." Link did in fact produce his notebook and write it down. "Police, a zoological society and didn't you say an apothecary cleaned up the Furies, Mia?"

"Yup." I glanced back and saw Link chewing on the end of his pencil.

Link took a deep breath, and I knew I was in for another onslaught of rapid-fire questions. "What other organizations do the Smyths have? Is the council part of a government agency or stand alone? What about the congregation? Who else is involved with that? What happens if you break a rule? Do you go to, like Smyth prison? Is there an exotic creature zoo? Do the Smyths have a mascot? I bet it's the Chimera. That thing was terrifying."

Mascot, I shook my head, of all the questions he could ask. "Let's see. As far as other organizations, if you think we need it we probably already have it."

"The council is its own separate agency but some of the members have been known to hold public office as well." Harris looked back at Link, smiling wryly. "It helps when we need some wheels greased to hide appropriating funds." Link laughed like Harris was joking.

"All those congressional bills have weird stuff in them," I pointed out. "Ever heard of a bill getting shot down that sounded like a good idea? Usually, it's not the front cover that the rest of Congress objects too. It's all the padding in the middle." Link made a sound of comprehension. "Our congregation, though, is more diverse. As for breaking the rules, our punishments typically come in the form of revoked licenses. We Smyths view the American prison system sufficiently nasty for everything else."

Going over his notes, Link checked off each question answered. He paused and I concluded before he could ask, "No zoo, no mascot." Poor kid looked mildly disappointed.

After that Link lapsed into contemplative silence. The four-hour drive down the coast to Jersey was pleasant enough. We made a couple of pitstops to fill up on gas and get snacks. My Volvo Amazon may have been known for her beauty but not quite the miles per gallon. When we crossed the Hudson River, Harris looked down at it sadly.

"What's wrong?" I flipped on my turn signal and changed lanes.

"Nothing," he forced a smile. I gave him a frown to indicate I didn't believe him at all. "Okay, fine. My mom lives out there."

"Ah, mermaid?" I was about 70 percent joking. The other 30 percent; hell, you never know.

"Waitress. Or at least she was. My dad, Tyler, saved her from a monster attack. In thanks she had me." Harris looked out the window with something like longing. I knew all too well the knight in shining armor act that was so common among Smyths. A lot of the next generation was born that way. The knight swoops in and saves the girl then, well, I'm sure you get the picture.

Harris cleared his throat before continuing, "I was two when she called him up and told him she couldn't take care of me anymore."

"Ouch," I started. "That had to suck."

Harris shrugged, "I don't remember so I couldn't tell you. Tyler did his best, I guess. Mostly he left me with his older kids."

That was also unfortunately on brand. Lots of kids. Lots of moms. My grandparents were a rarity. I could never find the appropriate time to ask about what happened to his brother, John. With Link snoozing in the back seat, I figured this was as close to a good time as any. It was like I could feel John's presence in his thoughts. "How did it happen?"

Glancing back at Link he lowered his voice to a husky whisper, "Demon."

I caught his gaze briefly. "That's why you went after Willow, isn't it?"

Not willing to admit to that, he looked down at his hands. "He was investigating something on his own. Kept leaving me and Link for days at a time. He wouldn't tell me what it was. One time he was gone for over a week. I went looking and I found him," his words caught in his throat.

I could tell he didn't want to talk about it anymore, so I didn't pursue it. Losing someone as important as a brother who operated more like a father must have been devastating. Sitting there passing by the place he last saw his mother probably didn't help his mood. We all had our skeletons in the closet, and it wasn't my business to go rooting his out.

7.2: A Scot and a gentleman.

The Pleasantdale Chateau had a chevroned brick driveway leading to a white stucco and natural stone accented main building. The grounds were blanketed in snow and lush with frost tipped flora. We parked and walked up to the entrance. At the steps my dad was shaking hands with an equally tall man. His broad chest and thick red beard were unmistakable to me from this distance, Uncle Alex.

My father might have had a complicated relationship with his brother, but I didn't. I don't want to brag but I was his favorite niece. He embraced me with a bear hug and swung me off my feet. "There's my little killer," Alex set me back on the ground. "My goodness, you're a full-grown woman now. And you got not one but two boys chasing after you. Couldn't pick between the lads, eh?"

"Nah, this is my hunting partner Harris and our trainee Link," I gestured at the boys, and they walked up to shake my uncle's hand. Harris had his head held high, probably proud that I finally admitted he was my partner.

Alex gave my father a wary look. "Link? Lincoln Monroe?" Dad gave him a curt nod. With an abrupt return to his cheerful state Alex clapped Link on the shoulder and announced, "Celeste will be thrilled you're here."

A squeal of delight bombarded us when we walked in. Celeste ran up and practically jumped into Molly's arms. Her blonde hair, longer than I remembered, had highlights that were on point. She gave us a smile that as usual brightened everything around her. Her seeming abject perfection could be kind of annoying, but she was the sort of person it was hard not to like.

Pulling away, she examined us all. "You guys!" she squealed. "I am so glad you could make it. Dad said not to get my hopes up because there is a zombie outbreak in Boston."

The smile on my face fixed. I might have started to look a touch insane. "Zombies? Boston," I whimpered. The drama of a full family event can cause massively entertaining memories, but zombies were my absolute favorite thing to hunt. They're not particularly hard to find but the creativity that a person can go into in order to kill them was endless. I swallowed my disappointment and tried to look hyped for the upcoming night of bachelorette pampering.

Celeste's voice broke through my preoccupation. "Did I overhear that Amelia Hamilton has finally taken on a partner?"

"Taken. Forced upon. You know same thing." I smiled too broadly to appear serious. Honestly the arrangement felt natural after all we'd been through.

Harris stepped forward and kissed her hand. "Pleasure to meet you."

He winked at her. Scoundrel. And to think that I was just feeling proud to call him partner. Before I could explain to the little cockroach that the girl was off limits a large man with sun kissed skin clapped him companionably on his shoulder.

"These must be the cousins I've heard so much about," the man nodded to me and Molly. "And you fine gentlemen must be the darlin' lady's escorts."

If Molly wasn't so besotted by the Scottish accent, she might have objected to being connected to either of the Monroe's. "Oh, my goddess, you must be Caelian." Turning to Celeste she had her hands clasped in front of her chest; I mean the way he looked at my cousin made even *me,* want to swoon. "Did you meet on your trip to Scotland last year?"

"No, Moll. They probably got into the same cab accidently one day and it was love at first sight." Molly rolled her eyes at me. I turned to the happy couple now holding one another around the waist. "No, but seriously, what's your meet-cute?"

Caelian answered, his Scottish lilt smooth as butter, "Celeste told me you were funny. You're right, we did meet in Scotland. This beauty was waitin' in the cue for a tour of Loch Ness. After I convinced her to join me for a cupa of coffee, I gave her a private ride on my boat."

I bet he did. The small fierce tiger of desire made a little 'rawr' in my mind. Caelian was a fully-fledged thirst trap; tall, handsome with the darkest and shiniest black hair I had ever seen. I could almost see how the gleam off the waters of Loch Ness ensnared these two.

Molly sighed; she was such a romantic. I'm not going to lie I could have listened to the guy read me the dullest of books and be totally satisfied.

Standing with his back straight Harris cut in. "So, what do you do?" I glared at him. No amount of peacocking could make him look more ripped than Caelian.

"I'm justa fisherman, nothing special." Something, in the way that Caelian glanced at Celeste, suggested there was more to that story. I was on vacation, so I didn't see the point in prying.

Someone cleared their throat behind us. We turned to see a timid man in black slacks and a vest over a crisp white button-down shirt. "Pardon me, Mr. McRannoch would you mind signing for the cake delivery?" Balancing the clipboard with his broad left hand he scrawled out a loopy signature. The Smyth Star topped the letterhead. Uncle Alex didn't leave anything to chance at a wedding in our family.

Following the vendor man in, my dad joined us. "Looks like you all have a lot of people who need your attention."

"I hate to admit it, but your uncle is right." Even as Caelian said it another attendant waited politely for a chance to cut in.

"Okay babe, I think I'll give these guys a little tour then start to get ready for tonight." Celeste rose on tiptoe to give him a soft kiss.

"Till my eyes are graced with your beauty again, my love," Caelian bent and kissed her hand effectively erasing the work Harris had done.

Taking Celeste by the elbow I steered her away. "Alright you two there is only so much romance I can handle. Even from a cute couple like you guys."

After a few more adoring glances Celeste took us through the venue. It was top to bottom luxury with old world charm. Curving wrought iron staircases and a fireplace the size of a minivan. The greenhouse was like a jungle of creeping vines. In the main reception area, the tables were being set up for the grand affair. I stared up at the domed ceiling thinking my cousin did a bang-up job on picking out the location.

Pausing before our separate rooms I dropped the main question of the hour, "Does he know?"

Celeste stiffened. Being the daughter of a Smyth didn't necessarily mean that she joined the practice like me. In fact, she taught 3rd grade in Albany. Anyone entering the family needed the insider info. Smyth or not, the Hamilton pedigree came with very large targets attached to our backs.

"He does." Celeste's clipped tone made it clear she didn't want to expand on that.

Whatever; not my circus, not my monkeys.

Seeing the subject securely dropped Celeste grabbed Molly's arm and coaxed her to join in the makeup application and girl talk portion of the afternoon. Thankfully, she didn't even bother to ask me to join.

"Not going?" Link's earnest expression made it hard to rebuff his question. A sarcastic remark at that point would have been tantamount to kicking a puppy.

"Not my bag, baby. I plan on pulling a full-on Diane Keaton tomorrow." Link just looked more confused. "Suit and tie. Though maybe not the tie." I rubbed my neck feeling the ghost of the noose-like garment.

"Hot." Harris had his eyes closed. Having previously seen his mental image of me I gave him a swift kick in the shins. He flinched, opened his eyes, and looked down at me appraisingly.

"You can fantasize about me all you like Monroe, but I won't have this glorious vision be replaced by some Barbie version." I gestured down my frame. Lumps, bumps, and perhaps too much in the trunk, I loved my body.

"Don't worry, Mi," Harris said with all seriousness. "You're perfect just the way you are."

I blushed and so did Link. "Um, good. Remember that." I covered the false bravado by trying my keycard on the door to my assigned room. The green light granted my access, and I took the reprieve to step halfway in. "I'll see you guys for dinner."

Harris smiled at me, and Link shuffled his feet awkwardly. I slipped inside and put my back against the closed door. *Smooth Hamilton. Real smooth.*

7.3: The rehearsal was a splash.

I came down the stairs to the ballroom. According to Molly, people usually dressed up for the rehearsal dinner. She wore a long flowy dress in a soft olive green. Trying to stay at least mildly true to form, I dressed up my black jeans with a rich purple blouse.

I found it shocking how much chaos went into getting six people to walk down a straight and remarkably short aisle. The minister looked bored as he stood at the head of the alter waiting. It seemed that Caelian didn't have any groomsman, so Alex's eldest son Sage filled in.

My other cousin, Fern, struggled with her three-year-old daughter, Rose. The little girl kept throwing flowers AT her mother not on the ground. Though the sweet baby reached into the basket for each handful I noticed that the vessel was completely empty. The bright flowers were not at all adherent to the bride's specified color palate. Little Ms. Rosey was already a wiz with earth magic. I looked around to see if any of the non-Smyth attendants noticed but I suspected this crew was chosen for its discretion.

Uncle Alex tucked Celeste's tiny hand into the crook of his elbow. The poor appendage looked like it might be crushed between his forearm and bicep. Father and daughter seemed like they were in their own world. Sweetly looking at one another with pride and respect. Uncle Alex kissed her on the cheek and placed her hand in Caelian's. When she stepped up beside her groom, they both beamed at each other. A moment of hushed silence stretched like a bubble of love engulfing us all. It was so pleasant no one seemed to mind the wait.

As the moment faded the minister cleared his throat. Before the proctor of events could begin, the groom doubled over and gripped his leg like something had suddenly stabbed him. I craned my neck to get a better look. A gush of red tinged water poured out of his pant leg and the fabric from his thigh downward clung to his skin, soaked. Celeste gasped. Caelian looked into her eyes and promptly disappeared in a splash of water. His clothes crumpled to the floor in the puddle.

I've seen some strange things in my time but that was a new one. Harris and I looked at each other but he seemed just as confused as I.

Link apparently missed the whole thing. "What's with all the water." I ignored him.

My dad's jaw was set. Molly started crying. A distraught Celeste collapsed into her sister's arms. Uncle Alex fumed directing staff members out of the room. Fern's daughter splashed in the puddle, giggling. For a solid three minutes no one said anything of substance.

"Good lord, does anyone want to explain what just freaking happened there?" I demanded. The spell of silence seemed to break.

"They took him," Celeste howled. "I thought I hid the tail well enough, but they must have found it."

Great, that cleared things right up.

"Tail?" squeaked Link.

My brain put the pieces together. Caelian was Scottish which gave me an area of origin to work with. Black hair, tail, lots of water clues.

Before I could voice my realization my dad did it for me, "A Selkie, Alex? You were going to let your daughter marry a sea creature?"

Uncle Alex straightened up to his full height squaring off with my dad. "Sage and Fern's mother was a tree Nymph as you might remember. And a damn fine woman, God rest her soul." The two in question stiffened glaring at my dad. Dad acquiesced with a nod. I never met my late aunt. She died before I was born but I've heard nothing but good things.

Alex apparently hadn't run out of steam, "Not to mention little brother, you knocked up, not one but two, witches. We don't throw stones in this glass house." Molly drew all the attention which made her blush furiously. She was the only practicing witch.

My dad stood up too and started forward toward my uncle. I made to step between them but again someone got there before me, Harris. "Slow down guys, the most important question is who took the tail? Selkies are peaceful right?"

"Correct." Uncle Alex turned toward Celeste. "Baby, show them the letter."

From the depths of her purse, she pulled out a sheet of delicate dried seaweed. The nori had some strange pearly writing on it. She handed it to Fern to read out loud owing to the loud hiccups punctuating her tears. "By order of the Trident Tribunal you are hereby commanded to cancel the upcoming wedding of Caelian McRannoch. His betrothal to Onda of Sturgeons Cavern is binding."

I think that the strangest revelation of the night for me was that the creatures of the sea were so organized. Tribunals, cease-and-desist letters, who knew?

Link stood up trying to see. "This Onda, is she another Selkie?"

"No." Celeste pulled herself together out of sheer fury. "She's a filthy, soulless mermaid." Interesting, turns out I was right about mermaids in the Hudson. "We chose Jersey because we thought it would be far enough away from the ocean. I can't believe they found us."

Now, as bad as I felt for my cousin, I knew that only one of the Smyths in the room was going to get to investigate this. "Nose goes," I promptly placed my index finger on the tip of my nose.

My dad smiled at me knowingly. Looking around the room I wasn't the only one quick on the uptake, Harris had his finger on his nose as well. "Looks like it's all yours," dad conceded. Internally, I jumped for joy. Externally, I gave Celeste a reassuring nod. This was going to be fun.

7.4: Turns out, you can go home again.

My cousin hid Caelian's tail in a storage unit in Hoboken. That made our first destination pretty obvious. We didn't even need to get out of the car to see that the shutters of the unit were torn apart in crude slashes and curled metal. Bits of grainy coral crunched underneath the tires as I rolled slowly past.

We all got out, but the only other clues left behind were some water spots and a few fragments. I picked up one of the blade-like scales and marveled at its iridescent surface.

"Now what?" Link kicked a loose pile of sand. As this wasn't a training exercise the answers fell solely on me, and I suppose Harris too. Sure, we could simply jump into the ocean but without knowing exactly where this Trident Tribunal kept their headquarters, we could search all our lives and never find it.

"I have an idea." Harris said but he didn't elaborate. Instead, he insisted on giving me directions to a local hole-in-the-wall diner.

A 'seat yourself' establishment, we chose a booth near the exit. In an unfamiliar place I always took account of a method for escape. A waitress in denim and a stained shirt with the restaurants logo on it turned in our direction. She had wispy curls of chestnut brown hair, wide hazel eyes, and beautiful mocha colored skin. There was no mistaking this woman's relation to Harris; from his smile to his high cheekbones, he was his mother's replica. He stared at her as if trying to imprint her image in his mind forever. In turn she seemed transfixed by him as well. It wasn't till someone bumped her on their way to another table that the woman moved at all.

Flipping over her order pad she opened her mouth to try to speak but nothing came out. Biting her lip, she closed her eyes and a single tear slid down her cheek. "Timmy, I need to take my 30," she called and ran out before the cook could respond.

"Was that your mom?" Link had his wounded puppy face on so I couldn't even make fun of him for the obvious question.

"She used to be. Come on, she owes me this." Harris stood up, roughly dislodging the wobbly table.

Outside we found the woman leaning against a wall near the rear of the building. Flies buzzed around the dumpster and rats skittered away from the sound of our footfalls. She had an unlit cigarette between her fingers as she hid her face behind her other hand massaging her temple.

"Hello Moira." The steely look in Harris' eyes softened but was not quite back to normal.

She looked up and lit the cigarette. "I quit; you know. Like two, no, three years ago." The embers sparked in the flecks of gold in her eyes. She didn't put the cigarette to her lips. The tiny curl of smoke coming from the tip did seem to give her some fiending satisfaction, though. "What do you want from me Harry?"

There was an icy bite in the way Harris responded. "It's Harrison or Harris if you like. Nobody calls me Harry anymore." Now I got why he snapped at Molly on the plane.

Moira flicked the tip of the cigarette and an ember floated to the ground. I could see her willpower straining. "I'm sorry, Harr...Harrison. I couldn't do it."

Harris let out an unamused scoff, "After 15 years, this is what I get. Sorry. Couldn't be bothered. Wow."

"Hey," I interrupted, admonishing him. "You took us here for a reason and I am pretty sure it isn't to torture your mother." Seeing his anger at her made me wonder if it was time to forgive my own mother for going and dying on me.

Harris glared at me but conceded, "No." He then turned to his mother again, "I came because of what happened to you. I know dad saved you from some sea creatures. I just need you to point out the way."

Moira's fingers lost their grip on the cigarette, and it fell to the asphalt. "You've become just like him, haven't you?" Harris' lips smashed together in a thin line. Then he raised his hands in a gesture that said, *what did you expect?*

She pulled another cigarette from the pack she'd stashed in her back pocket. "You're right. I gave you to your dad. I guess I should have seen this coming." She looked up with more determination. "I'm not helping you put yourself or any of these other kids in danger."

Before I could get too indignant about being called a 'kid,' Harris snapped back, "I only need one thing from you. Just one and you can't even do that?" Link made an awkward whimper. This exchange was getting messy.

Moira shook her head, steeling herself. "Fine Harrison." She sounded tired and emotionally spent. Her story came out more like a recital of facts: "I was at Weehawken Waterfront Park. It was overcast. I found a penny on the pier. I tossed it in the water. Figured I'd make a wish. It was just a penny, just a wish," her voice broke, and her eyes were fixed on the unpleasant memory.

"I'll remember that day for the rest of my life. It haunts my dreams. That thing came out of the water with crazy speed. There was nothing part-human about it except that it walked on two legs. There was nothing pretty about it. It took me under the water before I could scream. If your father hadn't been there, I probably would have drowned." Moira shook visibly. I wanted to hug her or get her a blanket.

"Thanks," Harris began. "That's all we need." His voice wasn't as harsh as it had been. I felt bad but it wasn't my place to try to build a bridge between them. We turned to walk away.

"I didn't want to let you go," Moira shouted.

Harris didn't turn around. I don't think he could face her. "Why tell me that?"

"I took you to the park one day. There was this tiny, stupid pond. We were playing so far away but I got talking to my friend. The next thing I knew, you were splashing into the water. I couldn't move. I just stood there and screamed. One of the other moms pulled you out. You were blue in the face. They got you breathing again but I couldn't even bring myself to go near the water. They had to take *you* to *me*." Tears were pouring down her face. She looked tragic.

Harris turned around and watched her sadly. There were several long uncomfortable minutes where he chose his words carefully. "I like who I am. I'm okay with how I got here."

It wasn't exactly forgiveness, but Moira took a deep relieved breath. My instinct normally would be to crack some joke about what a wonderful healing session that had been, but I kept it to myself. Sometimes the gravity of a situation needs to be reversed and sometimes it doesn't.

Moira gave her son a half smile and he responded with a small nod. Baby steps, I guess. Harris didn't seem as tense as when we got to the diner, so I counted that as progress. I watched his mother in the mirror as we drove away, but Harris kept his eyes on the road.

The drive to the park was silent and contemplative. I mostly thought about how I really wished I owned a harpoon. I wasn't all too fond of swimming.

Weehawken Waterfront Park was built like a YMCA. It had a lap pool, playgrounds, football field, the works. Most of which were closed for the night. The point of interest for my party was the pier. White rail guards surrounded every inch of the surface. Black benches sat down the middle and lampposts spread an eerie light over the fog layered water. The river lapped lightly below with an aroma like wet cardboard and sewage.

"How does someone go about getting the attention of the terrifying fish monsters Harris' ma...," Link stopped midsentence because of the glare Harris shot him. "I mean, that Miss Moira described."

I produced a handful of coins I'd rescued from the door of my Amazon. "Get wishing, I guess."

Divvying up the loot, we all got to plunking dead presidents into the water. I paused looking at the side profile of a really shiny Thomas Jefferson thinking this wasn't the wisest place for me to tempt fate. In daylight I was pretty sure I could see the exact place where my forefather got shot. Weehawken, New Jersey wasn't a good place for Hamilton's.

Just then I caught a glimpse of iridescent scales out of the corner of my eye. Before I could call out to the boys the fish-person bounded out of the water landing with incredible agility for someone with webbed feet. It grabbed me and dove off the pier.

7.5: Under the sea (scratch that) polluted river.

I died.

Or at least I thought so at the time.

My lungs felt like burning rocks in my chest. Beneath my breastbone, my heart slammed in protest. I tried to kick my captor's legs, but its sharp scales ripped into my jeans. Through my panic it felt like we took ages to reach the bottom. In reality my single breath was barely used up by the time the creature thrust me into some kind of air bubble. Of course, that didn't stop me from choking and spluttering. I didn't have time to worry about the boys because they were plunged in with me after a few seconds.

Through gasps Harris said, "Did we...come down here...with a...plan?"

Good question. Short answer, no. I'd worked too hard to let my 'know it all' mystique down now though. "Rule 7."

"Look seriously, only Linky has been studying that damn rule book," Harris croaked.

"Says the guy who knew about rule 6." I grumbled. The selective attention was frustrating.

My star pupil didn't let me down. "Make an offer that can't be refused."

"Exactly," I finally caught my breath. "We are here to negotiate."

Harris rang out the front of his shirt looking around at the literal curved bubble we were stuck in. "How? We're like a hundred feet beneath the surface. We don't have a lot of bargaining chips at hand."

"Two hundred," Link corrected. Both Harris and I looked at him confused. "The Hudson is two hundred and three feet deep to be exact but who's counting, right?" Link tried to laugh it off but neither Harris nor I could wipe the *who cares* off our faces fast enough.

"Listen, hostage negotiators have nothing better than, 'let them go because its illegal' on their side for an argument. If they can do it, so can we."

Looking around I noticed that our bubble didn't have bars or guards. I guess it's a reasonable assumption that your captives are not going to try to escape when they can't breathe underwater. It occurred to me that we could try to push off hard from the ground and swim up, but the depth sounded daunting. Plus, we were here for a reason. We had a wedding to save.

From outside the bubble, I saw a flash of scales and another fish-person came into view. Pausing outside our space she regarded us. She looked nothing like the creature before. Instead of legs she had a long thick tail like that of a dolphin but scaled like a fish. The upper torso was thin through the waist, and she wore a bra of clam shells held together with seaweed over a very impressive rack. Cool that something from the common mermaid stories still existed. Her arms were similarly covered in suckers as the first creature, but they ended in long pointed nails instead of claws. The face, closer to a feline than a human, had wide set black eyes and a pointed snout. Though clearly a strange mix of features, she was a knockout.

The scaled tail unfused into legs as it stepped inside. There was an almost too characteristic purr to her voice, "I'm Onda. I welcome you, Ms. Hamilton." Ah, she knew me. How nice. See, when I know what I'm dealing with and confident in my approach the Hamilton name can be a badge of honor. Right then, it was more like a stamp of execution.

"And you. Child of Tyler Monroe. You are most unwelcome." I felt like the temperature dropped ten degrees in the bubble. I sort of just realized that whatever Harris' dad did to save his mom probably didn't involve a peaceful transfer.

From some pathological need to keep the attention on me I said, "I'm here for Caelian McRannoch."

"Of course, Ms. Hamilton. I would expect nothing less from your, 'people.'" She said that last word like a grievous insult. Rude. "His blushing bride must be most distraught. But I have his tail and his promise. These are binding."

"Yeah, about that. In our culture when you put a ring on it, it's kinda binding too. Not to mention the astronomical catering costs, you know?" I may or may not have snorted at the end of that. I was very uncomfortable.

"It is no matter to us the cost of the pretender's wedding. If it is merely compensation you seek, we can petition the court. There are many riches beneath the sea." Onda's luxurious accent rolled r's like a rock polishing kit.

Very tempted, I wanted to declare it a fair offer and get back on solid ground, but I came here for something else. I asked for this, and I was going to win. "No sorry, jokes you know. Yeah, too many jokes. Um, anyhow, I really do need that groom back."

Onda glared at me for long enough that I started to wonder if she had already killed me, and this was my endless purgatory. Then she blew into a miniature conch she wore around her neck. It made a high-pitched squeaking noise. I cringed at the sound. In response to

Onda's whistle three guards appeared outside the bubble. "I suppose we must take this to the Tribunal."

7.6: Sandcastles and Legalese.

On the bright side this time we got to wear some magic breathing gel on our faces, so no one passed out. Judging from the length of the trip I estimated that the Tribunal was not in the Hudson. When my eyes began to burn, I guessed we must have reached salt water, likely the Atlantic. I closed my eyes; the speed made my stomach churn, and I was afraid of what my breathing gel would do if I threw up.

When we arrived at the Tribunal's headquarters, I chanced a look around. Before me an incredible structure of coral and glass dominated the seabed. The building reminded me of making sandcastles as a child; the smooth packed sides had strips of coral running up the walls. The decorated glass surfaces had designs of sea creatures, monsters, and battles. At the very top of what looked like a bell tower a golden trident glowed.

Each hallway inside the building seemed to sport a two-lane jetstream pushing visitors through efficiently. Onda and her lackies pulled us along the maze of passages taking so many twists and turns that I could confidently say I would never backtrack my way out of it. The creatures we passed gawked at us as if they weren't all brightly colored fishy hybrids.

Finally, we were pushed out in a flurry of bubbles into a large room. I wondered if the schools of small silver fish darting in circles above us were also conducting business or if the ocean had a class system like everyone else.

A creature with the head and front legs of a horse reared up on its orca tail and plucked a golden apple from a beautiful, gilded tree. Noticing us pass, Horsehead nickered in a way that sounded like a nervous laugh.

The center of the room held three thrones but only one was occupied. The creature in the middle seat appeared to be a merman. He bore the face of a Hammerhead shark and the same characteristic scaled fish tail. In front of him was a truly gorgeous dark-skinned woman with long braids that tied around her, modestly covering her human upper half. Her octopus' lower portion swirled agitatedly in the sand.

Hammerhead opened a mouth full of rows of sharp teeth and spoke in the most regal English accent that I had ever heard. "Your petition is denied. Additional sea otters would obliterate the local purple urchin population. All things must remain in balance, Boof." The name came out less like a word and more like a forced exhalation.

"Veganism is on the rise Lord Scalefin. The kelp forests must be protected. Sooner or later the court will have to accept it." Before his lordship could respond the woman took off in an explosion of ink.

If a hammerhead could look exasperated, this one did. "Next petitioner."

Onda conjured us our own personal bubble again and thankfully this one had chairs. I sank onto the offered seating. The coral and kelp furniture felt pokey and slimy at the same time, but beggars can't be choosers.

"Respected masters of the Trident Tribunal, please consider my plea." Onda addressed the court with confidence. The horse-headed apple eater left his snack and took the seat to the left of Lord Scalefin. "I accuse, Caelian McRannoch, of attempting to break his contracted betrothal to me."

Master Horsehead whinnied and Scalefin held up his hand, "I agree. This is a matter for all the masters of this court." Then he barked loudly. A plain seal swam in and took his seat on the right. Owing to his proximity to the bottom of the ocean I figured he was also a Selkie. No way a regular seal could breathe down here. The leaders assembled, Scalefin gestured for Onda to continue.

"McRannoch was recovered shortly before his wedding to a mortal land-walker." The horsehead member neighed in a way that I didn't think was strictly complementary and the Selkie banged his tail in what looked like a reprimand.

Putting up placating hands between his fellow masters, Scalefin said, "Bring forth the accused."

A cage made of what I assumed were whale bones was wheeled out on a chariot of sorts. Caelian's still looked human from the waist up, but his lower half was sleek, black with white spots tapering into a fin. He looked ragged with a bandage of kelp wrapped around his wounded tail.

Taking my cue from Onda I shouted, "Masters, Caelian was kidnapped this evening by his accuser." I wasn't sure my voice would carry through the bubble. The glare that Onda shot at me was confirmation that my message was clear enough. "He was even injured," I added, gesturing to his wrapped lower half."

The Selkie council member banged his own tail again and barked loudly. Scalefin responded, "Master Orck, this matter will be properly investigated however the accused does not have sufficient evidence to prove Ms. Onda had anything to do with it."

My 'Law and Order' brain kicked in. I'd seen enough episodes to know basic legal procedure or at least a highly dramatized version. "Your honor, may I be allowed a short recess to confer with my client?"

Scalefin slumped back on his throne. "The Tribunal will allow it."

The three masters started making noises at each other which I figured was normal for them. Onda swam off to the side, her arms crossed over her ribs and the chariot driver yawned. "Um, sorry to interrupt but can you let Caelian into the bubble we can't really breathe out there." Horsehead groaned and the chariot driver opened the cage.

When Caelian came near the bubble, we all gathered around him. "You shouldna' come. They may see this as an act of aggression."

I dismissed this notion. Acts of aggression were my specialty, but this situation called for a bit more finesse. "Well, welcome to the family. This is kind of what we do. Tell me about the contract."

"It wasna' me who signed it. I have a brother, twin. That's the trouble, we're identical. My blood is his blood. I canna' prove I didna' sign it." Caelian sighed heavily, his Scots accent growing stronger. "The fool musta' had second thoughts but you don't enter into a contract with a mermaid lightly. They're known for bein' vicious. They havena' got a soul you see."

"What if we can find him? Will they let you go?" I had many methods for hunting down creatures.

"Onda needs to wed tonight. Her father has died which leaves her dominion over Sturgeons Cavern. Mer-laws are a bit antiquated. Therefore, she isna' permitted to seize power without first being properly wed. If she doena' marry tonight her cousin will be granted lordship."

"I'm assuming marrying her and then getting a quick annulment won't work?" I ventured, without much hope. He shook his head.

Link popped up over my shoulder. "Can we see the contract?"

It was a good idea, so I relayed it to the Tribunal. Even though the request clearly irritated them they obliged. The document, on the same dark seaweed, appeared more pliable than the note Celeste had shown us. The writing on it seemed less formal than the other note as well.

Harris looked down at the contract with interest. There was a quizzical expression on his face like he was trying to figure something out. He mimed writing something in the air briefly before saying, "I have an idea." Since the first one panned out, I agreed to follow his lead.

7.7: Negotiation is an art, like literally.

Apparently, I'm not the only one who was a big fan of TV legal dramas. Harris put his hands behind his back and spoke in a deeper and clearer voice than I had ever heard before, "If it may please the court I request some of your sea-paper…um…stuff and a writing instrument." And he was doing so good before 'um' and 'stuff' slipped out, oh well.

They granted his request. Harris instructed Caelian to copy the words written on the blood oath document. The Selkie reached into our bubble and Link turned around so that Caelian could use his back as a writing surface. Curiously, my partner got his own paper and copied the words out as well. He then had the chariot driver present both documents for comparison beside the original. I didn't know if handwriting analysis could convince them, but it was worth a shot, I guess.

"Please consider the documents before you." The confidence in Harris' words got the Tribunal's full attention. "The letters 'o' on the note written by Mr. McRannoch are formed counterclockwise. The letters on my note and the blood oath were formed clockwise. The author of the blood oath is left-handed whereas Mr. McRannoch is a righty."

I lightly pushed him to get his attention. "What in the Sherlock Holmes was that?"

"I noticed when he was signing for the catering," Harris whispered. "Lefties can usually tell other lefty's handywork." Pun intended, I hoped.

"This proves nothing." Onda swam forward to see the documents herself. "He could have been coached."

"It's not easy to change your handwriting style. Not in the few minutes he was over here," Link argued.

Master Scalefin let the writing samples drift to the ground. "This evidence isn't exactly conclusive. I'm afraid the accused will have to honor his pledge."

The chariot driver moved to repossess Caelian. I couldn't let it happen. "I can fix this. If his brother signed the document, then I can scry for him."

"Finding Dylan wouldn't guarantee I could get him here in time," Onda spat.

This was exactly what I hoped for. An admission of guilt. Master Orck let out three sharp barks and a low throated growl. Apparently, hammerhead sharks can blush. The validation warmed my still soaked skin.

"Carry on then," Scalefin agreed.

I picked through the nori paper and shook my head. "I need something bigger and an easel."

With a half glance at his Selkie colleague Scalefin nodded, and the necessaries were provided. I selected the feather quill Harris used to write his note. Characteristic of an albatross, it had a dark tip fading to a white base.

Thinking back to my research on scrying, which was deep down in the vault of my memory, I considered what to do next. This type of freestyle scrying was usually used to get messages from the beyond. Letting a spirit take over your hand took a lot of trust and in the wrong situations a person could get lost in the process. What I had in mind took the concept about ten steps further than anything I've ever heard of. One thing I knew for sure was that I needed some kind of connection to the one I sought.

"Alright, I just need a drop of blood from Onda and Caelian into the ink pot. They obliged, skeptically. I couldn't blame them I barely knew what I was doing. Once the new ingredients were added the liquid took on a strange consistency; thick and undulating as if it were a living thing.

Sitting down, I examined the blank canvas and readied myself to Bob Ross this business. I took a deep breath trying to find my center. I had never done this type of scrying before. My witchy ways were rusty at any rate. I needed to do more than just find the missing Selkie, I had to pull him through the page.

In my hesitation I imagined eyes boring holes in my back daring me to fail. My heart pounded. Then I felt a calming force behind me. Soft hands touched my shoulders. As the thumbs brushed against the skin of my neck, I felt the tingling power that could only mean Link was drawn to me. His hands gently covered my eyes and just as I succumbed to the darkness, I saw the canvas in front of me glow in the blue light that could only be coming from him. The power, confidence and support made me feel like it was laughable to think I couldn't do what I had promised.

I began drawing large circles. Once the magic took over, I could feel my hand dashing across the page. I resisted the impulse to concentrate on my motions. Instead, I focused on freeing my mind. Intentions are powerful tools. With a dash of conviction, theoretically a person could draw anything out. Most people find the strength of their desire unequal to the sacrifices necessary to obtain their wish.

Putting philosophy aside, I reached deeper and began to feel the wave-like current of the ocean. As my spirit slipped into the astral plane, I could no longer feel my hand as it drew or my feet on the sandy seabed. In bursts of pulsating vision like that of a sonar beacon, I could see Caelian's brother.

With my eyes still closed I said, "I've found him." He turned to look at me. I wondered how I appeared to him because he didn't seem scared, just concerned. In my eagerness to get control of the situation I reached out and grabbed hold of the Selkie's tail. I could feel the surge of power being drawn from my connection to Link. Consequently, I felt the boy's hands fall away from my eyes. Vaguely I heard an echo of a thud nearby.

The sensation of being alone flooded me. "Someone anchor me." I choked.

The brother tried to book it. Fortunately, or unfortunately, depending on how you look at it I was firmly connected to him, so I went along for the ride. He was really fast. My stomach lurched at the speed. My hand solidified before me, and I knew I had what I asked for. Link must have come back to hold me to the Tribunal's cavern.

Bit by bit I reconnected my spirit back to my body dragging the struggling Selkie with me. When I opened my eyes, I watched as my clenched hand emerged from the paper pulling the renegade groom from the picture. Harris had his arms wrapped around my middle straining to hold me down. Though surprised it wasn't Link I was grateful. If he hadn't held on, I would have likely been sucked into wherever Dylan had been.

Owing to his seal tail the brother crumpled to the floor of our bubble. His futile efforts to exit and escape were kind of sad. The blubbery seal's scoot isn't nearly as graceful when half the body was humanoid. The chariot driver had him secured before he could say a word in defense.

I looked around and Link was getting shakily off the ground. As usual when we naturally did weird stuff he was confused and wary as if he had no memory of falling. If there wasn't a bunch of sea creatures around, he and I would be in for a serious conversation.

"Hello Dylan." Onda sidled up to him her arms crossed over her chest.

Dylan ignored her. "Good to see you brother. I am sorry she brought you into this."

"Tis fine. I do, however, have a bride of my own to attend to," Caelian replied. "If you get on to honoring your commitment perhaps you can even stand wi' me when I wed her." There was nothing specifically threatening in the way Caelian spoke, but the finality gave no illusions that things would go any other way.

"Aye, perhaps this fine court will grant us their authority to bind me to my intended," Dylan held out his hand to Onda. She still looked angry but softened by the crooked smile he flashed her. "Ya canna' be too cross wi' me, lass. The chase is what makes landin' a Selkie so favorable." He drew her in, tracing the line of her jaw with his fingers. Huh, mermaids can get goosebumps. "Once you've caught me, I'm yours for all the days of my life."

While potentially romantic, the concept of leaving your twin brother who would be forced to marry your betrothed seemed a touch callous. Then again, we were talking about cold blooded creatures. We stayed for the ceremony, mostly because I don't think we had a choice about it. It was nice for a 'justice of the peace' sort of wedding. With the bride satisfied we were permitted to go topside.

Exiting the frigid water Harris, Link and I looked like drowning victims whereas Caelian's black fin turned smoothly into trouser covered legs. His hair was perfect, and he didn't seem to have a drop of dampness. I had a lot of questions about that. Where did the pants go when he was in fin form? Did the clothes left at the wedding venue include pants? Could he take the pants off out of the water? If he had to pee... you know what, never mind.

7.8: Divorcees and pyramid schemes.

We got exactly 2 hours and 45 minutes' worth of sleep. By the time we made it back to the wedding venue it was nearly four in the morning. Celeste insisted on hearing every detail. The *thorough* thing was a purely Hamilton trait so I couldn't be too mad about it. The boys let me do most of the talking while they snoozed in their chairs but since they didn't see any of the scrying part, I guessed that made sense.

The ceremony took place at noon, but I drew the short straw and had to be Johnny-on-the-spot early on so that I could run interference for Uncle Alex. His ex-wife, Celeste's mom, operated like a heat-seeking missile programed to find him and unload her "opinions." I met my former aunt Brittney at the front door of the chateau. I had an extra-large cup of coffee in my hands and my eyes refused to open all the way.

"Goodness Molly, it's never too early to start working on your skin care routine." Brittney put a thumb under my eyelid pulling the loose skin from exhaustion down tight. "I have the perfect product for those racoon eyes." She pulled out a tube the size of a hotel shampoo bottle from her purse. "Just $29.95."

"I'm Mia, not Molly." I made to drink the coffee.

Brittney put the bottle back where she found it and grabbed the cup from my hands. "Just take me to my daughter, Hamilton." She took a tentative sip, made a disgusted face, and promptly tossed the cup in the trash. A sound like that of a squashed mouse escaped my lungs. Brittney rolled her eyes and stalked past me, her clutch purse tucked under her elbow and her hips swaying with jaunty purpose. Grumbling, I followed.

The flurry of activity in the bridal suite seemed chaotic but somehow the hairdresser and makeup artist managed to keep us all on track. I was seconds from digging into a bag of cheesy chips when my head was assaulted by a comb. I tried to protest but Celeste insisted. When I was finally released to go get dressed for the ceremony my hair was done up in two loose French braids and twisted into an elegant knot at the base of my neck.

With my sleek black slacks and matching blazer over a bottle green silk dress shirt I looked pretty good if I do say so myself. I had even acquiesced to letting the makeup artist put on some minimalistic eye shadow and a, close to natural, lip gloss. As I stood at the top of the stairs, I caught sight of Harris looking up at me. He had a smile that I don't think I had ever seen before. It wasn't wide, or giddy. Just happy. Harris offered me his arm as I made my way toward the ballroom. I noted that he wore the same suit from the winter formal, but his tie was striped black and green. I wondered if my father had something to do with that since it matched my outfit well. I tucked my hand into his elbow and walked with him to our seats.

My father got the unlucky job of walking Brittney down the aisle and escorting her to her seat. She squawked loudly when he "accidentally" stepped on her foot. I squeezed my lips together to keep from laughing. Because kids pick up on basically everything, instead of pulling a handful of flower petals from her basket little

Rosey threw a ball of yellow pollen into Brittney's face. I snorted unable to keep it in any longer.

Some of Sage and Fern's cousins from their mom's side began playing reed pipes that let out a woody hooting in the form of "Cannon in D." We all turned and watched as Uncle Alex led Celeste to the altar. Though my cousin didn't have a drop of magical blood she seemed to glow as if bathed in sunshine. Her honey blonde hair fell past her shoulders in ringlets. The ivory lace of her gown swished around her feet. Nothing compared to the expression on her face. Fiercely in love, she floated toward Caelian like an inevitability.

The minister performed a traditional handfasting. The bride and the groom faced each other and clasped hands while the minister wrapped and tied a ribbon around them binding them for life. They swore all the usual things; to love and cherish in good times and bad. Not having the strongest sense of what a functioning marriage would look like, I couldn't say for sure, but if any two people had a shot at making it these ones did. When they kissed, I joined in the whooping and catcalling.

I tried to play wallflower but my dad drug me out on the dance floor after we'd finished with our afternoon meal. The first song had an upbeat track that didn't leave much room for talk. Dad spun me, released me at arm's length then pulled me back in like a swing dancer. When the song changed to a slower waltz, he drew me in close and I rested my head on his shoulder. It felt good to be held. He smoothed a lock a hair away from my face and sighed, "This is nice. I always forget these things can be fun. I get too wrapped up in the notion that family drama would likely abound. Besides Ms. Holier-than-thou Brittney everything has been perfect."

I laughed, "At least she's not here now. Thank the goddess for Rosey. That Benadryl coma should keep Mommy Dearest out of our hair for the night."

Dad rested his chin on the top of my head. "Speaking of the goddess...do you think its time for you to join a coven? That scrying thing sounded impressive."

I stiffened and pulled away from him slightly. "I'm a Smyth. That's who I am and what I want to be."

"Its not *all* you are." Dad met my eyes and for the first time I thought he might start to talk about the mystery between me and Link. As if cued to come into sight Link passed by with Rosey standing on his toes and swaying with the music. "He's a good kid. I just wish he wasn't..."

I was so spellbound by my father's words that I didn't notice Harris standing right behind me. He tapped me on the shoulder, and I flinched. "May I cut in?"

"Of course," Dad smiled warmly at Harris and handed me over. I tried to catch Dad's eyes, but he was carefully looking away.

Harris put his palm on the small of my back and enveloped one of my hands in his other. "This shindig isn't half bad."

"'Shindig?'" I snorted.

"More elegant than that? *Soiree* work better for you, your highness?" He was too close to punch, so I shook my head unable to keep the smile off my face.

I looked over at my dad again and nodded my chin in his direction, "I think he was about to say something about the weird, me and Link, stuff."

Harris examined my face carefully, his expression one of cautious curiosity. "Are you sure you really want to know what he has to say?"

I considered that. I had a passion for the truth. I think most people do when it comes to facts that involved themselves but there were people who lived in complete ignorance of the supernatural and had blissful lives for it. "I think I do ... but maybe not tonight."

Harris caressed my cheek and tingles trailed his fingers. He lightly pinched the end of my chin and drew me close. We stayed that way through the next song. We would have remained on the floor longer but for the chinking of butter knives on the crystal glasses.

Caelian rose to his feet after giving Celeste an enviable kiss. "I just wanta' propose a toast to Harris, Link and Mia for helpin' me get back where I belong. Slàinte Mhath."

Everyone raised their glasses to us. I bowed my head in acknowledgement. The speech wasn't our only thanks. When the cake was cut, we each got an extra slice. And it was damn good cake.

Rule # 8: Don’t trust your fate to human organs.

8.1: Come get your mans.

How did I end up here? Sitting shotgun next to Molly we waited in a long line of cars. Raucous women were shrieking in the other vehicles. It was like a bachelorette party and a girls gone wild video had a baby. Our car was dead silent. Surprisingly, it wasn't because of Demi in the back seat. Molly was too nervous to speak.

I hated uncomfortable silences, so I turned on the radio, "Come on down to our 'Men for Miles' event. We have more than 350 of our city's most eligible bachelors lined up, waiting to be chosen this Valentine's Day for a date. Ladies, this is the event of the season. Our partners over at the 'Sirius' dating app have set up events at several local bars and restaurants. You can choose a romantic candle lit dinner at Turners Seafood..." *Not falling for that again,* I thought. "A trivia night over at Hamilton's Bar. Or if you're feeling adventurous a hot air balloon ride"

Guess what event Molly was planning to go to. If you picked home field advantage, you win. Harris and Link were already there saving us a table. All Molly needed to do was pick the least vile of the lineup we drove past. Her fingers were white knuckled on the steering wheel as she moved slowly forward. I told the girl she should have let me drive. Instead, she foolishly entrusted me with writing down the numbers of the men she was interested in. This gave me an opportunity to add a few surprises to the list.

Each man stood on the side of the road with a cardboard sign decorated in large stickers with both the logo of the dating app and the radio station's call numbers. The black digits in the middle made the whole mess so impersonal.

Molly kept sneaking glances at the men. Most of them looked flattered by the attention from the other cars where the women were busy objectifying them. There was a wide variety of ages and styles. Men in suits stood side by side with guys in flipflops and shorts. Molly tried to nod toward one of the latter. I put the clipboard firmly down. "Hell no, Moll. It's winter. Dude's either an idiot or trying to prove a point either way, ick."

Demi tapped me on the shoulder and pointed out a skinny kid with glasses and a large nose. I signed back to Demi reminding her that we were looking for someone Molly might like. I could be biased but I felt like the whole exercise was useless. None of these guys were going to be good enough for my sister. She was caring, beautiful and a damn good cook. What did number 65 have to offer with his messy cargo pants and ripped hoody?

"What about 72? Kinda cute, right?" Molly nodded toward a man with kind brown eyes and a firm jaw.

"Sure," I wrote the number down. "At least he's wearing appropriate winter gear."

After that, my sister loosened up. She caught me scribbling down number 102 who was a middle-aged man with a goatee that ended close to his belly button. "Absolutely not."

"Come on Moll, I bet he'd give you a ride on his motorcycle." I signed my words for Demi's benefit and let's face it mine too; she had excellent comebacks. Indeed, I caught her message in the rearview mirror. "Demi says, you'd be the queen of his trailer park." Molly raised her hand and brought her four fingers down to meet her thumb; ASL for 'shut up.'

A few of the other guys that were lined up looked decent, but I could tell that 72 was the clear winner. When we reached the end of the line Molly sent him a text via the dating app. My sisters' messenger ringtone chimed; it sounded like a bicycle bell. The screen illuminated her wide smile. Off we went on a forced triple date.

"How'd it go? Find someone to replace me?" Harris tried to sound unconcerned, but I noticed the straw of his soda was uncharacteristically chewed shut.

"Not me, but Demi slipped into a few DMs," I sat down beside him signing my words as was my normal custom around my best friend. Demi socked my arm, and I was told to shut up again.

"Wait you're not serious?" Link looked devastated. Demi walked over, kissed him on the cheek and took his hand in hers. I was taken aback by the PDA because I hadn't realized they were dating for real now. Demi and I didn't do the typical girl talk much.

By default, I sat next to Harris. Molly paced in front of our table till Mr. Brown-eyes arrived, spotted her, and waved. He walked over confidently but without the swagger of a man who thinks he's God's gift to women. He held out a thick, oil-stained hand, "I'm Keller, well Robert Keller but I never liked Bob, Rob or Bert so just Keller works better." He shook Molly's hand through all of this. My heart went out to the lad, clearly nervous too.

Molly went mute again, so I stepped in. "This is Molly, I'm her sister Mia. These guys are her, 'in case you are an ax murderer' friends: Link, Harris, and Demi." Molly turned to me, mortified.

She didn't need to worry; Keller laughed and patted the back of her hand. "Good, I was worried about that too. You never know who you could be meeting from the internet these days. To be honest I only signed up for this event because I wanted to meet a real person in real life. I'm so tired of catfish."

Keller joined our table blissfully unaware that not only did he have the Ax Murderer gang watching him, but our father was also tending bar. Best not to scare the guy too much though.

The coordinator of the trivia event stepped up to the microphone. She was a pretty little thing with sun-kissed olive skin and straight black hair. Her dark eyes were artfully adorned with black eyeliner. "Welcome everyone! Thank you for joining us at Sirius' first dating event. Are you ready to get Sirius?" A lot of the tables responded enthusiastically. Even Demi waved her hands in front of her twisting at the wrist in the ASL clap.

"To kick things off, I have your first trivia question. The lucky group to get this right will win a four-night, all-expense paid trip to The Ritz-Carlton in Miami Florida." I may or may not have joined in the cheering following that statement. When the noise died down, she continued, "Okay, make sure you write your answers before hitting the buzzer in the center of your tables. Which Egyptian goddess is known to be the representation of the star our company is named for?"

Harris snorted and shrugged. Keller and Link looked equally bewildered. I signed the question for Demi since it was hard for her to read lips with a microphone covering the MC's face. Molly got excitedly triumphant, "It's Nut, isn't it? Goddess of the sky?"

She was already reaching her hand over to the buzzer when I caught her wrist. Molly did a fair amount of research in learning about witchcraft, but I needed a wider range of expertise. "No, it's Sopdet. Goddess of fertility."

"You sure about that? The goddess of the sky sounds right," Keller agreed. It was cute that he wanted to side with Molly. Another night, I'll beat that out of him.

Molly smiled at him but nodded to me to ring the buzzer. Guess what? I was right, as usual. We won the trivia game as well. That wasn't all me, Keller turned out to be an expert in cars and rom-coms of all things. Molly may just have hit her personal jackpot. The rest of our group were no slouches either. Link dominated classical literature, Demi knew far too much about anime and Harris broke out as our sports expert. I answered every third question or so with my random knowledge.

In the end Molly secured herself a second date and I started looking forward to a summer break in Florida. While my sister went outside to say goodbye to Keller, I left her under the capable scrutiny of Rudy the bouncer and headed to the restroom. A few of the women from the event were freshening up their makeup and making sure their hair was still tamed. After emptying my bladder, I joined them at the sink.

I had my head down singing "Staying Alive" in my mind. Proper handwashing was essential for everyone, especially at a bar. One of the girls recognized me and said, "You're the one who answered the first question correct, aren't you?"

"Yep," I replied, not looking up.

"Bit young for an event like this," her tone made it clear that she didn't approve.

Before Karen could go to the manager, I wanted to have some fun. I looked up at her and my snarky retort caught in my throat. A shockingly large fashion choice dominated her eye, just the right one. The lid was heavily coated in black eyeliner that extended in a straight line from the outside corner of her eye nearly to her hairline. Her brow was thin, jet black and lightly curved with a straight tail that ran parallel with the mark above it. Emanating from the bottom lid a short level line reached her cheekbone and a second mark curved in a loop toward her ear. Strangely, it didn't look like make up. It almost looked permanent, like a tattoo. I couldn't tell if it was inspired by the Egyptian symbolism the Sirius dating site used or just a new trend, I wasn't privy to.

I blinked hard and the mark disappeared, replaced by the woman's inexpertly applied bright purple eyeshadow. She gave me a withering look. She must have decided that I wasn't worth it because she left. Maybe the Egyptian question threw off my equilibrium. In this town, in my life, I didn't think so somehow.

8.2: Unfollow your heart.

The sound of Molly's text message notification started to make me hate bicycles. The honeymoon phase of her budding romance in full swing, she floated through the house like cupid lent her his wings. I just wished she'd go spread her new love cheer somewhere else. I was busy being angsty.

Link's annoying attentiveness to Demi made me surly. Every day the two of them walked through our school halls, obscenely holding hands. The closest Harris ever got to me was to steal half my sandwich at lunchtime. Plus, after the Valentines event, my dad skipped town to investigate something without me. He left me in the care of my sister who seemed to have heart emojis permanently stuck to her eyes.

Saturday morning came; a day when I didn't have anything planned with the Monroe boys. When Harris rang the doorbell, it took me by surprise. His presence, though troublesome in its own way, was a relief. The clacking of Molly's keypad and her little giggles thrown in sporadically were making me nuts.

When I opened the door, I noticed he had something behind his back. "I got you a present," He bounced on his toes, positively giddy, then handed me the newspaper. The front cover had a circled story in the corner about a murder. I scanned the text and smiled.

Morbid, yes, but he really did know me. Link and Demi could hold hands all they liked. My guy got me a hunt.

"I already talked to Sheriff Field and got us VIP access to the crime scene. Go put some pants on Hamilton." Harris reached out and slapped my thigh. I realized I was still only in my night shirt and underwear. Hustling up, I got dressed and grabbed my keys.

Harris directed me to an apartment complex near the Willamette River. The media circus had left and only a single police car remained. The rookie officer led us up to the forensically cleared site removing the caution tape on the door so we could go in. We donned the ridiculous yellow shoe covers and gloves. The rookie didn't seem interested in looking at the carnage again though and stayed in the hall.

The tan carpet was soaked red, mostly surrounding the dining table near the kitchen. A half empty case of Mason jars sat on the counter smeared with blood as well. Prints marked a barefoot path around the table as if a person with smaller feet, probably a woman, had circled it multiple times.

Harris took a folder from the top of an entertainment center and handed me the crime scene photos. Now, I've seen a lot of death, gruesome ones at that but this looked straight out of a horror movie. The body of the man they had found was spread naked with his chest flayed open on the kitchen table. By the look on his face, he had been alive when the killer had begun what looked like a premature autopsy. I scanned the next few pictures to find that the killer had removed the man's organs and placed them in the missing Mason jars. His liver clearly didn't fit so it was cut and shoved into two, half his heart stuck out of the top of another.

I flipped through pictures of the suspect's hands, arms, and feet before coming to one of her face; 'speak to the manager' girl from the trivia night. Only this time she really did have the tattoo-like markings around her eye. I recognized it now, the Eye of Ra.

Harris peeked interestedly over my shoulder. "How'd I do?"

"Got a live one that's for sure." I put the pictures back.

"Oh man, does that mean you don't know what this is yet?" He seemed positively elated.

"I don't," I admitted, turning to him. "I know one thing for sure." I had his undivided attention. "Molly is in deep trouble."

On the drive back I couldn't help but wrack my brain for answers to this mystery. Nothing in the myths I've read about Sopdet indicated this kind of bloodbath. As far as I knew she didn't have anything to do with the Eye of Ra, at least not commercially so.

My silence seemed to be getting to Harris. "You okay?"

"Yeah, sorry. Thanks for this. It's a bit of a head scratcher."

"What makes you think that Molly is in danger?"

"The mark on that woman's eye. I've seen it before. In fact, I recognize that lady from Valentine's Day. I swear I saw that mark on her face that night but when I looked again it was gone. Can't be a coincidence, nothing ever *is* around here."

"Agreed. What does it mean though?"

"I don't really know but we can assemble the troops and find out."

Within an hour Link and Demi arrived. We wrangled a reluctant Molly, who was not fond of leaving her phone behind, and gathered in the library. Harris and I took turns filling them in with what we knew so far.

"You really think it has something to do with Sirius?" Molly ran her hands over her back pocket neurotically checking for her cellphone. The device was in quarantine at the moment. I didn't understand how a website had caused that murder, but I didn't like the concept of my sister obsessively browsing the app.

"Yes, I think the site has everything to do with this," I said. "Aunt Pippa, can you chuck us the works on Egyptian mythology?" Our resident poltergeist obliged but refused to make her form visible.

The books fluttered gently off the shelves and stacked on the tables. "Alright guys, from the top I guess." I plucked a large volume from the pile and dug in.

Hours later I wasn't the only person going cross-eyed by the mind-numbing tedium. Harris had his head propped up on his hand leaning far over a book. I kicked his chair and he fell face first into the tome. On reflection, it was likely this kind of behavior on my part that caused his less than amorous attention.

I flipped the page of a book revealing a list of all the Egyptian Goddesses. "Wait, what if it's not just about Sopdet?"

"Hmm?" Link looked up, his face losing the battle to keep his eyes open.

"The Eye of Ra is the feminine counter part of the god Ra. Sopdet isn't typically connected with it, but other goddesses are. One of them was Hathor, Ra's daughter, and the goddess of love. If you're going to invoke a goddess for a dating app, you don't choose Sopdet. Couples hooking up are not exactly looking for fertility help."

"True," Molly agreed. "But how do the goddesses of love and fertility inspire murder?"

I elaborated, "When Ra asked Hathor to become the Eye, she took on the aspect of the goddess of war, Sekhmet. She went on such a bloody killing spree that her own dear old dad had to drug her to get her to stop. The story is famous enough to be written in the tomb of King Tut. But maybe not enough to warn an entrepreneur from calling on Hathor/Sekhmet to bind up happy couples."

The imprint of his own hand was still marked on Harris' face. "You think the creator did this?"

"I think people do stupid things for money all the time," I replied.

Demi snapped loudly to get our attention. Waving her phone in the air she signed. "HQ is right here in Salem."

"Of course, it is," Link sighed. "Here we go again."

8.3: Beware of cultural appropriation, it can be deadly.

The headquarters for the Sirius dating company was in an austere building. The lobby with its water feature wall, marble floors and gold inlaid countertops screamed new money. Funds that I suspected were mostly borrowed as the site had only just begun attracting attention. The receptionist wore a pressed pant suit in the same lilac as the logo. Her name was even embroidered on her lapel, Jill. They spared no expense to look legitimate.

With a friendly, and very rehearsed greeting the receptionist said, "Welcome to Sirius, where serious people seek serious partners." Ick.

Molly, as the only genuine adult, strode up to the counter and put on her most authoritarian voice, "I want to speak with the CEO." I had to commend her it was a bold first request.

Naturally, Jill's training did in fact include the typical, "Sorry, she's occupied now. May I direct you to our handy specialists available 24/7 on the live chat feature of the website."

"No, Jill," I began. "If we wanted to speak to someone moonlighting as tech service from their day job scamming the elderly we would have stayed home." The girl's robotic smile faded from her face as she tried to consider how to respond.

As is with our generation her cell phone creeped up from the counter while she 'covertly' pressed the record button. Demi reached over and turned the damn thing off. Good, I was not interested in being the subject of a viral entitlement video. "I'm going to assume it's down that long hallway. Probably the biggest office we can find, right? Awesome, thanks a million, doll."

As Jill protested, we made our way to the furthest door, stamped helpfully with a marble slate identifying its occupant as 'CEO Lucile Martine'. Molly made to open the door, but my dramatic gasp stopped her. "Jesus, Mia. What?!"

I pointed to the hieroglyphs over the door. The first most striking feature was the Eye of Ra. Inside the eye were the symbols for the hoe, the viper (a bird) and a woman praying. Beside this perversion was the ever-popular Ankh, its classic teardrop head inverted over a capital T.

"It means 'Love conquers all,'" said a smokey voiced woman from the doorway of the room.

"It really doesn't," I whispered under my breath. I didn't want to thwart our opening into the realm of CEO Martine.

"Jillian called ahead and told me you were coming. I wish I had time to meet with all new clients like this, but my schedule would never permit it. It's lucky you came at such an opportune moment." Making her way around the desk, Lucile hastily exited out of her online shopping list. Then she dabbed at her mouth with a napkin that missed the smear of salad dressing at the corner of her lips. Otherwise, she was the picture of professionalism. She smiled pleasantly at us putting on her best 'I'm the boss' straight backed posture. "How can I help you?"

"You can start with this," Harris tossed her the stack of crime scene photos. She glanced down briefly and turned the whole pile over, looking slightly green. I put my hand on his arm, a restrictive gesture and whispered, "Okay bad cop, simmer down."

Lucile fiddled with her hair pulling it over one shoulder nervously. "Regrettable, obviously. Sirius has already donated handsomely to the Go-fund me page for the young man's funeral."

"Don't you think your company might be partly culpable for this?" Link's innate innocence softened his accusation.

"Of what? Some strange cult of 'warrior women?'" She looked flustered but also afraid.

Demi passed an index finger across her nose and brought her hand down on her wrist in the letter C, "Cult?"

I agreed. A cult suggested there were more attacks than we knew about. "You seem to be well informed."

"Listen," she began, giving up the hoity toity BS. There was something almost Bronx-ish about her accent. "Who cares if we had two murder-suicides out of our Beta testers. One of those girls only had four weeks to live anyway, not such a big loss." The passion in her justification was making her bold. "We also had three shotgun weddings and two other proposals. Our formula works. Sometimes crazy comes with love. It's intense."

I pinched the space between my eyes and sighed, "But why the hieroglyphs? People can get 'Sirius' without them."

Lucile's defensive posture softened. "Actually, that was an inspiration from my intern at the time. She's our event coordinator now." The woman looked like she had practiced this speech, ready to sit on a talk-show host's couch and spill the tea. "Mona is from the middle east and knows all about this ancient stuff. She designed our logo with all the pyramid pictures. It's the eye of...shoot...you know, uh, something."

My brain temporarily froze. The audacity of this woman to take at face value the language of an ancient culture she had no understanding of boggled my mind. I pulled out my phone and dialed up the Smyth cyber department.

A familiar voice greeted me, "Hey Geovanni. I got a website that's invoking a vengeful goddess can you shut it down?"

"Please Mia, give me something challenging for once," Geovanni responded, his voice playful.

"Sorry man, this is all I got right now. It's the Sirius, spelled like the star, dating site they are using unauthorized hieroglyphs." I gave a grimace of consolation to Lucile. The woman had half risen from her chair in alarm at what I was saying. Not being able to hear the other side of the conversation she teetered on the edge of her seat.

The clacking of his keyboard came from the background when he said, "How did you end up investigating that? Little above your age limit, isn't it?"

I rolled my eyes but of course he couldn't see that. "It was Molly. I guess she got tired of dating adrenaline junkies like you." Molly glared at me.

"Ouch. That was ancient history but still girl, that stings." I laughed; Geovanni had taken Molly to their homecoming dance in freshman year. They didn't really date though, more of a friendzone situation. "Okay, done and done," Geovanni interrupted my musing. "Tell Molly I'm sorry she got mixed up in all of this. I have a cousin she might like. He's an engineer."

"Ew. No thanks G, she has her heart set on this hook up." I winked at Molly. She didn't like that conjunction of gestures and phrases. "Do me a favor, can you cut the camera feed in the building too?"

"Please, I did that before I picked up the call. You really should turn your geo tracking off." I laughed. Geo, geo tracked me. Classic. "Alright girl, it's all done. Try not to get into too much trouble out there."

"No promises friend." I hung up the phone and turned to Lucile. "Your site will be down for the next 48 hours. Remove all evidence of the hieroglyphs from your letterheads to your mailers. If you don't, we will."

The CEO began to splutter, "Who do you think you are? I can't do that. Do you have any idea how much that would cost? We'd be ruined."

"Well, the next time you decide to snag part of someone else's culture you best know what you're doing. That sign out there doesn't say what you think it does. It says roughly 'Love is vengeance to the afterlife.'"

When Lucile leaned back in her chair, she looked small like the child she had once been. Part of me felt a touch sorry for her. She thought she was being cool connecting with younger people by bringing out something old. Very old. The dilemma now was how to protect those who had already been exposed to the message.

Leaving the frantic Lucile in her office, I shut the door and proceeded to use my telekinesis to mangle the hieroglyphs above it. Retrieving Molly's phone from my back pocket I noted the text message, voice mail and facetime notifications all indicating that Keller was still very interested.

"Okay Molly," I handed her back the precious. "Let's get you another date."

8.4: The three S's.

Keller took the bait immediately. On the way home Molly also got a text from event coordinator Mona. Though the Sirius app was currently 'down for maintenance' the stargazing event that was previously scheduled would go on as planned.

When we got home Uncle Wes called, "Hey kid. I know that boy of yours, Harris, marked you guys out for this investigation but it's getting kinda hairy down here at the station."

"It's Wes," I whispered to my companions. I put the call on speaker and handed Harris the phone so that I could translate for Demi. "It's Harris, sir. What happened?"

"We arrested three other women this afternoon. Two cases of assault and one for stalking. All three had that Egyptian symbol on their faces." Wes paused we could hear yelling in the background. "These women are practically rabid. Fought the whole time we tried to arrest them. One of the victims is getting three of his fingers amputated. I don't think I can get you guys in to interview them."

"That's okay Uncle Wes. We got a lead from the CEO. Looks like the event coordinator might be the source of it all. Molly's gonna get some field work in." My sister gave me the finger. "Well, at least she's gonna try to get *something* in."

Molly gasped and threw a pillow at me. "Evil little she-devil."

Wes laughed. Rough jobs breed rough humor. "Is it that stargazing event out on Cape Cod?"

"Yeah, is that alright sir?" Harris nearly fumbled the phone in his anxiety.

"It's fine son but it's out of my jurisdiction so you guys better keep your noses clean." We agreed and let my uncle get back to work.

"Okay Link," I got up and offered him a hand. "Let's gather our supplies."

As we left the room Molly shouted, "Please don't mess up my plants!"

Just off the kitchen I led Link through a door to the backyard and into our greenhouse. The glass door was adorned with the Smyth's nine-pointed star. "This is hands down one of my favorite places on the planet."

Link looked up at the gabled roof. The floor-to-ceiling windows gave the glow of mid-afternoon to the room. He examined the herbs overflowing on a baker's rack and brushed his fingers on the dried flowers hanging from the ceiling.

"To get rid of an attachment we are going to need to do a cleansing. Look around and find me the three things we need to do that." I sat back and watched as he moved around the room.

"We need the three S's: salt, sage and spice." I nodded encouragingly. "The first two are self-explanatory." He grabbed a bundle of sage from the ceiling and a can of salt from a shelf beneath the standing gardens. "That last one is tricky. Spice can be almost any dried herb. I think I'll grab lavender, for protection and it's associated with love so that's probably an extra boost. Oregano does the same. Um. Think Link."

"You're doing great, though you might need that lavender to help with the stress you're putting yourself through." I walked over to a glass fronted cabinet and pulled out two jars. The dried contents inside the first made a tinny rustling noise as I shook it lightly.

"Nettles drive out evil spirits." The second jar was filled with a reddish-orange powder. "Cayenne can break spells."

As I put our things into a paper bag, I looked up to see the sun-like white pedals surrounding a golden orange disc. The tiny flowers sprouted plentifully in a nearby trough, and it sparked something. "Hey Link, grab a few of those Chamomile flowers. If memory serves, the Egyptians dedicated them to Ra and used them for healing."

"How can that help?" Link handed me a few short stems.

"It couldn't hurt."

***

We made our way to Cape Cod just after an early dinner. Keller picked up Molly and we teens followed behind, in my Volvo. I saw Molly's abject embarrassment every time we pulled up beside her on the road. Bringing your little sister on the first date was one thing but this event was for couples who wanted to snuggle under the stars. Many things could happen in all that darkness. Unbeknownst to all the other couples I was afraid that some of those "things" might include bloodshed.

The drive, a little over two hours, wasn't fun. We didn't talk much; I mostly left my classic rock playlist on to keep out the tension. The four of us had been on a few outings together but this one seemed a bit more dangerous. Rampaging chimeras, missing grooms and youth stealing school counselors didn't have nearly the sinister aura of an angry goddess.

Cape Cod had a beach-town feel. Most of the buildings were white and lacking in the downtown height and glass fronts that we had passed in Boston. The tallest points visible were the many towering lighthouses. The water could be viewed glittering in the fading sunlight down every street.

Toward the 'elbow' of the Cape we crossed into the town of Chatham. Hardings Beach looked over a peaceful Nantucket Sound.

The water lapped spreading foamy bubbles across the sand. The wave retreated, sucked into the dark blue depths. Where the sky met the sea, a richly dark orange glow of the setting sun spread over the horizon. The sun was swallowed by the night sky to be reborn another day, or so the myths said.

Further back from the tide, wooden pallets were stacked, surrounded by white cushions, and adorned with candle filled lanterns. A fire burned brightly in the center. Mason jars decorated each space. After what I had seen yesterday morning, I wasn't fond of these sinister glass containers.

Given that Molly and Keller were the only two people who were invited, strictly speaking, the rest of us stood on the outskirts. Link took the jar of cayenne and not so covertly walked the perimeter spreading it diligently. Mona's dark hair glinted in the firelight as she went from couple to couple having them fill out a sign-in sheet of some sort. I knew we were barking up the right tree when Link completed the circle and Mona's spine stiffened. At the same time Link seemed frozen in place, eyes glowing.

"The jig is up," I whispered to Harris.

He reached out and grabbed my hand, gently. I looked down briefly before meeting his gaze. He let go and muttered, "Sorry."

"Come on over," Mona called. "The more the merrier." She had a friendly smile, but it was fixed on her face in such a way that the expression felt unnatural. We made our way to the event and Harris put his hands in his pockets to keep hold of the sachet that housed our herbs and salt. Given the right opportunity he would drop it into the fire.

Mona pulled her clipboard out from under her arm and handed it to me. One perfectly manicured set of fingers held tight to the top while she pulled out a pen for me to sign in. Glancing down, I noted three things that I didn't particularly like. First, my fool sister had already signed the document, with a little heart in place of her 'o' no less. Second, the top had the Sirius logo, complete with the very dangerous hieroglyphs. Third, if I tilted my head ever so slightly, I could see the paper glimmer and not with a glittering undertone. With magic. Owing to Mona's death grip I couldn't extract the paper and chuck it in the fire.

As I hesitated, wondering how best to incapacitate the woman in front of me, Link slipped the pen from my hand and signed. Satisfied, Mona pulled the clip board back. Before it left my sight, I saw that he had written his name next to mine and Harris' next to Demi. I looked at him concerned. He brought both hands in front of him, one slightly behind the other and closed each fist. ASL for; "Trust me."

8.5: Digestive tracts are not good at prophecy.

Trust him? That was a hard ask. The kid just signed us up for what I could only expect would be some kind of mass killing and possible suicide. He put his hand on the small of my back and led me to the opposite side of the table where Molly and Keller were busy making moony eyes at each other. Demi and Harris followed, though both looked markedly awkward and unsure about what was happening. I couldn't blame them I didn't know what was going on either.

"I'm trusting the process here, but having serious doubts, Link," I hissed at him.

"I know. It's just she'd have gone full feral on you, and I thought maybe you'd like to keep your neck intact," he snapped back.

First off, I was impressed he had the balls to bark at me. Second, I didn't like how oddly specific he was about what might have happened. "How do you know that?"

"Just a gut feeling." He waved me off.

"Bull. Rule 8 Link, your digestion has nothing to do with predicting the future. Spill," I crossed my arms over my chest.

Looking around to make sure no one was listening he said, "I think I had a vision again. All I know is this is about to be a massacre if we don't figure out how to stop it."

He had a point. You didn't need psychic powers to tell that this event was a powder-keg of emotion ready to blow. I turned to Harris hopefully. I wasn't watching him and couldn't be sure he had taken advantage of the distraction. "Did you deliver the package?"

"Of course, I did. Who do you think you're talking to," Harris smirked. He took one of the Chamomile flowers from the front pocket of his jacket and placed it behind my ear tucking the stem into my hair line. Perhaps it was the power of suggestion, or the aroma really did come through; the aroma of sage emanated from the fire.

Mona decided to kick things into high gear. With a snap of her fingers, ropes appeared on the pallets. "Have your partners lie on the tables and secure them with the available binding. This will be a night for the ages. Here beneath the stars, far from the influence of Ra, we will make a sacrifice to the goddesses of old."

Like sweet compliant Lemmings, half the group, mostly men with Harris included, volunteered themselves for slaughter. Even the same-sex and non-binary couples chose a victim and a torturer. I shuddered to think what that said about relationships in general.

Curiously, Link was the only one left unaffected. Those not laying down obediently tied up their companions. Mona weaved through, with her clipboard tucked safely in her wicker basket, handing out long metal rods with hooks on the end. When she passed Link, she tapped him on the shoulder and encouraged him to politely take his place. Which he did. More stunning was the fact that I took her instrument of torture without comment. I had to snap out of it before Harris and Link got brain scrambled.

I dug my nails into the sand grounding myself into something natural and real. It eased the heady sense of dizzy compliance I was slowly being dipped into. I visualized the scene I needed to happen. The binding document of sacrifice to the goddess had to be burned thus releasing us all from the horrific game of "find the gray matter." When my mind could literally feel the page beneath my fingertips, I flung out my hand towards the fire.

My telekinesis worked. I prayed the rest of the group would be too spellbound to notice. The paper fluttered lightly in the wind and then caught in the flames that consumed names ravenously. Some of the people around me began to shake off the enchantment, including Molly. For the others something still bound them to Mona's suggestion.

Suddenly, someone seized the back of my neck violently. My face was brought so close to the fire that I feared for the continuation of my brow line.

"Think you could just scatter some plants and push me out?" Mona's voice sounded tripled like three people talking in harmony. The other worldly noise sent shivers down my spine. The nails that clawed the back of my neck dug into my skin sending trickles of what I assumed was my own blood running down my collarbone.

The thing about enchantments was that it took a lot of magical effort which left very little strength for the physical. Mona's grip, though bitingly harsh, didn't have the oomph behind it to keep a well-trained specimen like me down for long. I rolled and managed to regain my feet. Glancing behind me I saw Molly and Demi working at the knots that bound up the boys. I only caught a glimpse of the rest of the crowd of blank-faced onlookers before Mona was at me again.

Her face had elongated, morphed to that of a lion's head. Eyes, large and slit pupiled, narrowed in on me with a single-minded stillness. From a short snout she opened a maw of sharp white teeth, and a low predatory growl came from deep in her chest. I noticed the hieroglyphs were tattooed on her arm. So that's how she remained in control. She safeguarded the goddess inside herself. Big mistake.

I spun toward the fire which was not what she was expecting. Reaching in, I grabbed the hottest log I could see. Ignoring the blistering pain that screamed at me to drop the damn thing I lunged for Mona. I'd like to say I promptly seared the correct portion of her arm and happily let go of the log but in reality, it took a few wrestled seconds before I got it dead on.

The enchantment broke as Mona screamed out. The goddess separated from her in an ethereal mist. Sekhmet's black hair shimmered, contrasting against a gold, collar necklace inlaid with yellow diamonds to match her fur. Her muscular body shown through the thin fabric of the broad-shouldered sheath she wore. A cord of braided gold hung at her waist. The most terrifying aspect was the weapon she carried. The khopesh had a thick leather handle with a deadly sharp curved blade that looked almost like a question mark.

The goddess hooked the weapon around Mona's throat and yanked upward. Instead of her head parting company from her neck, her body merely fell to the ground intact. Well, mostly. At the end of the blade, Mona's soul struggled for freedom. The goddess caught a glimpse of the flower behind my ear and nodded to me. I pulled it out and she let out a rattling purr. Then she disappeared, taking her prize with her.

I resisted the urge to run to the sea to cool my blistering hand. The salt would be excruciating on that. Instead, I held it close to my chest, willing myself not to cry. The rest of the group, now released from their single-minded task, began a crescendo of commotion. Arguments, tears, blame, pleading.

Harris skidded in the sand toward me after being released from his bonds. Taking one look at my hand he ran to the nearest ice bucket set out for the cocktails and came back with a napkin full of blissful relief.

Gingerly, he placed the soaked cloth into the palm of my hand, and I winced briefly before sighing. "I think you might need to pass me the keys, Hamilton. I doubt you can drive with this."

"In your dreams," I managed, gasping as the ice shifted.

Molly came over with Keller in toe. His eyes were wide and fearful. "Did that woman just turn into a lion?"

Molly's mouth fluttered open gaping like a fish out of water. Link, Harris and I all grimaced. Someone was bound to see what really happened. Most people would just put it down as an over-active imagination, but Keller seemed steady in his beliefs.

"She... didn't she? Wow. Then you just fought her." Keller turned to me his expression filled with wonder and excitement. "That was the coolest thing I've ever seen."

Relief followed by a tinge of exasperation crossed Molly's face. The secret was out but given Keller's reaction he was probably the Smyth's next recruit. I felt bad for my sister. Keller's hotness points took a marked dive. He shook his head then pulled Molly close. He then redeemed himself by giving her a very satisfying looking kiss.

All the other couples took off. Mona wasn't dead just catatonic. I figured we would just call in to the police on our way home. Let the locals deal with the cleanup. I actually did let Harris drive us home. And in an even stranger twist I felt comfortable enough with him behind the wheel of my baby to fall asleep.

8.6: You don't own me; I hope.

When we arrived home, Molly applied a healing poultice made mostly of aloe vera to my burn and Harris carried me up to bed. I woke the next morning to a deeply blistered palm. My sister also kindly left the aspirin open and next to my bed.

Sitting up I fumbled left-handed with my phone. I sent a quick text to Link asking him and Harris to come over. His premonitions grew more frequent the longer he worked with me. The time had come to face the problem head on.

Downstairs I found Harris already in the kitchen. I sat down on the stool beside him and yawned. "Spent the night, huh?"

Harris poured me a cup of coffee. "Someone had to look after you. Wes said your dad left for Miami right after Valentine's Day. Plus, I couldn't leave you with love struck Juliette no matter how good her healing magic is."

"Thanks." I held my mug up in salute. "Honestly she'd probably be force feeding me herbal tea if you weren't around."

Harris took a big gulp of coffee. "You know I better get back and make sure Linky gets a balanced breakfast before school."

"Firstly, its Presidents Day. No school, thank you ancestors."

"Oh sweet."

"Secondly, I already asked him to come over." Eyeing Harris speculatively I added, "You do know that donuts don't count as a balanced meal?" Harris gave me a sheepish grin.

When Link entered the kitchen only a few minutes later he did indeed have a pink box tucked under his arm. Apparently, my training would have to include the food pyramid from now on.

Link sat down on the stools with us. "How's the hand?"

"Stings but I'll live." I held the bandaged subject up for him to see.

For a moment the silence stretched between the three of us. Then Link broke his composure. "Those visions are getting worse. I can't control them. Most of the time they feel like a daydream. Like I'm just imagining things. It's weird."

"Link, I could literally be doing the dishes with my mind while we have this conversation." I gestured toward the sink with my wrapped hand and winced. "It's all weird around here, dude." He smiled weakly.

"I haven't had visions this strong since just after that day with the Wampus cat. Ever since we came to Salem, I feel like I see you in my mind all the time." Link had a nearly tragic look on his face.

"I'm hoping you don't really mean 'all the time,'" I joked but he clearly wasn't in the mood. "Why does it scare you so much?" I wondered if he felt the same way about the connection as I did. Part of me relished the added boost of power. I felt unstoppable. On the other hand, I didn't like the unconscious surrender it elicited.

A shadow of something I'd never seen passed over his face. His constant sunny disposition was suddenly marred by darkness. "Because it feels wrong. Inside me, something is wrong. Like evil. When I have visions, I feel like I'm protecting you because...because I own you."

Woah. Instinctually, I wanted to protest that no man owned me. But what Link was describing felt familiar. When we touched the bond was so much more than casual. I remembered our first handshake, how every inch of my skin had felt distinctly alive. The tango when he displayed a proficiency over the steps he didn't seem to have with Demi. How my body molded to his movements and suggestion without hesitation. Only then did I begin to speculate about the wisdom of my father's choice to let Harris and Link come to Salem. Not only that but to put our paths side by side.

"They're not telling us everything." My gaze was still unfocused in my contemplation. I could feel rather than see Harris' discomfort at my words. I looked him in the eyes and knew he held part of the mystery. How could he not? Surely, John confided in him. Trusted him to protect his son.

In a small way I felt betrayed. We'd all worked together these last few months and never once did Harris give me any reason to suspect he had a hand in this ploy. I addressed them both, but my eyes never left Harris, "I may not know what all this means but I know enough to guess it's not just some fluke. We have the same birthday, under the same blood moon. I'd be willing to bet Link was born just before midnight like I was. Powers that began the first time we touched. Strange, isn't it?"

Harris hung his head. He looked like he was coming to a personal decision. "All I know is that it's bad, like end of the world bad. I don't know why or how. Your dad does though. So did John."

"Can't say I'm surprised. Dad seems to know everything." I sighed, too exhausted from the day before to try to solve a puzzle with missing pieces.

"We could ask him," Link suggested.

I could hear the unspoken 'you' in place of that 'we.' "Go ahead Link. Tell me how it works out." After his minor slip at the wedding my dad seemed to reconsider his notion of telling me what he knew. When I tried to pry it out of him, he snapped shut more effectively than the jaws of an alligator when it tasted meat.

"I mean...I don't think... He probably wouldn't..." Link stuttered.

Poor kid looked helpless, so I came in for the rescue. "I can try but I've been down that road before and it's a very frustrating dead end. He doesn't talk about my mother, my birth, my powers, nada."

"I guess we have to trust they had a good reason." Harris offered.

"For keeping us apart or, letting us be together?" Link sounded morose as he massaged his temples.

I gave him a bracing smile. "Both."

Rule # 9: Know when to walk away, also when to run.

9.1: An inferno to reignite our partnership.

My father wouldn't spill the beans on what he knew about my connection to Link. Surprise, surprise. Nothing was more infuriating than being surrounded by people who know a secret that you don't. Especially, when it's about you.

Harris took Link on a trip for a few weeks. They got an independent learning contract at my dad's insistence. They came back mid-March seeming emotionally lighter than when they left. I sort of wished I was permitted the same license, but my own abilities had never given me the heebie-jeebies like Link's did.

For my consolation prize I got a rocking Easter gift. Dad came into my room holding a thick manila envelope and dropped it with a thwack on my desk. "What's this?" My fingers fiddled with the brass clasp.

"A mystery." Dad smiled down at me. His deeper tan made the crinkles at his eyes more noticeable. Though still salty that I didn't get to join him on his latest hunt, I did think the sun had done him good.

I pulled the documents and photographs marked with serial numbers indicative of a police investigation. "A murder-mystery," I said, intrigued.

"Could be," dad shrugged his shoulders. "If you're lucky this will get Link all the rest of his training hours, then you'll be off the hook as his teacher."

An interesting offer. In the beginning all I wanted to do was work alone again but I had gotten used to my squad. Those boys made hunting a challenge I hadn't had in a long time. "Thanks dad."

The boys came over for our usual pre-hunt research. Aunt Pippa sulked in the corner, irritated that her personal reading hour was being disrupted. They came into the library quietly, all of us acknowledging each other with curt nods. I didn't like all the doom and gloom. Apocalyptic events were a dime a dozen. So, what if Link and I seemed to be at the center of the next one? Hunting was my happy place, and I had no intention of letting it go.

With a flourish of my hands, I gestured toward the table laid out with the casefile documents. "We've been given premium access to the real deal."

"Because what we've been doing before now has been mere child's-play, huh?" Harris leaned against a bookshelf.

I smiled at him too relieved to respond with equal sass. "No, but it's been mostly reactionary. The few cases we've taken legitimately have been mild in nature." I patted the table lovingly. "This one is a straight enigma. I don't have any notes from other Smyths with suggestions on what we are up against. It's just us this time."

Harris sat down and Link shyly joined him still uncomfortable meeting my gaze. I figured one out of two wasn't all bad. Link picked up a police report and read through it quickly. "This looks like the first, chronologically, arson-suspected house fire." Link summarized. "The owners, Adam and Maria-Rose Gilbert were an elderly couple living with their adult son, Samuel. All three were killed in the blaze. Jeeze look at the pictures." The bodies were burned straight to the bone.

Harris examined the fire chief's report. "They suspect that some kind of major accelerant was used but they couldn't find traces of it. That's strange. Something that can cause this much damage should have left behind some evidence."

"If you think that's weird take a look at this." I pointed to another police report, this one from three days following the first. "Greta Vaughn, a 39-year-old female, was found in her car outside her workplace dead. Cause? Smoke inhalation. She'd just worked a twelve-hour shift at a warehouse. There was no evidence of fire in the car or her job. No apparent connection to the Gilberts. No next of kin."

"That's extra." Harris peered over the raised document in my hands. "Are we sure these two are connected? I get the whole 'where there's smoke there's fire' thing but sometimes people can walk around for a while before dying of smoke inhalation."

"Not twelve hours." I waved the paper at him.

Harris flicked it away. "As far as you know, *Dr. Hamilton,*" Harris teased.

Link poured over the next report and still had his nose in the papers when he said, "Looks like the elder Gilberts had a daughter. The woman, her husband, three kids, and even the dog were all found at a local park burned kinda like the grandparents. Witnesses at the park claimed they all spontaneously combusted, at the same time." He flipped the page over to see a photograph of the woman holding a small child both mother and baby were mere bones. He dropped the report.

"That one was yesterday," I added. We were all quiet for a moment.

Like a good student, Link broke the silence. "Let's figure out what this is?"

After a few excruciating hours of research, we each had a list of suggestions. Harris broke down first. The book bit wasn't his forte. "What about a dragon?"

Biting the end of my pen I shot that down. "Too big."

Harris scratched it off his list. "Phoenix?"

"Too friendly." I tasted the ink and stopped chewing.

"What's your suggestion smarty pants?" Harris slashed through another creature on his paper.

"Can't be a Chimera; you know, been-there done-that." I tapped my pen on my list. "Could be a Caorthannach but they are pretty rare and mostly in Ireland and Scotland. Though to be fair I didn't think I'd ever meet an Egyptian goddess, so I guess you never know."

"What the hell is a Cori-thank-notch?" Harris butchered the name. Granted it was a hard one.

"Caorthannach is like this witch-serpent hybrid lady who really likes to burn things. Mostly buildings though." I rolled my neck stretching out the kinks of nose-grinding research.

"The witch sounds like a maybe." Link looked me directly in the eyes: we both shivered. He absorbed himself in his own list. "What about the Cherufe: A Mapuche magma creature from Chile. Let's see, loves extreme heat. Oh no, they're like twelve feet tall. Probably not, right?"

Harris shook his head. "It's most likely just a Djinn."

"You might be on to something." I sat forward looking over our police files. "Three events. Could be the wisher is done."

"We can't just leave that to chance, can we?" Link looked genuinely worried.

"Of course not. We'll leave for Manchester after school on Friday. Gotta love Spring Break. The perfect time for a nice long investigation." I smiled, contentedly surrounded by books and gruesome photos of crispy former people.

Harris got up and stretched. "You got a jacked-up sense of fun, Hamilton."

9.2: Detective’s Hamilton and Monroe at your service.

When we arrived at the police station in Manchester, we were greeted by Detective Miles Overland. Yep, his parents seriously named him that. A fact that made me giggle the whole drive over. Standing before the detective I was glad I had gotten all that out of my system. A big man: his broad shoulders strained his button-down shirt’s seams. He had a stern angular face, topped with a buzzed crop of hair.

I’d suspected that Overland was handing us this case reluctantly by his demeanor, but his words caught me off guard, “I’m glad Mitch could spare you. Honestly, I hoped he’d come himself but the way I hear it you’re the next best thing.”

“Thanks.” I shook his offered hand.

“Come on in, I have the murder map up.” Overland led us to a room where a peg board sat surrounded by three tables and empty chairs.

The ‘murder map’ contained the collective evidence of the investigation thus far. Aside from what we had already seen in our welcome packet an old article caught my notice. Printed from what looked like a microfilm picture it had contrasting colors of grainy grays against a pure white border. Link and I gravitated to the document. Our fingers touched it at the same time.

With an awkward glance, I backed off and let Link read it out:

Twenty-three people dead in apartment fire. Infant miraculously found unharmed.

Horrific scenes from Friday's apartment fire have left residents of Litchfield seeking answers. As of yet no evidence of an accelerant has been found. Two-month-old Delano Gilbert is the lone survivor. His guardian, Rhonda Gilbert and her live-in boyfriend Brian Stock were found amongst the victims of this tragedy.

"That article is from sixteen-years-ago, but the crime is about the same," Overland said. "I'm going to get you guys some badges so you can do interviews if you want. I'll be right back."

"What do we think?" Harris examined the board. "The Djinn's either done or moved on."

"There are a lot of 'ifs' in that scenario. IF it's a Djinn. IF it's only one wisher. Given it seems to have a connection with the Gilbert family it could be a curse. Might make more sense." I shook my head, unconvinced.

"*Might* isn't that much better than *if*," Harris retorted. Touché.

Link traced a finger from the older article to the picture of the lone woman in her car. "We have two choices here. Focus on the pieces that fit or inquire about the one that doesn't."

I considered the picture of Greta Vaughn. One leg was still hooked outside of her sedan, as if she had just stepped in or out, as the case may be. Her graying brown hair fell loosely over half her face. Blue lips and fixed, staring, bloodshot eyes made my own throat constrict in sympathy. Air was one of the things in life people took for granted the most. Like the beating of our hearts, the automatic filling of our lungs was a function we didn't pay much attention to. It would be there until it wasn't. Maybe the answer lay on the coroner's slab with Greta Vaughn.

***

Link and Harris looked strange in button down shirts and slacks. Without the jackets they wore to the winter formal they did indeed look older. I used a copious amount of makeup that I normally don't bother with. My own professional attire aged me five years easy. By the look on the coroner's skeptical face, I needed every one of those years.

My complete indifference to the sight of a dead body helped legitimize our presence. The coroner was a tired looking woman in her mid-fifties. Her strawberry blond hair streaked with gray was done up in a bun on top of her head. Intelligent green eyes seemed to notice everything. The small portion of Link's shirt that wasn't tucked. The extra holes in my ears that, though empty of adornment, indicated I wasn't as prim and proper as my posture indicated. I couldn't help but think she'd make a good Smyth.

Introducing herself as Dr. Noreen Berkley she set to the facts, "We did find traces of particulates around Ms. Vaughn's mouth and under her nose. The shape indicated the matter was transferred from the hand of another individual though we didn't find any fingerprints or skin cells. Her lungs were scorched as if she inhaled the smoke rapidly before her esophagus could swell."

"So, it's going to be ruled a murder?" Harris apparently forgot to pretend to know what he was talking about.

Berkely narrowed her eyes at him. "I can't think of a natural reason for a healthy woman to suddenly die of smoke inhalation, can you?"

Harris merely sputtered incoherently. The doctor handed Link the woman's medical record. Before he could open it, his eyes began to glow. Seriously, these two were making my job ten times harder.

I stepped in front of Link, and he bowed his head. Thankfully, Dr. Berkley's attention was on Harris at the time.

I held out my hand and she took it. "Thank you for your time."

She nodded to me. "Let me know if you have any questions."

Immediately, Link stopped the doctor before she could leave. His eyes were mercifully back to normal. "Ms. Vaughn had a son? I thought she had no next of kin."

"The child was released into foster care. I'm told she signed away her parental rights." Dr. Berkley put her hands in the pockets of her coat completely at ease. "We don't typically inform next of kin in those type of situations."

"Right," Link breathed heavily. I wondered if the dead body thing was getting to him. He hadn't had to do that part before. Maybe he just needed a snack. My own blood sugar could have used a boost.

"Well, if there is anything else I'll be in my office." Dr Berkley left.

Once she was out of sight Harris turned on Link. "Dude, what's with you?"

Link looked up palely. "Her son is sixteen. Listed on her medical record as Delano Gilbert. And he was born..."

"On October 31st," I finished. Link nodded.

9.3: Not too shabby for a foster kid.

I should have known. The way Link and I seemed to gravitate toward the old article. We were recognizing a fellow member of our exclusive group. If I had to guess Mr. Gilbert got a special gift as well. This thought brought more questions than answers. The first of which was how to find him.

Back at the precinct we discovered that, naturally, Overland already had information on the youngest Gilbert available. The next day we set up an appointment with his foster family to have a meeting with the boy.

On the drive over Link filled us in on his thick social services file. "The poor kid's been through a staggering seventeen different foster homes."

"Bet we can guess why." Harris added from the back seat.

"Starts a lot of fires." I offered. I was still shaken by the notion that this kid might have been the murderer we were looking for.

"Yep, and he's violent, likes to run away. All around bad news." Link kicked his loafers onto my center console, and I smacked him. The brief contact sent a spike of tingles up my arm. There was something electric in the air since we discovered another person stuck in our mysterious situation.

"Harris, I think you need to take the lead here." I met his eyes in my rear-view mirror. If Link and I couldn't casually touch without magical consequences I didn't like the idea of either one of us taking the point position. Who knew what adding a third person with abilities might do.

"You got it boss," Harris agreed.

The house of the foster family was a cute, gray-slatted, ranch style. Numerous bikes and scooters littered the yard. The chorus of voices from young children sounded through the walls of the house. We had to ring the bell a good three times before a semi-harassed woman answered, one sweet girl clinging to her leg and two more kids peering at us from around her hips. When we introduced ourselves, she graciously invited us inside.

Sitting on the edge of a squashy couch I counted five children, the eldest of which looked around eight-years-old. "Mrs. Kirkwood, we've come to talk about Delano. Is he home?" Harris sounded surprisingly mature and in command.

The woman shook her head, "No Del's gone most afternoons at the library. Or at least that's what he tells us. He is good about coming home for dinner every night. Then again most teenage boys are ruled by their stomachs." She smiled indulgently at Link.

Harris quickly brought the attention back to himself before Mrs. Kirkwood could relate to Link's seemingly unavoidable youth anymore. "How long have you fostered Delano?"

Her kind bright eyes shone slightly with suppressed tears. "Going on four years. It's his longest period with a family. We don't usually take kids his age, but his story just pulled all my heartstrings. So many homes just giving up on such a bright kid. What a shame. In the beginning we did have trouble with his tendency toward F I R E," she spelled out shielding her mouth from the littles in the room. "But I have a degree in child development, and I know darn well how to manage attention-seeking behaviors. Once we began a regiment of positive reinforcement his problems seemed to disappear. We get the occasional flare up when he feels challenged but overall, he's a good boy."

Occasionally, you meet a person completely pure in their intentions and it helps you believe in humanity again. Mrs. Kirkwood was that. All the children under her care looked healthy and happy. They sought out her company and the littlest one was curled at her side cuddling.

Harris smiled at her warmly. "Do you think it would be okay if we took a look at Delano's room?"

"Of course, it's just upstairs. Given his history we have an open-door policy with him." She led the way to a room he shared with at least two other children. "It's kind of cramped right now. We're at max capacity. I just have the hardest time saying no to a placement. Del doesn't seem to mind when he's home, the little ones treat him like a grownup. He really has a wonderful natural authority. I've told him that will take him far in life. Strong wills make for strong leaders."

"You care for him a lot." I smiled at her.

"He's hard not to love." A thunk and the sound of wailing came from down the stairs. Mrs. Kirkwood turned toward the noise. "I'm so sorry, take your time up here I have to go see what that was."

The lack of child artwork clued us into which space belonged to the young man. His desk was neat and orderly. A single photo of him with Mrs. and what I assumed was Mr. Kirkwood was framed in the corner.

Harris leaned down to look at the articles taped to the wall. "Bunch of birth and death announcements from newspapers. Man, that one dates back at least 60 years. What is this chicken scratch he's written on there?"

I leaned forward and noted that his handwriting was damn near illegible. More obvious though were the articles indicating the deaths of the rest of the Gilberts. They were circled and slashed through with a red marker. With a gasp I suddenly realized what was happening.

Link put his hand on my shoulder, and I jumped. He became Mr. Glowstick-eyes again. Twice on a single hunt was a record. From the look on his face, he didn't like what he saw. "It's him," Link croaked. "He killed them all."

Harris looked at the two of us confused. "But why?"

Link shook his head; his vision didn't provide that answer. Unfortunately for us I already knew. "He's trying to sever his mortal coil."

9.4: Its Shakespeare, my darling.

"What?" Harris demanded.

"It's a concept that comes from Hamlet. 'To die, to sleep; To sleep, perchance to dream. For in that sleep of death what dreams may come. When we have shuffled off this mortal coil, Must give us pause, there's the respect, That makes calamity of so long life,'" I quoted.

"What the hell does that mean?" Harris was growing agitated.

Link answered, the ever-solid scholar, "In Hamlet it refers to death."

"Right," I began. "But it's more than that. It's the death of a person's connections to life. Some interpreted that to mean letting go of the pieces that bind you to earth to ease your death but that's not it. If you cut your connections to life, you become the opposite of human. Your frailty is replaced with invulnerability. Empathy with indifference. Transience with immortality."

"That doesn't sound so good," Link agreed, shocked.

Harris looked between me and his nephew. "Translation for the non-nerds in the room, please?"

"To sever your mortal coil everyone who really knows you, most importantly family must all be dead. The more people you kill with your own hands the stronger you become. The worst, most powerful demons are made this way." I felt a sudden tingle up my spine but couldn't be sure if I was freaking myself out or something otherworldly was the cause.

A voice from the doorway confirmed the sensation as the latter, "That is exactly what I was hoping for." Delano Gilbert leaned against the frame. Dark hair fell across his face shielding his disturbing black eyes. "Tell me more."

I didn't know if it was my imagination, but he seemed to radiate heat. Standing in a room with Link and Delano was like being the only attracting magnet amongst opposing ones. I could feel the friction between the boys.

"You seem to know enough about it already." I walked forward putting myself between Link and the newcomer.

Del eyed Harris with unguarded contempt. "I have my sources, but I'd like to know what a bunch of fake suits know about it. And why."

"That's a complicated question." I watched Del's expression trying to decern if the rabid kid might attack.

Casually, Del reached out a hand to me and I took it before I could consciously stop myself. Flames flickered lightly up his arm and surrounded our fingers. It didn't burn but my recent experience searing my own skin made me pull back in fear. That pissed me off. I didn't like showing that particular emotion to my enemy.

He moved toward me again, but Harris grabbed him by the arm. "Yeah, I don't think so, man." Smiling, Delano glowed briefly, and Harris let go shaking his fingers in the air as they steamed.

"Okay, let's chill out," I came between them. "You have questions. I have answers but I'm not doing the intimidation thing with you."

"What makes you think I won't just incinerate you right here, right now?" Del sneered.

"Because you can't," I held up my unblemished palm. It wasn't even red as Harris' had become. He had a lot of power but like with Link I figured that when it came to me, he wouldn't be able to use it to hurt me. As I'd known the kid for about a whole minute that was a bit of a gamble, but it felt right.

There was a flicker in Del's eyes that suggested he would really like to try, but he smiled and bowed sardonically. "Maybe we can take this outside," I suggested. I didn't like the idea of this guy losing control and killing all those sweet little ones alongside Harris and Link.

Del led the way to the backyard giving Mrs. Kirkwood a cheery wave as we passed. The way he looked at her was filled with love and respect. Given our brief meeting, and the knowledge of what he had done, the interaction felt odd.

In the backyard Del took a seat on the swing set and gave me an impatient gesture to keep talking. I considered how much I wanted to tell him about, well basically, everything. In getting him outside, I was simply stalling for time. This seemed like a good opportunity to play dumb. "You're the one attempting the severing you must think you know what you're doing?"

The grass between us grew brown and shriveled. I resisted the urge to back away. He considered me with a head cocked to one side like a child at a new game. Heat climbed my calf up to my inner thigh. Flushing embarrassedly, I gave the bold little jerk a nudge with my mind, and he fell out of the swing.

He jumped up out of the dirt and charged toward me. "How did you do that?" I pushed him back again, this time, with my hands.

Tiredly, Link explained, "The same way you set your fires. We were born under the blood moon as well. Something about that night changed us."

"Wait, I can do this," Del ignited his hands, "because of some basic hippy moon crap?"

"To be honest we don't really know." Link shrugged. "It's the only connection we have."

"I don't do connections," Delano growled, getting in my face. "When I found out all I had to do was to get rid of my family I was like, great! Sign me up. What did they ever do for me anyway?"

I backed up, disgusted. "How did you even find out about that? It's not like a person just picks up a copy of Hamlet and thinks 'mortal coil' huh, that's gotta mean patricide and all the other 'cides."

Del lit each finger individually letting the previous one extinguish staring lovingly at the flames. "A gift like mine doesn't go unnoticed. I've had, let's call them, mentors. Some demons are waiting for someone with the strength to challenge the leadership. Once I trash all my 'ties,' I won't just be immortal. My power will rule the darkness."

"Who's next?" I shivered at the dead look in his eyes.

"What do you mean? It's already done. My dad's sister and litter of brats were the last. The rest of the Gilbert's and Vaughn's are dead. I've made sure of it." Del's confidence peaked in the corner of his half smile.

My eyes darted to Harris, and I shook my head almost imperceptibly. That's not how it worked. If his family was truly all gone down to the last genetic connection, then he was being bound by something else. He'd need to sever that cord. After that his transcendence would be immediate.

I could almost feel the danger to the happy family behind me. In my mind I could see Mr. Kirkwood coming home from work and offering all the little kids hugs and shuffling his big hands through their tousled hair. Mrs. Kirkwood's wide smile would greet him as she swatted his roaming fingers away from the sauce that she would have been stirring on the stove. The final image was a wall of fire. I remembered the pictures of his aunt's children; burned to the bone. I wouldn't let that happen to the people behind me.

Perhaps it was my expression that clued Del into the truth. I could see his killer instinct falter as he realized what he had to do next. I strangely wished I could spare him this heart break. The family here had accepted him, taught him, and did what no one had ever done before, loved him.

"You can walk away." I hoped he would.

"I've come too far." A single tear rolled down his cheek. "Rhonda only took me for the state's money. When that apartment burned down, I lived but I was hospitalized for weeks. The bitch was starving me. I was only a baby."

"Just because someone wronged you in the past doesn't give you the right to take lives." I stepped an inch closer.

"You know I can't burn?" Del's eyes sure looked like they could. "One of my foster dads picked up on that by putting his cigarettes out on my arms. Social services only caught him after he left bruises holding me down while he did it."

"And Mr. and Mrs. Kirkwood? Did they ever do anything like that." I dropped my voice down to a low soothing hum like trying to calm a wild animal.

"Don't talk about my ma..." he cut off wiping tears from his eyes. "Don't talk about them like that."

"Bring me to the demon. I'm pretty good at making them mind their own business." I tried for a smile, but the corners of my lips merely twitched.

"They said people like you might try that. I am not a fool." The remainder of Del's tears steamed off his face. The air around him shimmered in a heat haze. His eyes blazed with tiny flames along the iris.

I centered myself then I shoved him with my mind as forcefully backward as I could manage. He flew a good ten feet and crumpled to the ground. "Harris, get the family out of here!"

"No way, I'm not leaving you." Harris came up to stand beside me.

Link's eyes glowed brighter than I'd ever seen them as he shoved Harris to the side. A blast of fire rolled over their fallen forms and smashed into the exterior of the house. The flames were alive. They spread with a single-minded obsession. Hungerly, they consumed everything in their path eating through the paneling at a rate no normal fire could have managed.

Getting off the ground Link shoved Harris toward the back door. "Know when to walk away. Mia's fireproof and I can see it coming. Go! Please!"

Reluctantly, Harris scrambled to the burning building. Standing beside me Link held out his hand. His glowing eyes were freakishly luminous, but I had to roll with it. I took his hand and felt my power triple. A blue pulsing light encapsulated us as if Link's power were binding our forms together. We squared off against Delano Gilbert.

9.5: Love cannot conquer all.

A spark of astonishment lit Del's expression. It's not every day that two people stand in your backyard glowing blue. I interlocked my fingers with Link's, amplifying our connection. Every blade of grass called to me. The twist of the metal chain on the swing waited for instruction. My mind reached out in a thousand directions on guard, listening for my decision to control the world around me.

"You really think you can scare me? Two can play at that game." Every inch of Del's skin erupted in flames. The fire crested toward us like a wave consuming everything in its path. A child's sand box melted sending the burned plastic noxious gas around the yard. Every second that passed the flames grew stronger. If I didn't cool off this inferno fast, he might explode.

I did the only thing that made sense and burst the waterline twisting the sprinklers toward him. The water evaporated in a mist that gathered around Del's flickering form. He laughed maniacally.

"You have to stop this!" I screamed over the roar of the flames.

For a split second the fire retreated, and a look of confusion passed over Del's face. Fiercely, he redoubled his efforts and the blaze rose high enough to obliterate the precious oxygen I needed to keep breathing. "You have telekinesis AND mind control? NO

FAIR!" His petulant child-like response would have been amusing under different circumstances. Staring down at flame boy with a pyre around him made the whole thing far more serious.

Strictly speaking, I didn't think I had mind control, but I still didn't understand all the ins and outs of these powers anyhow. I couldn't get enough air to respond so I called on the swing to disconnect and bind Del in place. The plastic seat never stood a chance, melting the second it encountered his body. The chains did their best to imprison him but in a burst of pure white light they too ran down his arms in puddles of molten steel. I blinked rapidly trying to rid my vision of the bright blind spot that stained my retina.

In retaliation Del sent a ball of flames in our direction. If it hadn't been for Link, I would have been fried crispy. Well, probably not, but he might have. We lay there panting. I could feel the sting of defeat rising like bile in my throat. On the ground Link turned to me still keeping my sweating palm interlaced with his own. He put the other hand on my cheek. If he wasn't giving up, then I wouldn't either.

Del wiped at a trickle of sweat that beaded on his forehead. Breathing heavy with the sustained effort of his power, his lips curled over his teeth in a snarl. He increased his flames and built himself a protective barrier.

In that brief moment of silence between us we heard an argument from the front of the house. Harris' deep reasonable tone spoke inaudibly before Mrs. Kirkwood shouted, "NO! WE CAN'T LEAVE WITH OUT DEL!"

Confident that we could not pursue him owing to the wall of fire, he stalked toward the house again. "She loves you; you know?" I called from the ground.

"And you love her too." Link pulled me to my feet.

"Don't give me that shit. I'm a dollar sign to these people. Just a paycheck. They don't give a damn about me, and I couldn't care less about them," Del dismissed.

"Then why do they bind you to your mortality?" I choked briefly on the smoke in the air, praying to hear sirens.

Mr. Kirkwood's voice joined his wife's screaming Del's name, clearly panicked. Our oppressor ran his fingers through his hair, his face screwed up in agony. "SHUT UP!" He fell to his knees and a blast knocked us to the ground, again. A plume of fire rolled over us. Examining Link, I was grateful that my apparent immunity seemed to be shared as well as his weird glow thing.

Del had his arms crossed over his chest. Tears evaporated from his cheeks as he rocked himself back and forth. "I have to do this," he rubbed his eyes like a sleepy toddler then straightened up and got to his feet. "I have to finish." His resolve was evident.

Back upright again, Link squeezed my hand showing me a vision. Just a simple picture. My face as he saw it through his eyes. The flames behind me. He shared his power with me but once upon a time I had taken it by force, even if it was an accident. The day we met. If I could do it then, could I do it now?

I drew the light around Link and I into myself. The glow in his eyes had even disappeared. It was mine. I reached a protective hand out in front of us squeezing Link's in effort.

Slowly the blaze retreated. Del watched in horror as the flames gathered back around him. He balled his fist and fought my intrusion, but I wasn't just borrowing his power. I was the one in the driver's seat. The flames traveled back forming a ring around his sneakers. It retreated up his legs and abandoned his fingertips. The remaining fire gathered in a collar of red, yellow, and blue around his neck, choking him. The primal force that had once spared him when he was an infant tightened around his throat, blistering skin that had once been invincible to its calling.

I wanted to stop. I want to say I at least hesitated, but I ended him quick. I wish I could call it mercy, but it wasn't. Killing him was convenient. I could have maybe found a witch to bind his powers. I could have let him cut the cord. I had choices. Rationalizing would have been the easy thing to do. Instead, I let go of Link's hand and stood shaking in the gathering dusk.

The thing about trauma is that it feels like it's happening to someone else. Or at least that's how it was for me. Everything was more vivid in my memories of that night and yet somehow disconnected. I could tell you with shocking detail about the colors of the flashing police lights against the scorched earth. How each rotation illuminated a new consequence of my actions.

I couldn't tell you what I said to the police or even how long the interrogation went. Time seemed to speed up then freeze in place to absorb things that may in retrospect be considered meaningless. Mrs. Kirkwood's scream of agony when she saw the body of her son could easily be dissected note for note as it rang out through my eardrums. A sound that conveyed so much more than shock and sadness. A keening, pleading with the past to undo its horrific mistake. No one would let her near the body, but she screamed for what felt like an eternity. In reality it was more like a few minutes. It would always be more than that when it haunted me later.

I remember looking at my hands in a way that I had never done before, like foreign objects. The traitors of my higher-minded self. I wanted them gone in some irrational way. That was until Harris took one away from my glare. He held it gently as he encouraged me back to my car. Before I could slip into the passenger seat I broke. I went weak in the knees my chest heaving with wracking sobs. My body crumpled in on itself trying to protect my vulnerable shattered spirit.

Harris held me, stroking my hair and whispering things I will never remember. Slowly the agonized sounds stopped bubbling up from the torment inside me. I was left with a deep ache in my chest and tears that flowed continuously down my cheeks for many of the miles between Manchester and home.

Rule # 10: Destiny is just a suggestion.

10.1: No easy answers.

It took me two days till I was ready to ask the questions that had come after finding Delano Gilbert. Harris and Link were keeping their distance. I sought my dad who was in his study with reading glasses resting precariously on the tip of his nose. He didn't like anyone to know he needed them, but he and I had no secrets. At least that's what I thought.

Removing the frames, he looked up at me. He put down the screen of his laptop as I slumped into the chair opposite him. My posture and abject silence over the last few days made it clear that I was trapped in circular thoughts about what I had done.

"You ready to talk about it?" Dad's expression was open for once. His guard appeared down but I wondered just how far he was willing to let me in.

"I don't think I have a choice anymore, do I?" My body felt heavy with mental pressure.

"Probably not. Knowing you I'm surprised it took this long." Dad studied me looking for some change of heart, I think. When I didn't say anything, he continued, "That thing with the fire kid wasn't your fault."

"Don't do that. It was literally my fault." I felt queasy as the vivid image of Del's blistered throat flashed across my vision.

"There's nothing I can say to make this better, is there?" I shook my head and dad sighed. "Maybe it wouldn't have been like this if we had just paid more attention to the other ones. I don't know. I'm sorry Mia. Taking a life isn't easy no matter what the circumstances are."

We were getting to it now; I could feel it. The chance to walk away was in my court. My dad waited for me to decide. There was a strong part of me that wanted to stop. Go back to the fun. Reject this intrusion into my life and keep finding monsters to take my self-loathing out on. That was the easy path. But I've never been fond of easy. I would face my demons and carve them out if necessary.

Taking a deep breath, I steadied myself. "How many others?"

Dad looked me dead in the eyes searching for weakness. To see if my resolve wavered in the slightest. I suspected that he had rehearsed this conversation with himself many times over the years. "Ten."

That meant ten other people potentially out there with abilities as destructive as Delano's. "Explain. Please. I'm begging you." My voice broke. My emotions tipping over like a glass filled to the brim. One small tremor and I'd be done for.

My pleading struck something in him. "It's probably time, I suppose. You're not the only one I owe answers to, though."

No, I was not. Link deserved to know why we could do these extraordinary things. Why we shouldn't have been permitted to be near each other. Though, that part I was beginning to understand. The power we all displayed when the three of us were together was something I'd never experienced before. Clearly, the answers to these questions would come at a cost. One my dad had been unwilling to pay until now. As before, I wanted to hesitate because no sane person intentionally seeks out harm. Instead, I texted the Monroe boys to come over ASAP.

***

Looking at Link, I thought he seemed as broken as I felt. My dad brought out a large black box and placed it on the dining table where Link, Harris and I were gathered. We were all silent; my dad didn't know where to begin and I didn't know what to ask. There were too many things on my mind. I feared what this added burden might do to my sanity. Committed, I intended to see it through.

Clearing his throat, Dad began, "Seventeen years ago the Smyths got wind that a prophecy was about to be enacted. There are thousands of known prophecies and most of the time they don't come to much. This one had the Wiccan community in an uproar. Seers across the country started reporting omens. Some kind of massive energy emergence. You must understand that when these things happen, it's not easy to prevent them. Everything in a prophecy is vague and could generally apply to thousands of different situations."

"But here we are." The exhaustion that plagued Link seeped out in his cadence.

"Yeah." Dad rubbed his face uncomfortably. "Well, in a nutshell it talked about the birth of a set of children born under a blood moon. Each would be 'bound by magic' into "the hands of the divine' and 'blessed by the blood of the damned.'" He let that sink in. "Three circumstances that would give them 'gifts.'"

I stared at him, my expression pleading for more. "What does all that mean?"

"I can only speak to what I know and that's you, Mia." Leaving my gaze he addressed the boys, "Her mother knew exactly what Mia would become, though, she didn't clue me in at all. I wouldn't know if I hadn't followed her the night Mia was born."

He painted the picture well. Under that bright blood moon, he found my mother lying on the ground. Candles illuminated the clearing that she had chosen in Highlands Park. The circle where she set up the ritual had a time slowing spell to keep him at bay. As he tried to span the distance, Dad's movements were painfully exaggerated. A man, dad had never seen before knelt at her side. He glowed in a bright white light that nearly rendered the candles unnecessary. The labor came to completion and the man prepared to guide me into the world.

"He was an angel." Paled by the memory, my dad somehow looked older. "That was the first and the last time I'd ever seen one. He swaddled you in a blanket, dipped his strange long fingers into a chalice nearby and spread a line of dark crimson across your forehead. Then he let a few drops drip into your mouth. The bastard had the audacity to smile at me when he placed you on the ground. Then he disappeared in a blinding flash of light. By the time I made it through the spell your mother was dead, and you were crying."

I couldn't speak. The story sent gooseflesh up my arms. The part about the blood was kinda gross but the rest made it hard to pass off so easily. I'd always known my mother died in childbirth but the mental image of her lying dead beside me sent a sharp pang through my heart.

"Do you think she knew what she was sacrificing?" I couldn't help it, tears welled in my eyes.

Dad reached over and brushed one away before it could fall. "I do. I'm sorry baby."

Link sat up straighter in his chair. "What about me? Did my dad tell you anything?" I was grateful to Link for the intrusion. It gave me a chance to regain my composure.

"He told me everything," dad nodded. "Some things were similar, like the chalice and the blood but he said the woman who delivered you was normal as far as he could tell."

Harris sat forward with his elbows resting on the table. "You had to have told the council."

"I did," dad agreed. "John and I went together. A few months after you were born, I found the prophecy your mother had hidden away from me." He patted the box again like it contained her ashes, but I suspected it was merely her aspiration.

The heartbreak in my father's expression told me that my existence had not always been assured. "They wanted us dead." I guessed.

He thought about it for a moment. Shaking his head he said, "They wanted you eliminated." Potato-patato if you ask me. "Because the prophecy mentions thirteen children, we got them to agree that unless all of you could be found the threat would still be out there."

"They couldn't find us all?" This didn't ring true to me. We were all born on the same day. Granted that equated to at least ten-thousand babies in the US per day alone. But a few years of digging with the Smyth resources at hand would probably find most of them. Delano was one state over and setting fires since infancy.

"They never tried." Dad's face said it all. My father, Mitchel Hamilton. I could imagine that conversation. A council of over-the-hill bureaucrats and two of the Smyth's most famous sons. Monroe and Hamilton would never allow the casting out of one of their own.

Link's complexion grew rosier as the conversation went on. He seemed to be regaining his natural boyish curiosity. "So, what does the prophecy say?"

10.2: Fun fact: prophecies don't rhyme.

I loved facts. I was sufficiently nerdy to find it base level insulting when I got even one wrong answer on a quiz. My competitive nature kept me from accepting mediocrity. This time something inside me wanted to put my hands over my ears and hum loudly till this part was over. My feelings of being trapped must have registered on my face because my father waited for me to give a nod before he responded to Link's question.

Dad recited from memory, "'Daughter of the seventh son. Mother, maiden, and crone. Reborn in flesh, immortal indemnity of soul. The sacrificed Selene presides. Of each the tribes of Jacob, a chosen to oppose. By hand of God and blood of death the Adversary bound.'"

We were all silent for a long time. Then Link said, "Why doesn't it rhyme?"

Taken aback by the question, my father sat down at last. It looked like a relief. "They usually don't. Plus, that's just the translation from ancient Greek."

I put my figurative scholar hat on, "Okay, 'daughter of the seventh son.' That's gotta be me." My dad nodded in agreement as the seventh son of his father.

"'Sacrificed Selene' that's the blood moon," Link added.

Harris leaned in taking a stab, "The 'tribes of Jacob,' like his descendants, there were twelve of them. Does that mean including Mia or not?"

"From what I know, not," dad answered.

Harris slouched, seemingly pressed down by the prophecy. "That means there's thirteen of you guys."

"Twelve, now," I corrected, morosely.

"Crap, I'm sorry I didn't mean to…" Harris trailed off not knowing what to say.

"What's the rest, Dad?" I met his eyes and knew he wished he didn't have to keep going. "It's not the end of the world to predict the birth of a few weirdos." My joke fell flat.

Dad paused, cleared his throat, and recited again, "'The shining one by covenant will bless the daughter's womb. Bring to life a son, of heaven, earth, and torment of which is crowned to rule.'"

"Okay, that kinda rhymed." Link looked mollified.

Harris cuffed him on the back of the head. "Not the point, dude."

I sat back in my chair feeling nauseous again. Eleven bachelors vying for the chance to gift me with a devil child. Literally the devil, since the 'shining one' and the 'adversary' were both early texts to describe Lucifer. Thankfully, I didn't have to explain that to the boys. My dad made the necessary connections.

Grasping at straws Harris reasoned, "Well, 'maiden,' it can't happen if she's not a…" he seemed to realize what he was suggesting and shut up.

"Are you volunteering to get the job done, Monroe?" I snapped.

Harris spluttered an apology, but my dad cut in before we could snipe anymore, "'Maiden' in this context doesn't mean what you think it does. The 'mother, maiden and crone' phrase is a traditional way of describing the goddess of magic. Given the rest of the prophecy it seems as if the goddess is somehow connected with Mia."

In the stunned silence, Dad opened the black box on the table. I peered over the rim to see a browned and torn piece of woven papyrus. The incomprehensible letters stretched across its surface. Drawn by the same magnetic pull Link and I both reached our hands toward the glass encased document. When our fingertips touched the tingling intensity sparked between us again. This time we both met the sensation apprehensively. All our hard-earned familiarity was gone; sunk into the words written thousands of years ago. The truth sliced through our friendship like the blade of a samurai. Sharp, deadly, and unforgiving.

Harris' voice broke through my thoughts. "How do we stop it?"

"There's nothing in the prophecy that indicates how it even starts," dad said. "Until you guys met that fire kid, I thought the powers could only begin if Mia encountered one of the boys. That's why John and I agreed to keep you apart. After Mount Mitchell, we realized it was more important than ever."

"So why invite them to stay after John died?" Looking at my dad I realized I had crossed into one of those moments where you suddenly find out that your hero isn't perfect and even adults don't have all the answers.

"I promised John that I would protect Link. If the council got wind that you boys were on your own, I have no doubt that some kind of accident would have been arranged." There wasn't even an ounce of irony in my dad's delivery.

I always considered the Smyths to be the good guys. Not only had my idol been tipped off his pedestal but my pride in my heritage fell shattered beside him.

"What do we do now?" Link's voice sounded small, the enormity crushing his bright spirit.

"That's up to you," dad began. "John and I shielded you as long as we could. It seems that now you all are being drawn to each other. I suspect one way or another the others will come. I'm not giving up.

I'll keep looking for some way to stop this from happening. Now that the event seems to be drawing closer, I think it's time you both find a way to fight back."

With that heavy burden added to our list of worries the Monroe's took their leave. My dad came back into the dining room after walking the boys out. He grabbed my hand and squeezed it. He might not know how to stop this thing, but he would never abandon me. His love remained constant no matter what I might become. I held on to that. He may no longer be the infallible man I'd looked up to all my life, but this version felt more honest and somehow more comforting. My mother gave me magic. My father gave me everything else.

10.3: It's all Greek to me.

I dreamed that I was in the Kirkwood's backyard. Just me, Del, and the blackened earth beneath us. He stepped up close to me and ran a finger caressing my cheek. Little arcs of flames dance down my jaw.

When he spoke, his voice was deeper and rough as if the collar of deadly fire I had ended him with scorched his vocal cords. "I wonder what it would have been like if we'd met before it was too late."

"Better for you I expect." The dead didn't scare me. He couldn't intimidate me now.

He laughed like a branch snapping in two. "I think I would have liked you, Amelia Ann Hamilton."

I'd never told him my name but then again this was my subconscious. "Not sure I could say the same." Tough words but I still couldn't seem to back away from him.

"I just hope the chosen one doesn't turn out to be that weak little glowstick." Del laughed unkindly.

Link may not have Del's raw power, but he was not one to overlook. "At least he's still alive."

"Ah, well for as long as you let him be, my queen." Del kissed my hand and as the dream faded the flames from his lips remained on my skin.

Suddenly, my fingers were being beaten savagely by a pillow. I groggily looked toward my attacker to find Demi in a state of panic. I crossed my flattened palms in an upside-down T-shape. ASL for, 'Stop.'

Demi pulled the pillow away but raised it in defense. My fingers were still ablaze. The air in my lungs vanished. Panic engulfed me. I shook my hands trying to douse the flames, but they wouldn't stop burning. I couldn't tell if my general state of anxiety kept me from feeling the pain or if there wasn't any.

I felt a sharp flick to the forehead. Demi had dropped her pillow and held her fingers ready to deliver another blow to my brows. I calmed slightly but the fire didn't budge. "It's magic. Control it," Demi signed.

I stared at my hands breathing heavily trying to quench the hyperventilating. Of course, that made it worse. I got another flick, "Okay. I'm trying."

I closed my eyes and thought about how I first started to use my telekinesis. Trust me, there were a lot of accidentally slammed doors in the beginning of that mess. I didn't like being out of control, so I willed my power to obey. I tried the same with the fire. When I opened my eyes, the flames were gone. My fingers were mercifully unblemished.

Demi threw the pillow at me. "What the hell was that? And who said you could skip off and try to die in another state? Do you have any idea how worried I was? Dreaming of ashes and volcanos and all other nonsense. Then Link came over yesterday and told me everything. A prophecy, devil babies, more kids with powers?"

I grabbed hold of her hands stopping the flow of admonitions. Then I turned them over frantically hoping I hadn't burned her. She was fine though. I sighed in relief.

Demi pulled me in for a bone crushing hug. She let me go and signed, "I'll come back this afternoon. I promised to meet up with Link for breakfast. We can discuss whatever the hell that was with your flame fingers later."

"Sure, I'll see you then." She left and I sat down on my bed examining my palms. Had the fire been just a manifestation of my dream? I didn't think so somehow. I'd taken it from Del. I'd taken it and turned it back on him. It was mine now for better or for worse.

I got humanized with a shower, my favorite jeans, and a large mug of coffee then barricaded myself in the library. Pippa helped me find a book on Greek gods and goddesses. I stared at an illustration of Hecate trying to figure out how we were connected. Depicted in her three-aspect form, the heads of the mother and the crone framed the maiden in her thorny crown. Grecian gods didn't pull my interest any more than all the other myths.

I was fascinated by all aspects of history and studied all sorts of mythology, but nothing had ever caused me to gravitate toward this particular goddess. I had even refused to join my sister's coven even though I was the daughter of a witch and could easily perform spells I felt worth my time. Whose bright idea was all this anyhow?

I know I usually provide all the answers but none of this made sense to me. My suspension of disbelief was strong considering what I did on a daily basis, but wrapping my mind around that prophecy was hard.

Behind me Harris knocked, standing in the doorframe. "Can I come in?"

I nodded and pushed my seat back from the table where Hecate's beautiful, marbled face stared unseeingly out. Harris regarded the textbook then grabbed a seat, spun it around and sat with his arms folded over the backrest. I smiled remembering the first time he'd come into the bar. Though, the tables were now reversed. I knew before he said it, that this was goodbye.

"I can't let it be Link," he answered, cued by my mute nod of surrender.

"I know." I tried not to cry but my nose tingled in the beginnings of tears.

Harris reached out and caressed my cheek. "He's saying goodbye to Demi, but I figured it would be best if I came here alone."

I pressed my face into his palm feeling its warmth so much more comforting than the dream touch of Delano Gilbert. Harris stood up and I walked with him to the door. He pulled me in and held me.

"Take care of each other," I whispered.

"Don't go looking for trouble." I could tell it was more than a passing suggestion. He didn't want me to go find those other boys. He didn't want me lost to words over 4000-years-old. After kissing me on the forehead, he left. I felt that kiss for hours after.

Shutting the door, I made my way to my room and sat behind the laptop on my desk. I didn't want to disappoint Harrison, but I had to know who else was out there. I needed to see if I could stop this prophecy from coming to fruition and I didn't know how long I had. Google would help me find them. After that it was a matter of how to remove this curse.

None of us asked for this. I felt honor bound to rectify that mistake. I knew I'd have to navigate this search through my father's rules. I knew I was looking for a needle, or ten, in a haystack. But I come from House Hamilton, and we don't know how to quit.

www.ingramcontent.com/pod-product-compliance
Lightning Source LLC
Chambersburg PA
CBHW070613310726
48982CB00001B/70

9798990351905